What Cannot be Taken

Brad Raby

Copyrights

To my patient wife, for those long moments of silence she endured.

Chapter 1

CHAPTER ONE: THE RIVER Sarah

He'd been looking at me all morning the way a man looks at something he's been planning.

I recognized it eventually. Took me until after the second coffee — because I am not at my sharpest before the second coffee, and also because nobody had looked at me that way in approximately twenty years, and I'd let the habit of recognizing it go the way you let go of things you've decided you'll never need again.

But there it was.

That particular quality of attention. Patient. Unhurried. The look of a man who has already made his decision and is simply waiting for the world to catch up.

I put my cup down.

"What," I said.

"Nothing," he said. The way men say nothing when it is very much something.

"Daniel."

"Finish your coffee," he said. The look still there. Steady as weather.

I finished my coffee.

He stood up and held out his hand.

"Put your shoes on," he said. "I want to show you something."

The path behind the cabin I'd walked a dozen times. I knew the root that catches your toe, knew where the tree line opened and the light changed quality, knew the sound of the land shifting from tended to older and wilder.

What I didn't know was what was at the end of it.

He'd never taken me this far.

His hand in mine. The June morning doing what June mornings do in northern Michigan when they're being generous — warm without demanding anything of you, the air clean enough to taste, everything green and committed to it. The kind of morning that makes a person think the world has been preparing itself without their knowledge.

The path narrowed. Grass high on both sides, brushing my calves through the white cotton.

Then the willows appeared.

Four of them. Ancient and unhurried as the river itself, their long branches sweeping down to make a room — a private room, green-gold and moving with the breath off the water. And underneath them, hidden from every direction except this one, a bend in a river I hadn't known existed.

I stopped.

He stopped beside me.

I looked at the willows. At the river catching light between their curtains. At the grass beneath them, long and sun-warmed and secret.

Then I looked at him.

He was watching me with that expression. Patient. Certain. The face of a man who has been holding something in his hands for weeks and is finally setting it down.

"You planned this," I said.

"I showed you a river," he said.

"You planned this entire —"

"I showed you a river, Sarah."

I looked at him for a long moment. Then I looked at the white dress. The white cotton dress he'd handed me three weeks ago without explanation, without ceremony, just — here, folded soft, and then nothing. As if it were simply a thing that needed to exist in my possession and the reasons would sort themselves out.

"The dress," I said.

Something moved through his eyes. Not surprise. The satisfaction of a man whose patience has been rewarded.

"What about it," he said.

"You knew I'd wear it today."

"I didn't know anything," he said. "I hoped."

This man.

This specific impossible man who had bought a white cotton dress and said nothing and waited three weeks for a Tuesday in June.

I looked at the river again. At the willows making their green cathedral. At the long warm grass where the light came through in pieces.

Then I smiled at him.

Not sweetly. The other kind.

His breath changed. Just slightly. Just enough.

I let go of his hand and walked to the water's edge.

The cold found my feet before the rest of me was ready for it.

I stood there a moment, just that — the cold working up through my ankles, the current pressing in like something with an opinion. After twenty years of managing everyone else's comfort, there was something almost reckless about a sensation that demanded nothing back. Just: feel this. I did.

I didn't look back at him. Didn't need to. I could feel him watching.

Good.

Let him watch.

I walked in deeper.

The water rose to my calves and the cotton lifted and spread around me, white on the dark water, and I heard him behind me — still not moving, still watching — and I did not look back.

Deeper.

To my knees now, the dress clinging from hem to mid-thigh, the white cotton doing in cold river water exactly what wet white cotton does in morning light, which is considerably less than it does when dry. I was very much aware of that. I was not remotely unhappy about it.

I stopped.

Looked back over my shoulder.

He was standing at the edge with his arms crossed and that look — the hungry one, the one that still surprised me sometimes, because there is a difference between a man performing desire and a man actually feeling it, and Daniel had never once in all our months together performed a single thing.

"Cold," I said.

"Is it," he said.

"Very," I said.

I turned back to the river and walked in deeper.

The water hit my thighs and I gasped — couldn't help it — the cold finding skin that hadn't expected it yet, the dress plastered now from waist to hem, the white cotton in filtered willow-light doing what I'd known it would do from the moment I'd felt his eyes on me that morning while I pulled it over my head and understood, finally, all at once, why he'd handed it to me three weeks ago and said nothing.

He'd been thinking about this.

Three weeks he'd been thinking about this.

I waded in to my waist, the dress spreading around me on the surface, and I turned to face him.

He was in the water.

I hadn't heard him come in. He moved quietly for a man his size — the kind of quiet that comes from a long life of paying attention to things, of knowing when the moment requires stillness and when it requires moving without announcement.

He was looking at me. At the dress. At the places where the dress had stopped performing its customary duties.

"Hi," I said.

"Hi," he said. Voice carrying a quality I had learned to notice.

I liked that. Considerably.

He came to me through the current. Stopped close enough that the water moving around him reached me first, a small advance party, and his hands found my waist beneath the surface — warm against the cold, impossibly warm, the warmth of a man who has been standing in a June morning waiting to touch you.

"I've got you," he said.

"I know," I said.

He lifted me.

One hand beneath my shoulders, one beneath my knees, the river releasing me into his arms the way water releases things it was only holding temporarily. For one suspended moment my feet left the bottom and the current took the weight of everything — the twenty years, the invisibility, the woman who had learned to take up less space — and I felt the specific lightness of something put down that had been carried too long.

The current still moved around us. The willows overhead made their quiet green sound. The morning had arranged itself, patiently, into exactly this.

I went horizontal in his arms.

The cold moved through every inch of the cotton and I looked up at the willows and the pieces of blue sky between them and felt his hands beneath me and thought —

This is what it feels like.

Not the cold. Not the water. Not even him, exactly.

The being held. The actual, deliberate being held by someone who wanted to and had built a Tuesday around it.

I closed my eyes.

That's when his hands changed.

Not position. Quality. They went still in a way that was different from still — the stillness of someone who has felt something unexpected and stopped to be certain of it.

I opened my eyes.

He was looking at me. The hunger still there, but behind it now something more careful had arrived. Something that didn't have a name yet. Something that was going to require one.

"Daniel," I said.

"I know," he said.

"What do you know."

He stood me up slowly. The dress fell against my skin. All of it. The cold having formed strong opinions about every part of me, and those opinions not remotely private in the morning light through the willows. His eyes moved down once — one long, deliberate, entirely unashamed look — and then back to my face. The focused restraint of a man who has decided what this moment deserves.

"Something's different," he said. "In you. The last few weeks — like you were always a frequency I could tune to, and now the signal is—"

"Stronger," I said.

He looked at me a moment.

"Yes," he said.

The river moved around us both. The willows moved. I put my hand flat against his chest — here, just here, feeling his heart — and held it there.

"I feel good," I said. "Better than I have in maybe ever." I looked up at him. "Is that a problem."

His hand came up and covered mine. Pressed it against his heart.

"No," he said.

One word. Carrying everything he wasn't ready to say yet.

We came out of the river.

The grass under the willows was warm from the sun — long and soft and private in the way of things that became themselves without anyone's permission. He spread his jacket on the ground and turned to look at me standing there in the wet dress, the cotton clinging to every decision the cold water had made about my body, the willows moving overhead, the river talking to itself around the bend.

I looked at him looking at me.

Three weeks he'd been thinking about this morning.

I reached for the hem.

His breath changed again — that same almost-imperceptible shift I was learning to listen for, the sound of a patient man reaching the end of his patience.

"Sarah," he said. Low. Not a protest. Something else entirely.

"Nobody's here," I said.

A long look. The willows between us and the world.

"No," he said quietly. "Nobody's here."

The dress came off over her head. The June air found her. His hands found her. The warm grass received them both.

She had been invisible for twenty years.

Here, under these willows, with this man — she was the most visible thing in the world. And she let herself be seen. Completely. Without management. Without the twenty years of practiced smallness. Without checking first whether she was allowed.

It felt like the first honest thing she had done in longer than she could calculate.

His hands on her were different from before — she felt it, and he felt it too, she could tell by the way he went still sometimes in the middle of everything. Not stopping. Receiving. The way a musician goes still when he hears a note he didn't know was in the composition, making sure he has it right before he continues.

The willows moved.

The river talked to itself.

The morning did what it had been planning all along.

Afterward.

Her back against his chest. His arm across her. The June afternoon making no demands.

She looked up through the willows at the pieces of sky.

"You bought that dress on purpose," she said.

"I bought you a dress," he said.

"Three weeks ago."

"I wanted you to have it."

"You wanted me in it," she said. "In a river. On a Tuesday."

The corner of his mouth.

"I wanted you to have it," he said again.

She laughed. Real. Unmanaged. The laugh she'd been finding more of lately — the one that didn't ask permission first, didn't check the room, didn't apologize on the way out the door.

He pulled her closer. His arms holding something he didn't fully understand and had decided to hold anyway.

She felt that. The difference between those two things.

"You're not finished," he said quietly.

She looked up.

"Becoming whatever this is," he said. "You're not finished."

She thought about Emma's hair. About Marcus's hand, the one that had been giving him trouble for years, moving easier lately. About Janet and the glasses she kept reaching for that weren't there anymore.

"No," she said. "I'm not."

He pressed his mouth to her hair. Not a kiss exactly. Something more deliberate than a kiss. A statement.

She exhaled — slow, quiet, the breath of a woman who has been holding something in her chest for longer than she knew, and is only now, here under these willows, setting it down.

I know. And I'm here. Whatever this is, I'm here.

She filed it. Next to the other things she'd been filing.

They dressed slowly.

Her back to him. The dry dress from the bag he'd thought to bring — of course he had, of course — the cotton soft and warm against skin that had been in a river and in June grass and in his arms, and she felt him watching her and she did not rush.

This man. This specific impossible man.

She was going to be in considerable trouble with this man.

She was already in considerable trouble with this man, and she found she did not mind even slightly.

She pulled the dry dress over her head. Turned.

He was watching her with that look. The patient certain one. The one that still surprised her.

"Ready," she said.

"Yes," he said.

The way he said it.

The path back. His hand in hers. The root that catches your toe if you're not watching. The place where the tree line opens and the light changes quality.

The county road appearing through the trees.

And a dark car parked a quarter mile down. Engine off. Still. The quality of stillness that had nothing to do with someone enjoying the countryside.

She kept walking. Hand in his. Didn't break stride.

Noted it the way she was learning to note things now — the way you note weather. Not alarm. Information. Filed it next to the footsteps before she heard them, the phone before it rang, the knowing that arrived quiet and certain and without asking permission.

The car was still there when they reached the driveway.

Gone when she checked from the kitchen window.

She put the kettle on. Said nothing. Tonight was still theirs.

The file could wait.

Chapter 2

CHAPTER TWO: THE MORNING AFTER Sarah

I woke before him.

That's new.

For twenty years of marriage I woke to an alarm because Tom needed the alarm and the alarm needed me and the whole machinery of that life ran on schedule regardless of what any individual body wanted to do.

Daniel sleeps like a man with a clear conscience.

I lay there watching the morning come through the curtains and listening to him breathe and thinking about the river. About the grass. About his hands going still in the middle of everything. That registering. That note he hadn't known was in the piece.

I thought about that for a while.

The jeans were in the chair where I'd left them.

I pulled them on standing at the window while Daniel still slept. Got them to my hips.

Looked down.

Stood there for a moment with the morning light coming in and the waistband loose around me in a way it hadn't been three weeks ago. My hands registered it before my brain did — the absence of the familiar resistance, the fabric simply not finding what it expected to find. And something moved through me that wasn't alarm and wasn't vanity and wasn't any of the feelings women are supposed to have when their bodies change.

Just — interest.

Like my body was making a statement it had been drafting for a long time and had finally decided to send.

I held the waistband out with two fingers.

Two inches. Maybe more.

I looked at myself in the mirror on the back of the door. The woman looking back was not the woman who had walked into that coffee shop six months ago. Same face. Same hair. Same eyes that Daniel said saw things other people missed.

But something had been turned up.

Some dial I hadn't known existed.

I stood there looking at myself for a long time.

"Sarah."

His voice from the bed. Sleep still in it.

"I'm here," I said.

He found me in the mirror. Looked at me standing there holding my jeans away from my waist with two fingers.

He sat up. Crossed to me without saying anything. Stood behind me looking at my reflection.

His hands came to my waist. Slid inside the gap. Warm. Certain. The hands that had been under the water yesterday feeling something the water hadn't. He felt it now. Different under his palms.

He looked at me in the mirror with that careful expression. The one I was learning. The one that meant he was deciding how much of what he felt to say.

"How long," he said.

"I noticed last week," I said. "But probably longer."

He nodded slowly. His hands still at my waist. Inside the gap.

"Does it frighten you," he said.

"No," I said. Surprising myself with how true it was. "Does it frighten you."

He looked at me in the mirror for a long moment.

"Ask me again in a month," he said.

We didn't talk about it over coffee.

We talked about Marcus's gathering on Thursday. About Emma's text that had arrived while we slept — *something happened, call me* — that I'd answered with *calling in ten* and then sat with the phone in my hand for a moment feeling the edges of what Emma's something was before I dialed.

Not good edges. Not terrible. Significant.

Emma answered on the first ring.

"Janet's prescription changed again," she said. No preamble. Emma operates like Daniel that way. "Her optometrist called it unprecedented. She's twenty-twenty now. She's been wearing glasses since she was nine years old, Sarah."

I looked at the window. The county road visible between the trees. No car this morning.

"Did she tell the optometrist anything," I said.

"She said she'd been doing eye exercises." Emma's voice dry as August. "The man wrote it down. Actually wrote it down."

"Good," I said.

"Is it."

"Isn't it."

Emma quiet for a moment. "Marcus called me last night. After you left the barn last week. He wanted to talk about—" She paused. Choosing. "About the pattern. About what's been happening to all of us since you came back."

I waited.

"He's been running these gatherings for eleven years, Sarah," Emma said. "Eleven years and nothing like this. Nobody's eyesight improved. Nobody's—" She stopped again. "He wanted me to know he's not alarmed. He specifically said not alarmed. Which is what you say when you are."

"I know," I said.

"What are we supposed to do with this."

I looked at Daniel across the kitchen. His coffee. His careful face. The hands around the mug that had been under the river water yesterday feeling something.

"Keep going," I said. "Same as before. Thursday. The barn. All of us together."

"And if it keeps accelerating."

"Then it keeps accelerating," I said.

Emma made a sound. Half laugh. Half something else.

"You're different," she said. "From six months ago. You know that."

"I know," I said.

"Good different," she said quickly. "I want to be clear about that. Good different." A pause. "Just — more. More of whatever you always were."

I thought about the jeans. About Daniel's hands in the gap. About the river.

"Yeah," I said. "I think that's right."

He was watching me when I hung up.

"Janet," I said.

"I heard," he said. The cabin being what cabins are in the morning — intimate in ways apartments aren't.

I sat down across from him. We looked at each other over the coffee cups the way people look at each other when something is happening that neither of them has adequate language for and they're both deciding whether to try.

"Daniel," I said.

"Sarah," he said.

"Something is happening."

"Yes."

"To me specifically. But also to the others. Since I—" I stopped. "Since I came back. Since the barn. Something in the group is—"

"Different," he said.

"Accelerating," I said.

He nodded. Looked at his coffee. Looked back at me.

"Marcus called me too," he said. "Last night. While you were sleeping."

I waited.

"He said—" Daniel turned the mug in his hands. "He said he's been feeling something building for weeks. Like a frequency getting stronger. And he thinks—" He stopped.

"What does he think," I said.

"He thinks you're the reason it's building." He looked at me carefully. "He doesn't mean that as pressure. He was specific about that. He said it's not something you're doing. It's something you are. Something that was already—" He paused. "He used the word catalyst."

The word sat between us on the kitchen table.

I looked at my hands. Ordinary hands. The hands that had held my jeans away from my waist this morning. The hands that had been in the river yesterday. The hands that had reached for Emma's call before it came.

"Catalyst for what," I said.

Daniel shook his head.

"He doesn't know," he said. "That's the part that kept him up last night."

I went outside after.

Sat on the back steps with my second coffee, both hands around the mug, the warmth of it the most ordinary thing in the world. Birdsong. Wind in the trees that had been there before any of us and would be there after. The path to the river visible from where I sat, the willows just showing at the far edge.

The morning quiet enough that I could feel my own heartbeat.

I'd been sitting there maybe ten minutes when I felt it.

Not the phone this time. Not footsteps. Something larger.

A shift in the quality of the air. Like pressure changing before weather arrives. The morning still bright and clear — no storm coming, nothing meteorological to explain it.

But something coming.

I sat with it. Let it arrive without reaching for it or pushing it away.

It came in pieces.

A car. Dark. Not the one from yesterday. Different plates. Same stillness. The same quality of attention that had nothing to do with someone enjoying the countryside.

Parked on the county road.

Not visible from the back steps.

I knew it was there anyway.

I sipped my coffee.

Didn't go look.

Knowing was enough. Knowing and staying was different from knowing and reacting. I was learning that. The knowing arrived clean and factual and what you did with it was the part that required thought.

I thought.

Two days in a row wasn't coincidence. Different car, same position, wasn't coincidence. Someone was establishing a pattern. Not trying to hide it entirely — if they wanted to hide it they'd vary the position, vary the timing. This was deliberate visibility. A message delivered in the language of parked cars and notebooks we never see.

We know where you are.

I finished my coffee.

Went inside.

Daniel looked up from the table.

"There's a car on the county road," I said.

He went very still.

"Different from yesterday," I said. "Same position."

He started to stand.

"Don't," I said.

He looked at me.

"Don't go look," I said. "That's what they want. Reaction. Evidence that we know. Evidence that we're—" I sat down. "Frightened."

He sat back down slowly. Looked at me across the table.

"How do you know there's a car," he said carefully. "You've been on the back steps."

I met his eyes.

Didn't answer.

Watched him work it out. Watched his face do the thing it had done in the river — the registering, the note he hadn't known was in the piece arriving again, slightly louder than before.

"Sarah," he said. Quiet.

"I know," I said.

"How long has—"

"A while," I said. "Getting stronger."

He looked at his hands on the table. My hands on the table. The space between them.

Then he reached across and covered my hands with his. I felt the weight of them — not just warmth this time, but ballast. The specific gravity of a man who has decided something and is telling you without words.

Not frightened.

Not yet.

Something before frightened. Something that was paying very close attention.

"Thursday," he said. "We talk to Marcus."

"Yes," I said.

"All of it."

"All of it," I agreed.

His hands over mine.

The car on the county road doing what it was there to do.

Both of us at the kitchen table deciding the same thing without saying it.

Not small.

Not going back.

Not eve

Chapter 3

CHAPTER THREE: THURSDAY

Sarah

The barn smells like old wood and lantern oil and something underneath both of those things that I've never been able to name.

The first time Marcus brought me here I thought it was just a barn. Weathered boards. Mismatched chairs arranged in a loose circle. A woodstove in the corner that threw more heat than its size suggested. Nothing remarkable.

Then the people arrived and I understood.

It wasn't the barn.

It was what happened in the barn when these specific people were in it together. The quality of attention. The way conversation moved differently here than anywhere else. The way nobody performed anything. Nobody managed their impression. Nobody said I'm fine when they weren't or laughed at things that weren't funny or made themselves agreeable at the expense of being true.

Eleven years Marcus had been running these Thursday nights.

I'd been coming for six months.

And something had changed.

I felt it walking in — not metaphorically. The way you feel a room that's been holding heat all day, a warmth that gets into the chest before the mind registers it. Something had been building in here, quiet and patient, and tonight it was closer to the surface than it had been.

Daniel felt it too — his hand tightened slightly on mine at the door before he released it and we came in separately the way we usually did. Not hiding. Just — keeping what was ours to ourselves while we were here. The group knew about us. They knew everything eventually. But there's a difference between known and displayed and we both preferred known.

Marcus was at the woodstove.

He looked up when I came in. That look again. The one he'd been giving me for three weeks. Careful. Measuring. Not unfriendly — Marcus is constitutionally incapable of unfriendly — but serious in a way that had a question underneath it he hadn't asked yet.

Tonight he was going to ask it.

I could feel that too.

Emma was already there. She'd saved me the chair beside hers the way she always did and handed me coffee the way she always did and looked at me over the rim of her own cup with the look that meant she had things to say and was deciding the order.

"Janet's here," she said quietly.

I found Janet across the circle. Sixty-something. Reading glasses perpetually perched on her head for twenty years because her arms weren't long enough to hold things far enough away. The glasses weren't there tonight.

She caught me looking. Touched the top of her head where they should have been. Smiled. The smile of someone who keeps reaching for something that isn't there anymore and finding the absence more remarkable than the presence ever was.

"Twenty-twenty," Emma murmured beside me.

"I heard," I said.

"Her optometrist is writing a paper apparently."

"About what."

"He doesn't know yet," Emma said. "That's why he's writing it."

Marcus called the gathering to order the way he always does, which is not calling it to order at all but simply sitting down and going quiet in a way that invites everyone else to do the same.

The circle settled.

Twelve people tonight. Usual faces. The quiet man called Robert who spoke rarely and precisely. Diane who had been coming eleven years, almost as long as Marcus, and carried that history in the way she sat — like someone who had learned to be patient with the pace of important things. Tom — different Tom, not my Tom, a Tom I'd chosen to reclaim the name from in my own mind — who worked nights and came to Thursday gatherings still half-asleep and woke up incrementally over the course of the evening in a way that was quietly fascinating to watch.

Daniel in the chair across the circle from me.

Not looking at me.

Which meant he was very aware of me.

We'd developed a whole language of not-looking.

Marcus looked at each of them in turn. The slow survey of someone taking inventory not of attendance but of something less measurable.

Then he looked at me.

"Something's happening," he said. To the group. But to me.

Nobody disagreed. Nobody looked surprised. That was the thing about this group. You didn't have to convince them that something was happening. They'd all felt it. Had been feeling it for weeks. Had been not-saying it the way you don't-say things when the saying of them makes them real and real things have consequences and consequences require decisions.

"I want to talk about it," Marcus said. "Openly. All of it. Whatever anyone has noticed."

Silence.

Then Diane: "My garden."

Marcus waited.

"I have a black thumb," she said. "Twenty years in that house. Nothing survives me. I've killed succulents." A pause. "Three weeks ago I planted tomatoes. I don't know why. I never plant tomatoes. I was at the hardware store for something else entirely and I walked out with six plants and potting soil and I have no explanation for that." She looked at her hands. "They're already eight inches tall. I've never grown anything eight inches tall. My neighbor asked what I was doing differently and I told her I'd been getting more sleep."

Quiet laughter around the circle. Not dismissive. The laughter of recognition.

"My sleep," Robert said. One of his rare contributions, delivered with the precision of someone who has considered the words before releasing them. "I've slept poorly for fifteen years. Two hours here. Three there. Medication that helped sometimes." He paused. "Six weeks ago it changed. I sleep seven hours. I wake rested." He looked at his hands. "I told my doctor. He adjusted my chart and told me bodies do surprising things." A pause. "He seemed personally affronted by it."

More laughter. Warmer this time.

Marcus was listening with his eyes moving slowly around the circle. His left hand resting on his knee. The hand that had been curled and careful for three years. Resting flat now. Open. Easy.

I watched it.

He caught me watching.

"Six weeks," he said quietly. Answering the question I hadn't asked.

Six weeks ago I'd come back.

The door opened.

Cold air moving through the barn and with it two women I didn't recognize.

Then I looked again.

I recognized one of them.

Rachel. The nurse. I'd seen her twice before at the edges of gatherings — quiet, watchful, the particular stillness of someone deciding whether to trust a thing before committing to it. Dark hair. Practical hands. The look of someone who had been carrying something heavy for a long time and had gotten very good at not showing the weight.

The woman beside her I'd never seen.

Sixty. Maybe older. White hair loose around a face that had good bones underneath something that had been through considerable difficulty. She was wearing clothes that didn't quite fit — slightly too large, slightly wrong — the way clothes are wrong when someone else chose them for you. She moved carefully. Not infirm. Careful. The way you move when you've learned that the world sometimes shifts under your feet without warning and you've adjusted your relationship with gravity accordingly.

She stopped just inside the door.

Looked at the circle of people looking at her.

Her eyes went around the room.

When they reached me they stopped.

Something moved through my sternum — not pain, not quite — the physical sensation of a connection made at a frequency I didn't have a name for yet. Like standing at one end of a taut wire and feeling someone touch the other end. My breath steadied itself without my permission. My hands in my lap went still.

She knew something about me.

I knew something about her.

Neither of us knew what yet.

Marcus stood up. Crossed to them. The way Marcus crosses a room — unhurried, certain, the movement of someone who has decided something and is simply closing the distance between decision and action.

He reached them. Looked at the woman with the white hair. She looked back at him.

Something passed between them that the rest of us weren't privy to. Quick. Wordless. The recognition of people who have been through the same specific thing from different sides of it.

"I'm Marcus," he said.

"Grace," she said. Her voice careful. Like something she was learning to use again after not using it.

He offered his hand. She looked at it for a moment. Then took it.

His left hand — the one that had been curled and careful — holding hers with a steadiness that three months ago it wouldn't have had.

She felt that. I could see her feel it. Her eyes went to their joined hands and back to his face and something in her expression shifted. Fractionally. The way ice shifts before it decides to melt.

"Come sit down," he said.

She came.

Rachel sat beside me. After a moment she leaned slightly toward me and said very quietly: "Thank you."

I looked at her.

"For asking," she said. "At the facility. For the question you asked me that I couldn't answer then."

I remembered the corridor. The woman who had told me she couldn't see anymore. The question I'd asked Rachel that had felt too large for that fluorescent hallway.

Do you ever wonder if they're right to keep her here.

"How is she," I said.

Rachel looked at Grace across the circle. At Marcus sitting beside her. At their hands — his left, her right, still connected in the particular way of people who have just found something solid and aren't ready to let go of it yet.

"Getting there," Rachel said.

Then quietly: "She's the bravest person I've ever met."

The gathering moved differently tonight.

The conversation that usually built slowly found its depth faster. The things people had been circling for weeks coming out more directly. Janet's eyesight. Robert's sleep. Diane's tomatoes. Three other people with smaller stranger things they'd been sitting with privately — a sense of direction that hadn't failed them once in six weeks, a dream that had told them something true, a moment of knowing so clean and clear they'd written it down before it could be explained away.

Grace said nothing. Listened to everything. Her face doing something gradual and private. Like a room filling slowly with light from a source you couldn't identify.

Halfway through the evening Marcus poured tea. Brought her a cup. His left hand steady on the saucer.

She watched the hand.

"How long," she said. Quiet. Just for him.

"Three weeks," he said.

She nodded. Understanding something the rest of us were only adjacent to.

"Mine will come back," she said. Not question. Not quite statement.

"Yes," Marcus said. Equal certainty.

He sat back down beside her. Close enough that their shoulders almost touched. Neither of them moved away.

After.

The group dispersing into the cold Thursday night. Cars starting. Voices carrying in the dark. The particular warmth of people who have been honest with each other in the same room moving back out into a world that requires more careful management.

Daniel found me at my car.

We stood in the cold with the barn light behind us.

"Grace," he said.

"Yes," I said.

"What Rachel did—"

"Yes."

He looked at the barn. At the light through the old boards. At the shadow of Marcus and Grace still inside — two people not rushing whatever was beginning between them.

"She could lose everything," he said. "Rachel. What she did is—"

"Yes," I said. "She knows."

He looked at me. The cold between us doing nothing to diminish the warmth of him standing close.

"Are you alright," he said.

I thought about the wire pulled taut between me and Grace when she'd looked at me from the door. The knowing that had arrived in the barn larger than it arrived anywhere else. The word catalyst sitting on the table in my kitchen this morning. The car on the county road.

The jeans in the chair.

His hands in the gap.

"I'm more than alright," I said.

He searched my face. Found what he was looking for. Reached out and tucked a strand of hair behind my ear — simple, deliberate — his fingers trailing along my jaw after, just for a moment, before he dropped his hand.

The charged ordinary moment.

Added to the collection.

"Let's go home," he said.

I looked back at the barn once. Grace and Marcus inside. Two people finding each other in the wreckage of what had been done to them. Rachel's courage sitting in the air like something that had changed the composition of it. Twelve people carrying their impossible quiet changes back out into the world.

And something else.

Something I'd felt building all evening and hadn't named yet.

A frequency. Getting stronger.

I got in the car.

We drove home on the county road. No dark car tonight.

Which was almost worse.

Because the dark car was information. The absence of it was a question.

I sat with that question, and with Grace's face at the door, and with Marcus's left hand steady on a saucer, and with Rachel's quiet *she's the bravest person I've ever met* — all of it settling into my chest like stones finding the bottom of still water.

Heavy. But mine. Every bit of it mine now.

I reached across and put my hand on his knee.

He put his hand over mine.

We drove home in the good silence. The kind that doesn't need filling. The kind that knows what it is.

Chapter 4

CHAPTER FOUR: WHAT RACHEL KNOWS Rachel

The night shift has a sound.

Not silence — people think hospitals go quiet at night and they don't. They go different. The particular acoustics of a building running on reduced staff and fluorescent light, where every footstep carries farther and the absence of daytime noise makes the sounds that remain more distinct. The cart wheel that needs oil. The ventilation system cycling. The specific quality of a door closing on a ward where people are trying to sleep and mostly aren't.

Rachel had worked nights for six years.

She knew every sound in this building the way you know the sounds of a house you've lived in long enough — not by listening for them but by noticing when they're wrong.

Nothing was wrong tonight.

She stood at the medication cart outside room 14 and did what she'd been doing for nine months.

She looked at the chart.

She looked at the pills in the small paper cup.

She looked at the number.

Then she looked down the corridor toward room 14 where Grace Ellison, sixty-three years old, former high school English teacher, had been admitted nine months ago on a 5150 hold initiated by her two adult children who had described her behavior as delusional, erratic, and a danger to herself.

Rachel had read the intake paperwork the day Grace arrived.

She'd read it the way she read all intake paperwork — efficiently, clinically, extracting the relevant medical information and filing the rest.

What she hadn't been able to file was the look on Grace's face in the first photograph. Not the admission photo — the one the daughter had included, presumably to illustrate the before. Grace at a backyard gathering of some kind. Summer. Laughing at something outside the frame.

Radiant was the word that had arrived in Rachel's mind and declined to leave.

Not happy exactly. Something larger than happy. The specific luminosity of a person who is completely present in their own life.

Rachel had looked at that photograph for longer than was strictly professional.

Then she'd looked at Grace in room 14.

The same woman. Technically. Same face, same white hair, same hands — a teacher's hands, Rachel had noted, the particular calluses of someone who'd spent decades holding chalk and pens.

But the light was gone.

Not medicated-away gone. Not sedated-flat gone. Something more specific than that. The light had been present and then something had happened — not a breakdown, Rachel had decided within the first two weeks, whatever the chart said — and the light had been interrupted. Like a power line in a storm. The source was still there. The capacity was still there.

The current had simply been cut.

Nine months ago Rachel had noted this clinically, professionally, and moved on.

Eight months ago she had started paying attention.

Seven months ago she had started asking questions she didn't write down anywhere.

Six months ago she had started with the doses.

She looked at the number in the cup.

Looked at the chart.

Made a decision that was the same decision she'd been making for six months, incremental, careful, the kind of decision you could almost convince yourself wasn't a decision at all because you made it so quietly and so slowly that it never felt like a line being crossed — just a long walk in one direction that you'd started so gradually you couldn't identify the moment it began.

She adjusted the number.

Put the cup on the tray.

Walked to room 14.

Grace was awake.

She was usually awake when Rachel came. Had started being awake at this hour approximately four months ago, which corresponded with nothing in her chart and everything in Rachel's private observation log that she kept in a notebook at home and would burn before she let anyone read it.

She was sitting up in the bed with her hands folded in her lap and her eyes on the window that showed her nothing but her own reflection and the dark beyond it.

"Ms. Ellison," Rachel said.

"Grace," she said. She'd been asking Rachel to call her Grace for three months. Rachel had been resisting for professional reasons that were becoming increasingly difficult to defend.

"Grace," Rachel said.

Something shifted in the woman's face. Small. The fractional acknowledgment of someone keeping careful track of small victories because small victories were the available kind.

Rachel set the tray down. Did what she was there to do. Noted the responses, the clarity of Grace's eyes tonight — better than last week, better than the week before, the return of something measured and present in her gaze that had no pharmaceutical explanation Rachel was willing to write in a chart.

"You slept," Rachel said. Not question. She'd checked.

"Some," Grace said.

"Better than Tuesday."

"Yes." Grace looked at her hands. The teacher's hands. "I dreamed."

Rachel made a note. "About what."

Grace was quiet for a moment. "My classroom," she said finally. "The good year. The year I had the junior class that actually wanted to read." A pause. "I dreamed it the way it actually was. Not distorted. Not the way dreams usually are." She looked up at Rachel. "I haven't dreamed anything true in nine months."

Rachel wrote it down.

Kept her face the way she'd trained her face to be in this corridor — professional, attentive, offering nothing that could be noted in someone else's chart.

But her hand, writing, was not entirely steady.

"That's a good sign," she said.

Grace looked at her with those eyes that were getting clearer every week.

"You think so," Grace said. Not asking whether Rachel thought it was medically positive. Asking something else. Something that had been building between them for months in the particular way things build between two people in a small room in the middle of the night when one of them is pretending not to know what she knows.

"Yes," Rachel said. Meeting her eyes. Giving her that much. "I think so."

Grace nodded. Looked back at her hands.

"My daughter called today," she said.

Rachel waited.

"She wanted to know how I was progressing." The word progressing delivered with a delicacy that contained considerable weight. "She said the doctor told her I was responding well to the treatment plan."

Rachel said nothing.

"Am I," Grace said. "Responding to the treatment plan."

The corridor outside was quiet. The ventilation system cycling. The cart wheel that needed oil somewhere on the floor above.

"You're doing well," Rachel said carefully. "Your numbers look good."

Grace looked at her for a long moment.

"My numbers," she said.

"Yes."

Another long moment.

"Rachel," Grace said.

It was the first time she'd used Rachel's name. In nine months of nightly visits she had always said the nurse or just looked at her directly with those increasingly clear eyes.

Rachel went very still.

"Whatever you're doing," Grace said quietly. "Thank you."

Rachel picked up the tray.

"Get some sleep," she said. Professional. Steady. The voice she used when she needed to leave a room before her face did something that would be difficult to explain.

She was three steps down the corridor before she stopped.

Stood there.

The fluorescent light above her making its faint sound. The cart wheel somewhere above. Her own heartbeat doing something irregular that had nothing to do with her cardiovascular health.

She thought about the woman in the photograph. Radiant. Present. Completely alive in her own life.

She thought about what had been done to that woman.

What was still being done.

She thought about the questions she'd stopped writing down. About the medication numbers she'd been adjusting for six months with the careful patience of someone who understood that you don't correct a slow wrong with a fast fix. About the notebook at home that she would burn before she let anyone read it.

About the gathering she'd been to twice at the edges. The barn. The circle of people who didn't perform anything. The woman — Sarah — who had looked at her in a corridor three weeks ago and asked a question too large for that fluorescent hallway and had clearly already known the answer.

Do you ever wonder if they're right to keep her here.

No, Rachel had thought, standing in that corridor with her professional face on and her hands steady and her heart doing what it was doing now.

No. I have never once wondered that.

She walked back to the medication cart.

Looked at the chart.

Looked at the corridor.

Made a different kind of decision.

Not incremental. Not the long slow walk she'd been taking for six months.

This one had a date on it.

Thursday.

She was early to the barn.

Pulled into the gravel lot with Grace in the passenger seat — Grace who had walked out of the facility at 2am in clothes Rachel had brought from her own closet, slightly too large, slightly wrong — and sat for a moment with the engine running looking at the old weathered boards and the light coming through them and listening to the woman beside her breathe the specific breathing of someone who has just been given back the air.

"You don't have to go in," Rachel said.

"I know," Grace said.

"We could just—"

"Rachel." Grace's voice. Quiet and clear and carrying something that hadn't been in it nine months ago or eight months ago or last week. "I know what I want to do."

Rachel looked at her.

The bones in that face. The white hair loose because Rachel hadn't thought to bring a hair tie and Grace hadn't asked for one. The eyes in the dark of the car finding Rachel's with a steadiness that made Rachel's chest do something complicated.

"Okay," Rachel said.

They got out of the car.

Walked to the barn door.

Grace stopped just outside it. Rachel stopped beside her. The cold air. The light through the boards. The sound of voices inside going quiet as they pushed the door open.

And then the barn full of faces turning toward them.

Rachel felt it — whatever it was that happened in that barn, the frequency she'd felt at the edges twice before — felt it fully for the first time, standing in the doorway with Grace beside her. It moved through her like warm water. Like something her body recognized before her mind did.

She looked for faces she knew.

Found Sarah's immediately.

Watched Sarah's expression as her eyes went to Grace and something moved across her face — not surprise, not quite — the recognition of someone who has been expecting something without knowing they were.

And then Marcus was crossing the room.

Rachel had seen Marcus at the two previous gatherings. Had noted him the way she noted things she didn't have immediate categories for — carefully, without conclusion. Steady man. Patient. The particular stillness of someone who had been awake for a long time and had made his peace with what that cost.

He came to them.

Looked at Grace.

Something moved between them that Rachel observed from three feet away and could not have described in clinical language if her career depended on it.

She watched Grace look at his left hand when he offered it.

Watched her take it.

Watched Marcus's face in the moment Grace's hand was in his — a man receiving something he'd stopped expecting, recognizing it precisely, not rushing a single thing.

Rachel exhaled.

She hadn't known she'd been holding it.

She found a chair beside Sarah. Sat down. And after a moment, because she had been carrying it since 2am and her body was tired and the barn was warm and whatever moved in this air was doing what it did — she leaned slightly toward the woman beside her.

"Thank you," she said. "For the question you asked me."

Sarah looked at her.

"How is she," Sarah said.

Rachel looked at Grace across the circle. At Marcus beside her. At the two of them not moving away from each other.

"Getting there," Rachel said.

She watched Marcus pour tea. Watched his left hand on the saucer — steady, open, nothing like what she'd seen in him two months ago at the edges of things when that hand had been careful and curled.

She watched Grace watch the hand.

Watched something in Grace's face decide something.

Rachel had spent nine months reading faces in fluorescent hallways. She knew what a decision looked like when it arrived.

This one looked like morning.

After.

The parking lot. Cold. Cars leaving. Rachel stood beside her car with her keys in her hand and the full weight of the evening and the night before it and the nine months before that settling into her shoulders all at once.

She'd just committed a felony.

She knew that. Had known it at 2am standing in the corridor outside room 14 with the decision already made. Knew it now with the cold finding the back of her neck and her keys in her hand and the barn light behind her.

She was not, she noted with some clinical interest, as frightened as she'd expected to be.

What she was was tired.

The particular exhaustion of someone who has been quietly doing the right thing for a very long time in very small increments and has just done a large version of it all at once and needs a moment to let her nervous system catch up with her conscience.

She was standing there doing exactly that when the voice came from her left.

"You know what you just did."

Not a question.

She turned.

The man was leaning against the car beside hers with his arms crossed and the particular stillness of someone who has been there long enough to be part of the landscape. She hadn't seen him arrive. Hadn't seen him inside either. He existed in the barn the way certain people existed in certain spaces — present without announcing it.

Forty, maybe. Dark jacket. The posture of someone who had spent time in situations where posture was not optional. Not threatening. But the kind of not-threatening that came from discipline rather than absence of capability.

He was looking at her with an expression she couldn't immediately categorize.

Not judgment.

Not alarm.

Something more like recognition.

"Yes," she said. "I know what I did."

He looked at her for a long moment. The cold between them. The barn light. Her keys in her hand and the full freight of the evening in her shoulders.

"David," he said.

"Rachel," she said.

He nodded. Looked at the barn. At the light through the old boards. At the door where Grace and Marcus were still visible inside, not rushing whatever was beginning between them.

"The woman you brought," he said. "She was a patient."

"Yes."

"And you—"

"Yes."

He was quiet for a moment.

"That took a while," he said. "To decide."

"Nine months," she said.

Something moved across his face. Quick. There and gone.

"Okay," he said. Just that. The single syllable carrying a weight she didn't have the energy to fully assess right now.

He pushed off from the car.

Stood in front of her. Not close. The correct distance. The distance of someone who understands that a woman standing alone in a cold parking lot at night after the night she'd just had does not need a man invading her space. Someone who had thought about that. Who thought about things like that.

"There are things you should know," he said. "About what comes next. About how to protect yourself." He paused. "About how to make sure what you did tonight doesn't get undone."

Rachel looked at him.

The tiredness still there. But underneath it something else arriving. Something her body was registering before her mind had fully processed the evening or this man or the particular quality of attention he was paying her — the kind of attention that sees the whole person, not just the situation.

She was a practical woman.

She noted it.

Filed it.

"Okay," she said.

The corner of his mouth moved. Not quite a smile. Something that might become one under the right conditions.

"You should eat something first," he said. "You look like you haven't since yesterday."

She hadn't.

"There's a diner," he said. "Open all night. Good coffee."

Rachel looked at her keys. At the barn. At this man who had appeared from the edge of things and was offering her coffee and information and the specific steady presence of someone who knew what to do after the kind of night she'd just had.

Practical, she reminded herself.

Be practical.

"I need to check on Grace first," she said.

"I know," he said.

She went back inside.

Marcus had Grace in a chair by the woodstove and was telling her something quiet that was making her face do what Rachel had been waiting nine months to see it do — open, present, the light not fully back yet but clearly, unmistakably, on its way.

Rachel stood in the doorway for a moment.

Just that.

Then she turned around.

David was still there.

Of course he was.

"Okay," she said. "Coffee."

He fell into step beside her. Not too close. The correct distance.

They walked to his truck.

The cold doing what cold does in northern Michigan in the dark — honest about itself, no pretense, just the actual temperature of the actual night.

Rachel thought she could work with that.

She thought she could work with a lot of things she hadn't expected at the beginning of this evening.

She did not examine that thought too closely.

Not yet.

The diner was warm and bright and smelled like coffee that had been on since morning and pie that had been good at noon and was still acceptable at midnight and Rachel slid into the booth across from David and wrapped both hands around the mug the waitress brought without asking and felt the warmth move through her palms the way the barn's frequency had moved through her earlier.

Something her body recognized.

Before her mind did.

She looked at him across the table. This man from the edges of things who had been watching and had seen what she'd done and had said *okay* like it was sufficient and it had been.

"Tell me what I need to know," she said.

He told her.

She listened the way she listened to things that mattered — completely, without interrupting, filing everything and asking the three precise questions at the end that told him, she could see, something about who she was.

He answered them without hesitation.

When he was done she looked at her coffee.

Looked at him.

"Why are you helping me," she said.

He considered the question with the seriousness it deserved.

"Because what you did was right," he said. "And right things need protecting."

Rachel looked at him for a long moment.

The diner warm. The coffee real. The night outside doing what northern Michigan nights do in the dark — indifferent, cold, enormous.

She was, she noted, no longer quite as tired as she'd been in the parking lot.

That was probably information.

She filed it where she was filing things.

"Okay," she said. "Then let's talk about what comes next."

He nodded.

The corner of his mouth again.

Closer to a smile this time.

Rachel decided not to notice.

She was, after all, a practical woman.

She noticed anyway.

Chapter 5

CHAPTER FIVE: THE KNOWING BEGINS Sarah

The phone rang at 7:14 on a Tuesday morning.

I knew it was Emma before it rang.

Not the second before, not the half-breath of premonition that could still be explained away as coincidence or pattern recognition or the brain doing what brains do when they've catalogued enough data to start making predictions.

A full minute before.

I was standing at the kitchen window with my coffee watching the tree line and the county road beyond it and thinking about nothing in particular when it arrived — clean, quiet, factual as weather — Emma is going to call.

I watched the second hand on the clock above the stove.

Watched it.

At 7:14 the phone rang.

I let it ring once before I picked it up. Some instinct I didn't examine suggesting that answering on the first ring might require an explanation I wasn't ready to give.

"Emma," I said.

A pause.

"I was going to say good morning first," she said.

"Good morning."

"How did you—" She stopped. Reconsidered. Emma was good at reconsidering. "Never mind. Can you come Thursday early? Before the gathering. Marcus wants to talk to the three of us."

"Yes," I said.

"I'll tell him." Another pause, smaller this time. "Sarah."

"I know," I said.

"Do you."

"Yes."

She was quiet for a moment. Emma's silences had textures. This one was the texture of someone standing at the edge of something large trying to decide if the ground was solid.

"Okay," she said finally. "Thursday. Six o'clock."

She hung up.

I stood at the window with the phone in my hand and the coffee going cool and the tree line doing what tree lines do in northern Michigan in the morning — holding the dark a little longer than the open sky, keeping its own counsel.

The county road was empty.

I noted the emptiness the way I'd been noting the cars. Both were information. The car said *we see you.* The empty road said *we're letting you think we've stopped.*

I didn't think they'd stopped.

I put the phone down.

Picked up my coffee.

Thought about Emma's voice and the minute before it arrived and the clean factual quality of the knowing — not a feeling, not intuition, not any of the soft imprecise words people used when they wanted to describe something real without committing to its reality.

Just — knowledge.

Arriving without a source.

Like light arriving without a visible sun.

Daniel noticed on Wednesday.

We were in the kitchen again — the kitchen had become the place where the important things happened between us, some domestic gravity that made it the room where neither of us could perform anything — and I was making eggs and not looking at him and he was reading something and not looking at me and the cabin was doing its cabin thing, holding us in its easy intimacy, when he said:

"You did it again."

I turned the eggs.

"What did I do."

"You moved to the left before I reached past you," he said. "I was going to reach past you for the pepper and you moved before I got up."

"I heard you shift in the chair," I said.

"You were at the stove. The eggs were making noise."

I turned the eggs again.

"Sarah."

"Daniel."

"How many times this week," he said.

I thought about it honestly. The eggs needed an honest answer and so did he.

"I've stopped counting," I said. "Small things. The phone. Your coffee cup before you ask for it. Emma's call yesterday." I turned the eggs one more time and took them off the heat. "Once — just once — the car on the road before I could possibly have seen it."

The kitchen was quiet.

The eggs cooling.

"Tell me about the car," he said. His voice careful. The voice he used when he was managing something large by taking it in small pieces.

I put the plates on the table and sat down across from him.

"Three days ago," I said. "You were in the shower. I was in the bedroom and I knew — the same way I knew about Emma's call — I knew there was a car on the road. Dark. Still. I went to the window and there it was." I looked at my eggs. "It was gone before you came out of the shower."

He looked at his plate.

At his fork.

At some middle distance that wasn't either of us.

"Did you consider telling me," he said.

"I'm telling you now," I said.

"Wednesday."

"Yes."

He picked up his fork. Put it down again. Looked at me with the expression I had the most complicated relationship with — the one that was love and fear occupying the same space without apparent conflict, neither one canceling the other out.

"Does it hurt," he said. "When it happens."

The question surprised me. Not because it was wrong but because it was so specifically right — the question of someone who had been sitting with his fear long enough to move through it to concern.

"No," I said. "It doesn't feel like anything. That's the strange part." I thought about how to say it accurately. "It just — arrives. The way you know it's raining without looking out the window. You just know. The knowing has no texture, no drama, no—" I stopped. "No announcement."

He looked at me for a long time.

"Marcus," he said.

"Thursday," I said.

He picked up his fork.

We ate our eggs.

The cabin held us in its quiet.

Outside the morning was doing what mornings do when they're not required to perform anything — just being the morning, honest, unhurried, the light coming through the trees at the angle particular to this time and this place and no other.

I watched Daniel eat.

Watched him process the thing he was processing in the methodical way he processed things — not avoiding it, not rushing it, just working through it at the pace it required.

I had learned to love that about him.

The patience with difficulty.

The willingness to stay in the room with things that were uncomfortable until they became, if not comfortable, at least known.

"Ask me again in a month," he'd said about whether it frightened him.

We were at three weeks.

I didn't ask.

But I watched his hands on the fork and thought about how those hands had gone still in the river water and I thought — he's closer to an answer than he thinks he is.

It happened three more times before Thursday.

Once with the coffee — his cup empty, him reading, me knowing before he moved or shifted or gave any physical indication that the cup was empty and he wanted more. I poured it. He looked up. Neither of us said anything.

Once with Emma's second call — Wednesday evening, not the content this time but the fact of it, the phone sitting on the counter and me looking at it thirty seconds before it lit up. I turned away before it rang. I didn't want to watch myself know things.

And once that wasn't small at all.

I was in the garden — we'd started calling it a garden, the patch behind the cabin where Daniel had planted things in April with the optimism of someone who had decided to be attached to this place — and I was pulling something that had gotten out of hand and not thinking about anything except the dirt and the specific satisfaction of removing a thing from where it had decided to be against your wishes.

The sky was clear.

The county road invisible from where I was crouching.

And then the knowing arrived. Not clean this time. Not the quiet factual certainty of the phone or the coffee cup. This one had a different quality — rougher, urgent, the difference between weather arriving and weather that has already decided what it's going to do.

A car.

But not parked this time.

Moving.

Slowing.

I stood up.

Stayed in the garden. Didn't go to the road. Everything in me going still the way prey goes still — not fear, something older than fear, the animal intelligence underneath the thinking mind that knows when something is being assessed.

The car slowed to almost stopped.

I felt it.

Then it continued.

I stood in the garden for a long time after.

The dirt on my hands. The thing I'd been pulling still in my fist. The sky overhead the same clear blue it had been before the car.

Nothing had happened.

And yet.

I went inside and washed my hands and stood at the kitchen sink looking at the water running over them and thought about the difference between surveillance and whatever that had been.

Surveillance watches.

What I'd just felt was something being evaluated.

Something being measured against a threshold.

I dried my hands.

Made tea I didn't drink.

Called nobody.

There was nothing to say yet. Nothing specific enough to say. Just the knowing and the quality of it and the fact that the quality had changed in a way I didn't have language for and wasn't sure I wanted.

Daniel came in from outside an hour later.

Looked at me at the kitchen table with the untouched tea.

Looked at my face.

Sat down across from me.

"Tell me," he said.

So I told him.

He listened the way he listened — completely, without interrupting, his hands flat on the table, his eyes on my face the whole time.

When I finished he was quiet for a long moment.

"Thursday," he said.

"Thursday," I said.

His hands moved across the table and covered mine.

The weight of them. The ballast of them. A man who had decided something and kept deciding it every time the thing got harder.

We sat there for a while.

The tea going cold between us.

The afternoon light moving through the kitchen the way light moves when it isn't in a hurry.

Both of us sitting with the fact that the file was getting thicker and the knowing was getting stronger and Thursday was still two days away and the quality of what was watching them from the county road had shifted in a way that neither of them had adequate language for.

Both of us not saying that.

Both of us knowing it anyway.

The particular intimacy of two people sitting in a kitchen at the exact edge of something they can't see yet and choosing — actively, quietly, without ceremony — to stay.

I thought about the first morning.

The jeans in the chair.

His hands in the gap.

Ask me again in a month.

One week left on that month.

I looked at him across the cold tea.

He was already looking at me.

"Whatever it is," he said. Not finishing the sentence.

He didn't need to.

"I know," I said.

"I mean it."

"I know you mean it," I said. "That's the part that keeps me here."

Something moved through his face.

He turned my hands over in his.

Looked at them. The hands that knew things before they happened. The ordinary hands that had become something he was still learning the dimensions of.

He pressed his mouth to them.

Not a kiss exactly.

The same thing he'd done in the river.

A statement.

I filed it.

The file getting heavy now.

Getting ready.

Thursday coming.

Chapter 6

CHAPTER SIX: WHAT DANIEL HOLDS Sarah

He almost asked me on a Monday.

I felt it coming three days before he said anything — not the phone-before-it-rings kind of knowing, something older and more personal than that. The specific atmospheric pressure of a man carrying a question he hasn't decided whether to release.

I recognized it the way you recognize weather you've been watching build.

I didn't say anything.

I waited.

We'd been living in the particular sweetness of new domesticity — the kind that arrives after the first strangeness of sharing space wears off and before anything has had time to calcify into habit. His coffee cup on the left side of the drain board. My books in three different rooms because I never finish one before starting another and he had stopped mentioning it. The path to the river worn a little more visible each week from the frequency of our going.

Good days.

The kind of days that feel like something you've been owed for a long time finally arriving.

And underneath them, steady as a second heartbeat, his fear.

Not of me. I want to be precise about that because imprecision here would be a disservice to both of us. Not of me, not of what was happening, not even exactly of what was coming — though that was in it too.

Fear of losing it.

All of it. The coffee cup on the left side. The books in three rooms. The path worn visible by the frequency of our going.

Fear of what I was becoming — not that it was wrong, not that it was frightening in itself — fear of what it made possible. What it made probable. Fear wearing the face of love, which is the most convincing disguise fear has ever found.

I understood it.

I held it gently, in the part of me that held things quietly while I waited for him to find his way to saying them.

Monday arrived.

We were in the kitchen.

The light in the morning had a particular quality that week — late October finding its angles, the sun lower and more honest, coming through the window at the slant that turned ordinary things gold. His coffee. The grain of the table. His hands around the mug.

I was at the counter with my back to him.

He shifted in his chair.

Opened his mouth.

I felt it — the gathering of breath before words, the particular quality of air in a room where something important is about to be said.

I turned around.

He was looking at his coffee.

"Daniel," I said.

"It's nothing," he said.

It was not nothing.

I came and sat across from him. Left my coffee on the counter. Sat down with my hands flat on the table and my eyes on his face and waited with the patience of a woman who has learned that some things cannot be hurried without being broken.

He looked at his coffee.

At the table.

At his hands.

Then at me.

"I want to ask you something," he said. "And I need you to know before I ask it that I already know it's the wrong question."

I waited.

"Is there a way—" He stopped. "Is there any possibility of—" He stopped again. Looked at his hands. Something moving through his face that was complicated and honest and cost him something to let me see. "I was going to ask you if there was a way to slow it down."

The kitchen was quiet.

The light doing its gold thing on the table between us.

"To slow it down," I said.

"Yes." His jaw tightened once. "I know. I know what I'm asking and I know why it's wrong and I know—" He exhaled. "I know exactly what I'm asking you to do and who I'm asking you to be while you do it and I hate that I almost asked it."

I looked at him for a long moment.

This man.

This specific impossible man who had bought a dress three weeks in advance and planned a Tuesday around willows and cold water and warm grass and had the foresight to bring something dry for afterward.

This man who was sitting across from me in the October light telling me the truth about his fear before he let it become a request.

"You didn't ask it," I said.

"I almost did."

"Almost is the whole thing, Daniel." I reached across the table. Put my hand over his. "Almost means you caught it. Almost means you knew what it was before it got out."

He looked at our hands.

"I'm afraid," he said. The simple version. The one underneath all the other versions.

"I know," I said.

"Not of you. I want to be—"

"I know," I said. "I know exactly what you're afraid of."

He looked at me.

"Tell me," he said.

"You're afraid of losing this," I said. "The coffee cup. The books in three rooms. The path to the river. You're afraid that whatever I'm becoming is going to require something of me that doesn't include—" I paused. Found the precise word. "This. Us. The ordinary Tuesday of us."

He was very still.

"Yes," he said.

"That's not a small fear," I said.

"No."

"It's not a wrong one either," I said. "It's just — not mine to resolve for you. I can't tell you what's coming. I can't promise you the shape of it." I turned his hand over in mine. "I can tell you that I'm here. That I'm choosing here. That I've been choosing here every day since the coffee shop and I haven't stopped."

He looked at our hands.

At the window.

At the light that was doing what light does when it's being honest.

"Ask me again in a month," he said.

"You keep saying that," I said.

"I keep meaning it differently," he said.

I looked at him.

"How do you mean it now," I said.

He was quiet for a long moment.

"I mean — ask me again in a month and I think the answer will be different." He met my eyes. "I think I'm working my way toward something. I'm not there yet. But I'm moving in that direction."

"Toward what," I said.

The corner of his mouth.

Not the hungry one this time.

Something quieter than that. Something that had been earning itself for weeks and was only now ready to show its face.

"Toward not being afraid of what you are," he said. "Toward being—" He paused. "Proud of it. I think that's where I'm going. I'm not there. But I can see it from here."

The light on the table between us.

His hands in mine.

The kitchen holding us the way kitchens do when they've witnessed enough to know what matters.

I didn't say anything.

Some things don't need a response. Some things need to be received without addition — held exactly as they are, not built upon, not decorated, just taken in and kept.

I kept it.

That night, it was not the river.

The river had been revelation — the first honest thing, the visibility after twenty years of practiced invisibility, the body discovering what it felt like to be wanted without management.

This was something past revelation.

This was residence.

The specific intimacy of two people who have seen each other's fear and stayed anyway. His hands on her not exploring now but knowing — the difference between a man learning a landscape and a man who has learned it and moves through it with the ease of familiarity and the reverence of someone who understands the privilege of being allowed.

She felt the difference.

It was considerable.

There was a moment where he went still.

Not the river-still. Not the note-he-hadn't-known-was-there still.

He pulled back just far enough to look at her face in the dark.

Just — looked.

The way you look at something you have been afraid of losing and are, in this specific moment, not losing.

She looked back.

Neither of them said anything.

The moment held itself.

Then he came back to her and something had shifted — some last remaining held-back thing released — and what came after had the quality of a man who has made a decision and stopped negotiating with himself about it.

She felt that.

Filed it.

Next to the dress and the river and the hands in the gap and the mouth pressed to her hair.

The collection growing.

One true thing at a time.

After.

She lay in the dark listening to him breathe.

His arm across her. The window showing her the dark and the stars and the October sky that had no opinion about any of this and was beautiful anyway.

She thought about the almost-question.

About what it had cost him to catch it before it got out.

About what it meant that he had.

Twenty years of marriage to a man who never caught anything before it got out. Who let every fear become a sentence and every sentence become a wall and every wall become the architecture of a life she'd slowly disappeared inside.

This man caught it.

Held it up.

Looked at it.

Told her what it was before he let it speak.

That was not a small thing.

She turned her head and looked at his profile in the dark. The jaw. The specific way he slept — on his back, one arm out, the clear-conscience sleep she'd noted that first morning and noted every morning since.

She put her hand flat on his chest.

Felt his heartbeat.

Here. This specific place. Something underneath his heart that hadn't been there before. Starting to change. She'd felt it in the river. Had noted it and filed it and not said anything because some things needed time before they needed words.

She felt it now under her palm and thought — whatever is happening to me is happening to him too.

Not the same. Not identical.

But adjacent.

The frequency getting stronger.

Not just in her.

In both of them.

In the barn.

In Marcus's hand and Janet's eyes and Diane's tomatoes and Robert's sleep.

She lay in the dark with her hand on his chest and felt the beating of something that was more than one heart in one man and thought about the word Marcus had used.

Catalyst.

Not source.

Catalyst.

A catalyst doesn't create the reaction.

It makes it possible. It lowers the threshold.

The reaction was already there. Had been there. In all of them — eleven years of quiet Thursday gatherings, of people finding their way to that barn and sitting in that circle and not performing anything and waiting without knowing what they were waiting for.

She had arrived and the threshold had dropped.

Not because of something she'd done.

Because of something she was.

Something she was still becoming.

You're not finished, he'd said. *Becoming whatever this is.*

No.

She was not finished.

She lay in the dark and felt that truth settle into her bones — not frightening, not thrilling, just true, the way important things are true, without decoration — and she thought about Thursday and Marcus and the question he was going to ask and what her answer was going to be.

She already knew her answer.

She'd known it since the river.

Since the jeans in the chair.

Since the first morning she'd woken in this bed and watched the light come through the curtains and felt — for the first time in longer than she could calculate — like someone who was living her actual life.

Not a managed version.

Not a careful version.

The actual one.

She was not going back.

She was not slowing down.

She was not going to be made small again by anything or anyone — not by the cars on the county road, not by the fear in the eyes of people who needed her to be less than she was, not by the almost-questions of the man she loved who was, by his own account, finding his way toward proud.

She was going to find out what she was.

All the way to the end of it.

Whatever that meant.

Whatever that cost.

She closed her eyes.

His heartbeat under her palm.

The October dark outside.

The file getting heavy and ready and full of things that were about to require action.

She slept.

For the first time in weeks, she slept without filing anything.

Her body knowing, even in sleep, that she was exactly where she was supposed to

Chapter 7

CHAPTER SEVEN: THE DOOR
Rachel

The decision didn't arrive dramatically.

That's the thing nobody tells you about the moments that change everything — they don't announce themselves. They don't arrive with the weight you'd expect given what they're going to cost you. They arrive quietly, in the middle of an ordinary night, while the ventilation system cycles and the cart wheel needs oil somewhere above you and you're standing in a corridor you've stood in four hundred times before.

It arrived on a Wednesday.

2:06 in the morning by the clock at the nurses' station.

Rachel was on her third round of the ward, the one she did not because protocol required it but because she had learned over six years of nights that the ward had a rhythm and she was part of it, and deviating from her own internal schedule produced a low-grade unease that wasn't worth the comfort of sitting down.

She stopped outside room 14.

The way she always stopped outside room 14.

Listened.

Quiet inside. Not the quiet of sleep — she'd learned to distinguish them, the breathing of someone actually asleep versus the breathing of someone lying in the dark waiting for morning because morning was the only thing that moved in a place like this.

Grace was awake.

Rachel stood in the corridor with her hand not quite touching the door and thought about the woman in the photograph. The backyard. The summer. The laughing at something outside the frame.

Radiant.

She thought about nine months.

About the incremental adjustments she'd made with the careful patience of someone who understood you don't correct a slow wrong with a fast fix — each one small enough to be unremarkable, each one logged in the notebook at home that she would burn before she let anyone read it, each one a quiet argument with a system that had decided Grace Ellison's light was a symptom requiring management.

She thought about Thursday.

About the barn.

About Sarah's face when Grace had walked through the door — that recognition, the taut wire between them that Rachel had felt from three feet away, the quality of two people who know something about each other that neither of them has language for yet.

About Marcus crossing the room.

About Grace's hand in his.

About the way Grace had looked at his left hand on the saucer — steady, open — and something in her face had decided something.

Rachel stood in the corridor.

The ventilation system cycled.

The cart wheel somewhere above.

She thought about what David had told her in the diner. The careful precise inventory of what came next — the patterns, the escalations, the specific ways the system reached back when it decided someone had gone too far outside the lines. His three cups of coffee to her one, not from nerves, she'd decided, but from the habit of someone who ran on less sleep than most and had made his peace with it. The way he'd answered her three questions without hesitation or qualification.

The way he'd said *right things need protecting* like it was a principle he'd arrived at through experience rather than theory.

She thought about her job.

Her license.

The apartment she'd worked six years of nights to afford.

The career she'd built on the specific foundation of being someone who could be trusted in the difficult hours when other people were asleep.

She thought about all of it with the clinical thoroughness she brought to things that mattered, laying it out, examining it, giving it its full weight.

Then she thought about nine months.

About what had been done slowly and carefully and legally to a woman whose only crime was being too awake for the comfort of the people around her.

About the photograph.

About radiant.

She pushed open the door.

Grace was sitting up.

The window showing her nothing but her own reflection and the dark beyond it, the same window she'd been looking at for nine months, the same dark. But something was different tonight in the quality of her stillness — less the stillness of someone enduring and more the stillness of someone who has been waiting and has heard, finally, the sound of what they've been waiting for.

She looked at Rachel.

Rachel looked at her.

"Get dressed," Rachel said. "Wear layers. It's cold."

Grace looked at her for a long moment.

In nine months Rachel had never seen her cry. Not at intake, not during the family visits that left her staring at the wall for hours after, not during the assessments or the adjustments or the long slow institutional process of being managed.

She didn't cry now.

What her face did was quieter than crying and considerably more difficult to witness — the expression of someone who had been told so many times in so many ways that the door was locked and has just heard the sound of a key.

"Okay," Grace said.

She got up.

Moved to the small closet where her things were kept — not many things, the wardrobe of someone whose life had been reduced to what fit in a space this size — and Rachel set the bag she'd brought on the bed and Grace looked at it and looked at Rachel and understood without being told that the clothes in the closet were staying here.

She dressed in what Rachel had brought.

It didn't quite fit. Rachel was smaller through the shoulders, longer in the leg. The clothes were wrong in the specific way clothes are wrong when someone else chose them for you — which Grace understood, Rachel realized, better than most.

It didn't matter.

Grace zipped the jacket.

Looked at Rachel.

"Is there anything you need to take," Rachel said. Quiet. Professional. The voice she used when she needed to keep her own chest from doing what it was doing.

Grace looked around the room.

At the window.

At the small table with the book she'd been reading in pieces over three months because concentration was one of the first things to go and one of the last to come back.

At the photograph on the nightstand — her classroom, the good year, the junior class that actually wanted to read. Someone had brought it in the first week thinking it would comfort her and it had done the opposite for reasons Rachel understood now that she hadn't then.

Grace picked up the photograph.

Held it for a moment.

Set it back down.

"No," she said.

They went into the corridor.

Rachel had thought about this part.

Had run it in her mind a dozen times over the past week the way you run things when the cost of being wrong is everything — the stations, the cameras, the night staff, the specific geography of who was where between room 14 and the side door that opened onto the parking lot.

She'd done her rounds.

She knew where everyone was.

She walked the way she always walked — purposeful, unhurried, the particular pace of someone who belongs exactly where they are and is simply moving through their own domain. Grace beside her matching the pace, taking her cues, the instinctive collaboration of two people who have just agreed on something without discussing the terms.

Past the nurses' station.

Janet on nights — Janet who was new enough to defer and tired enough not to question, who looked up from her paperwork and Rachel gave her the nod that meant everything's fine, routine, nothing to see, and Janet gave it back and went back to her paperwork.

Past the corridor junction.

Left.

The exit sign at the end throwing its red light on the linoleum the way it always did, indifferent, reliable, just a sign doing what signs do.

Rachel pushed the door open.

The cold came in immediately — northern Michigan in the dark, honest about itself, no pretense, just the actual temperature of the actual night hitting them both at once.

Grace stopped on the threshold.

Just for a moment.

Rachel watched her take it in — the cold, the dark, the open sky above the parking lot, the specific quality of air that had not been filtered through an institutional ventilation system.

She watched Grace breathe it.

In.

Out.

The breath of someone reacquainting themselves with the texture of the actual world.

Then Grace stepped through the door.

Rachel let it close behind them.

They stood in the parking lot in the cold. Rachel's car was where she'd left it, pulled close to the building, backed in the way she'd been backing in for a week in preparation for exactly this moment and not letting herself think too hard about what that meant.

She unlocked it.

They got in.

Rachel sat for a moment with her hands on the wheel and the engine not yet running.

In the passenger seat Grace was very still. Not the facility-still, not the managed-quiet of a woman in a room she couldn't leave. Something different. The stillness of someone in the first moments of a thing they haven't had time to process yet, whose body is ahead of their mind, who is sitting in a car in a cold parking lot at 2am in clothes that don't quite fit and is, for the first time in nine months, free.

Rachel started the engine.

"Are you alright," she said.

Grace looked at her.

In the dark of the car her eyes were clear. Clearer than Rachel had ever seen them — the medication doing what it had been doing less of for six months, the clarity coming back in the specific incremental way Rachel had been watching and documenting and not writing in any chart.

"Yes," Grace said.

Then, quieter: "Thank you."

Just that.

Two words.

Rachel put the car in gear.

She had been a practical woman for thirty-four years. Had made practical decisions. Had built a practical life on practical foundations — the license, the apartment, the career, the trust she'd accumulated across six years of difficult nights.

She had just done the most impractical thing she'd ever done.

She found she had no regrets.

None.

Not even the small preliminary kind that arrive before the full weight of a decision lands. She went looking for them, clinically, the way she checked a patient for symptoms — thorough, honest, not wanting to miss anything.

Nothing.

Just the cold outside and the heater coming on and the woman beside her breathing the breathing of someone who has just been given back the air.

"We're going somewhere," Rachel said. "People I want you to meet."

Grace looked at the road ahead.

"The barn," she said.

Rachel glanced at her.

"Sarah told me," Grace said. "Three weeks ago. She came to see the woman in the next room and she stopped in my doorway and she looked at me—" Grace paused. "She looked at me the way people used to look at me. Before." A pause. "She didn't say anything about a barn. But I knew."

Rachel drove.

The county road dark and empty, the headlights finding the white lines and the tree line and nothing else.

"What did she say," Rachel said.

"She asked me if I could still see," Grace said. "I told her I couldn't. Not anymore." She looked at her hands in her lap. The teacher's hands. "She said — and I have thought about this every day since — she said: *it's still there. The seeing. It doesn't go away. It waits.*"

Rachel drove.

The heater doing its work.

The dark outside doing what northern Michigan dark does — enormous, indifferent, full of stars that had been there before any of this and would be there after.

"Is that true," Grace said. "Do you think that's true."

Rachel thought about the barn. About the frequency she'd felt standing in the doorway with Grace beside her — the warm water feeling, the body recognizing something before the mind did. About Marcus's hand on the saucer, steady, the hand that had been careful and curled three months ago now open and easy.

About David in the parking lot.

Right things need protecting.

"Yes," Rachel said. "I think it's true."

Grace nodded.

Looked back at the road.

They drove in the quiet that had earned itself — not the absence of things to say but the presence of something that didn't need saying. Two women in a car at 2am in northern Michigan, one of them a nurse who had just committed a felony for the right reasons and was not looking for forgiveness, one of them a teacher who had been told for nine months that her light was a symptom.

Both of them on their way to a barn.

Both of them, in their different ways, going home.

The gravel lot was empty when Rachel pulled in.

She'd called Marcus from the car — three rings, his voice immediately alert the way it was alert, she suspected, at any hour, the voice of someone who had been awake in the important sense for a long time and didn't require much notice.

Bring her, he'd said. Nothing else. *Bring her and come.*

The barn light was on.

They got out of the car.

Walked across the gravel.

Grace stopped at the barn door.

Rachel stopped beside her.

The cold. The light through the boards. The sound of voices inside going quiet as they sensed the arrival — that specific barn quality, the attunement, the group feeling things before they had reason to.

Grace stood at the door and Rachel watched her feel it.

Whatever moved in this place — the frequency, the thing Rachel had no clinical language for and had stopped trying to find clinical language for — Grace felt it from outside the door. Rachel watched it move through her. Watched her shoulders change. Watched her chin come up slightly, fractionally, the posture of someone remembering something they'd been told they'd imagined.

"Ready," Rachel said.

Grace put her hand on the door.

Looked at Rachel.

"I've been ready for nine months," she said.

She pushed it open.

The warmth of the barn came out to meet them.

The faces turned.

And Sarah's found Grace's across the room before anyone spoke, before Marcus stood, before anything — that wire pulled taut between them, that recognition, that frequency finding its frequency.

Rachel felt it from beside her.

Felt Grace feel it.

Watched something in Grace's face do what Rachel had been watching for nine months — the light coming back. Not all at once. In pieces. The way the best things come back, carefully, honoring what they cost.

Then Marcus was crossing the room.

And Rachel exhaled.

She hadn't known she'd been holding it since the corridor outside room 14.

Since the photograph.

Since nine months ago when a woman arrived with the light interrupted and Rachel had looked at her and thought — radiant. That's the word. That's what she is underneath whatever has been done to her.

Radiant.

She was right.

She found her chair beside Sarah and sat down.

The barn warm around her.

The frequency doing what it did.

And for the first time in six years of difficult nights Rachel felt the specific exhaustion of someone who has done something that cost everything and was worth every bit of it lift — just slightly, just enough — and underneath it something she recognized from a long time ago.

Rest.

Not sleep.

The deeper kind.

The kind that comes when the conscience and the action are finally, after a very long time, the same thing.

She sat in it.

Let it be.

The barn holding all of them.

Grace and Marcus across the circle.

The light coming back.

Chapter 8

CHAPTER EIGHT: THE TEA

She came through the barn door like someone who wasn't sure the floor would hold.

Marcus was at the small table in the back corner — the one he'd put there three years ago with the electric kettle and the mismatched mugs and the tin of Earl Grey nobody had requested. He'd set it up on a Tuesday afternoon without knowing why, the way you sometimes do a thing before the reason for it arrives. He understood the reason now.

He heard the door and turned.

He knew her face. Not from meeting her — he had never met her. From Rachel's descriptions over the past four months, which had been precise in the way of someone reporting something that mattered. *Her eyes,* Rachel had told him once, sitting in this same barn, her voice careful and tired, *look like she's been somewhere very far away and isn't all the way back yet.* He had nodded then without fully understanding. He understood now, looking at her standing in the doorway with the afternoon light behind her and the particular stillness of someone who had learned to be very careful about where they stepped.

He didn't move toward her. Didn't speak. Didn't do the thing people did when someone fragile appeared — the rushing forward, the bright voice, the performance of welcome that was really about making themselves comfortable with her discomfort. He stayed where he was and let her take in the barn. The space. The high windows with their slanted light. The chairs arranged in a loose circle that wasn't clinical, wasn't institutional, wasn't anything that required her to report how she was doing to someone with a clipboard.

She looked at the circle of chairs for a long moment.

She looked at him.

He picked up the kettle.

"Tea," he said. Not a question. Not an offering wrapped in the careful helpfulness of someone who needed her to perform okayness. Just the word. The plain fact of it.

She crossed the barn.

Her footsteps on the old wood floor were quiet and deliberate, the steps of someone relearning how to take up space. She pulled out the chair across from him and sat down and put her hands flat on the table — both of them, palms down — as though she needed to feel something solid beneath her.

He set the mug in front of her. His left hand doing it without the small managed wince he'd carried for thirty years and then one day, eighteen months ago, simply set down and never picked back up. He noticed the absence of the wince the way you notice the absence of a sound you'd stopped hearing — only when it's gone long enough to miss.

She wrapped both hands around the mug and looked at the steam rising from it.

He sat down across from her and poured his own.

The barn held the quiet without any particular effort. It was good at that. Old wood and afternoon light and the smell of the place — not hay exactly, not anything you could name precisely, just the accumulated honesty of years of people being real inside it. Some buildings carry that. Most don't. This one did.

"Rachel talks about this place," Grace said. Her voice was careful. Not weak — careful. The voice of someone who had learned that words could be used against you and was relearning that they didn't have to be.

"She's been good to us," Marcus said.

Grace looked at her tea. Something moved across her face — gratitude and grief arriving together the way they sometimes do when you've been without something long enough that getting it back hurts. "She's been good to me," she said quietly. "Better than she should have risked."

"Rachel decides what Rachel risks," he said. "Nobody talks her into anything."

The corner of Grace's mouth moved. Not quite a smile. The memory of one, maybe. "No," she said. "She doesn't give you the chance."

They sat with that for a moment.

Outside a car passed on the road. Neither of them looked toward the sound. Later Marcus would think about that — how neither of them looked. How some part of both of them was already attuned to the difference between a car passing and a car stopping.

"Your hand," she said.

He glanced at it. "What about it."

"Rachel mentioned it. That it hurt for a long time and then stopped."

"Thirty years," he said. "Then stopped."

She studied his hand on the table between them. Not with the clinical interest of the people who had surrounded her for the past however long it had been. With the interest of someone recognizing something. "When," she said. "When did it stop."

He considered giving her the short answer. Decided she deserved the real one. "About the time the group started changing. People shifting in ways I couldn't explain. The barn feeling different on Thursday nights." He paused. "I didn't connect them at first. Then I did."

She nodded the way people nod when they're confirming something internal rather than agreeing with something external.

"I used to know what I was," she said. She said it plainly, without self-pity, which somehow made it worse. "Before. I had a sense of it. Not words for it — I don't think there are good words for it. But a sense." She looked at the high windows. The light had moved while they'd been sitting. "They were very thorough," she said. "The people at the facility. They had a whole system for it. Medication and language and structure and the specific patience of people who have done something many times before." She stopped. Looked at her hands around the mug. "I could feel it going. Like being walked backward away from something. Slowly enough that you almost don't notice."

Marcus said nothing. He knew better than to fill that space.

"It's still in there," she said. "What I was. I can feel it the way you can feel something in a dark room — you know it's there, you can almost touch it, but you can't quite see it yet." She looked at him. "Does that make any sense or does it sound like exactly the kind of thing they said was the problem."

"It makes complete sense," he said.

Her shoulders dropped a quarter inch. The specific release of someone who has been braced against not being believed for long enough that being believed requires a physical response.

He drank his tea. Said nothing more. Some things you confirm and then leave room around.

The barn door opened and Emma came in — the woman whose roots were coming in darker, who had stopped wearing her glasses three weeks ago and seemed to see better for it. She stopped when she saw Grace. Looked at Marcus. He gave her nothing, which she understood, because Emma was good at reading what a room needed. She went to the kettle, poured herself tea, and settled into one of the circle chairs with a book she didn't open.

The presence of a third person in the room changed something — made it more ordinary, less weighted. Grace seemed to feel this. Her hands loosened slightly on the mug.

"Rachel says Thursday nights," she said.

"Thursday nights," Marcus confirmed.

"I'd like to come. If that's — " She stopped. Looked around the barn. The circle of chairs. Emma in the corner with her unopened book. The light in the high windows going gold now, late afternoon pressing toward evening. "If that's something people just do," she finished. "Without having to be invited."

"You're already here," Marcus said.

She looked at him. Really looked, for the first time — not the careful surface assessment she'd been giving him since she walked through the door, but the real look. The one that goes past the face.

He let her look. Didn't perform anything. Just sat there in the particular way he'd learned over years of sitting in this barn with people who were finding their way back to themselves — still, present, not requiring anything of her.

Whatever she saw seemed to be enough.

She looked back at her tea.

"Okay," she said quietly.

They sat in the fading light while Emma pretended to read and the kettle ticked as it cooled and somewhere outside on the road that ran past the barn a car that had been there for the past forty minutes sat with its engine off and its windows slightly dark and its driver doing something with a phone, or appearing to, and neither Grace nor Marcus nor Emma knew about the car yet.

But Marcus's left hand — the one that had stopped hurting eighteen months ago — rested on the table between them, and Grace's eyes, which Rachel had said looked like someone who had been somewhere very far away, were a little less far away than they had been when she walked through the door.

That was enough for now.
That was, in fact, everything.

Chapter 9

CHAPTER NINE: THE WATCHER

Sarah noticed the car for the first time on a Wednesday.

She'd been standing at the kitchen window with her second cup of coffee, not looking at anything in particular — the way you stand at a window in the morning when your mind is still deciding what kind of day it wants to be — when it registered. Black sedan. Parked at the far end of the road where the gravel widened slightly before the tree line. Facing the cabin.

She stood there looking at it.

It didn't move.

She finished her coffee. Rinsed the mug. Went about her morning. Checked the window again forty minutes later when she came back through the kitchen.

Gone.

She filed it under nothing. A turned-around driver. Someone checking a phone. The thousand ordinary reasons a car sits on a road for forty minutes and then leaves. She was good at filing things under nothing. She'd had years of practice at it — the long marriage had required a fluency in not seeing what was inconvenient to see, and the habit didn't vanish just because the marriage had.

But she noted it. The way you note a sound in an old house — probably nothing, probably the wood settling, probably the thousand ordinary explanations that are almost always right.

Almost.

Thursday night she drove to the barn.

The group had been gathering for three weeks since Grace arrived and the atmosphere had shifted in a way nobody had named but everyone felt. Something had completed itself. A frequency finding its last note. Grace sat in the circle now with the particular stillness of someone relearning how to occupy space without apology, and Marcus sat across from her with the particular stillness of someone trying very hard not to be obvious about where his attention was, and the rest of them watched this with the fond discretion of people who understood that some things needed room to become what they were going to become.

Rachel arrived late, which wasn't like her. She came through the door with her coat still on and her keys in her hand and the expression of someone who had been moving fast and hadn't quite stopped yet.

David was already there. He'd been coming earlier lately — before the others, helping Marcus set out the chairs, making tea, doing the small logistical things that were really just reasons to be in the barn before anyone else arrived. Sarah had noticed this. She suspected Rachel had noticed this. She suspected everyone had noticed this except possibly David, who struck her as a man more comfortable reading other people's situations than his own.

He looked up when Rachel came in.

Something passed between them. Not words. The specific look of two people who have been through something together and are still processing which category to put it in.

Rachel sat down. Unwound her scarf. Said: "There was a car behind me for six blocks."

The barn went quiet in the particular way it went quiet when something important arrived.

"Same car the whole six blocks?" David said.

"I tested it. Three turns. It stayed with me."

"Then?"

"Then it didn't." She looked at her hands. "Turned off on Maple. Gone."

David looked at Marcus. Marcus looked at the door.

Sarah looked at her own hands in her lap and thought about the black sedan at the end of her road on Wednesday morning. She'd filed it under nothing. She took it back out of that file now.

"I saw a car Wednesday," she said. "At the end of my road. Black. Parked facing the cabin. Forty minutes, then gone."

The barn held that for a moment.

"Why didn't you call me," David said. Not accusation. Just the precise question of someone recalibrating.

"I thought I was being paranoid."

"You're not being paranoid," he said.

Emma, who had been sitting with her hands folded in her lap and her unfocused gaze that saw more than it appeared to, said quietly: "There was someone parked outside my building Tuesday morning. I noticed because the engine was running the whole time I was walking to my car. When I drove out he didn't follow me but he watched me go." She paused. "I also thought I was being paranoid."

Grace had gone very still across the circle.

Marcus looked at her. "You don't have to — "

"The day Rachel brought me here," Grace said. Her voice was steady in the way of someone who had decided something before she spoke. "There was a man in the parking lot of my old building. I assumed he was waiting for someone. But he looked at Rachel's car when we pulled out. He looked at it the way you look at something you've been told to look for."

The circle sat with this.

Seven people in a barn on a Thursday night, each of them having separately noticed something and separately filed it under nothing, now looking at the shape those separate nothings made when you put them together.

It was not a comfortable shape.

Daniel's hand found Sarah's under her chair. She didn't look at him. She felt his thumb move once across her knuckles — the small language of someone saying *I'm here* without interrupting the room.

"They're not watching one of us," David said. "They're watching all of us. They've mapped the group."

"How long," Marcus said.

David considered his answer with the care of someone who understood that honesty in this particular moment was more important than comfort. "Long enough to know the address of everyone in this room. Long enough to know Rachel drives six blocks to get here. Long enough to know Emma's building and Grace's old building and the road that runs past Sarah's cabin." He paused. "This isn't new. This is us noticing something that has been in place for a while."

The barn was very quiet.

Outside the wind moved through the tree line with the particular sound of late season — the leaves nearly done, the branches starting to show, the world getting spare and legible the way it did every year when the cover fell away. Sarah had always liked this time of year. The honesty of it. Nothing hiding behind anything.

Right now she would have preferred more leaves.

"What do we do," Emma said.

"We keep meeting," Marcus said. He said it without drama, without a speech built around it, just the plain fact of what they were going to do delivered in the same voice he used to say pass the tea. "We keep meeting and we're careful and we don't do anything that makes their job easier." He looked around the circle. "We've been here before. Some of us longer than others. This is what it looks like when they decide you're worth watching. It means something is working."

Grace looked at him across the circle.

He looked back.

Neither of them looked away for a moment longer than the situation required, and when they did look away it was with the slight adjustment of people recalibrating the distance between themselves and something they hadn't planned on.

Rachel saw it. Sarah saw it. Emma saw it. David, to his credit, also saw it and had the good sense to look at the floor.

After the gathering broke up Sarah stayed to help stack chairs. Daniel and David carried the folding table to the back wall while Marcus walked Grace to Rachel's car — a short walk across gravel that somehow took longer than the distance required.

Sarah watched them through the barn door. Marcus's hands in his jacket pockets. Grace with her collar turned up against the October air. The gravel between them and then less gravel and then almost none.

She couldn't hear what they said. Didn't need to.

Rachel appeared beside her. They stood together in the barn doorway watching Marcus and Grace in the parking lot saying something quiet to each other in the cold air.

"How long," Sarah said.

Rachel smiled without taking her eyes off them. "Longer than either of them knows yet."

Daniel came up behind Sarah and put his hands on her shoulders and she leaned back into him and the four of them — the two in the barn doorway and the two in the parking lot — occupied the same October evening, the same cold air, the same particular sweetness of being alive in a world that was also threatening them, which was, she was beginning to understand, simply what being alive looked like if you were paying attention.

She drove home with Daniel's hand on her knee and the familiar road dark and familiar and then — there, at the end of her road, just at the edge of her headlights' reach — the black sedan. Same position. Facing the cabin.

She stopped in the road.

Sat looking at it.

It sat looking back.

She took out her phone and photographed it. Plate and all. Sent it to David before she'd consciously decided to. Then she pulled into her driveway with the deliberate steadiness of someone who had decided a thing and was acting accordingly, got out of the car, went inside, made tea she didn't drink, and sat at the kitchen table while Daniel moved around the cabin quietly doing the small evening things people do when they are trying to be normal in an unnormal situation.

After a while he sat down across from her.

"It was there again," she said.

"I know. I saw it."

"They want us to see it," she said. "That's the point. If they just wanted to watch us they'd be better at hiding."

Daniel looked at her. "When did you figure that out."

"Just now," she said. "In the driveway."

He was quiet for a moment. "So what is it then. If it's not just watching."

She thought about the circle in the barn tonight. Seven people who had each seen something and each said nothing until they were in a room together. Seven people who had been watched separately and hadn't known they were being watched together.

"It's a message," she said. "They want us to know they're there. They want us to be afraid enough to stop."

Daniel looked at the window. The road beyond was dark now, the sedan invisible in it, present or not present, no way to tell. "And are you," he said. "Afraid enough to stop."

She looked at her hands on the table. The ordinary hands of a woman who had spent twenty years making herself small and had stopped doing that and apparently someone had noticed and was now sitting at the end of her road in the dark to remind her what small had felt like.

"No," she said.

Daniel nodded once. Got up. Put the kettle on.

They didn't talk about it again that night. But when she finally slept she slept deeply and without the anxious half-wakefulness that had followed her through the long years of the marriage, and in the morning when she stood at the kitchen window with her coffee the road was empty and the sky was the particular pale grey of early November pressing down on the last of the color and she felt — beneath the fear, underneath it, steadier than it — something that had no name yet but that she recognized the same way you recognize a piece of music you haven't heard since childhood.

Not gone. Never gone.

Just waiting for her to be quiet enough to hear it.

Chapter 10

CHAPTER TEN: SOMETHING IS HAPPENING

The knowing started small enough to dismiss.

Tuesday morning, phone on the counter, coffee not yet ready, and she knew it was going to ring before it rang. Not hoped, not anticipated — *knew*, the way you know your own name, clean and without effort. She was reaching for it before the first sound came out of it. Rachel's voice on the other end saying *are you up* and Sarah saying *yes I just picked up* and Rachel saying *I know, I heard* and neither of them mentioning the reaching.

She filed it under coincidence.

Wednesday, Daniel coming up the back path from the woodpile, and she knew he was coming ten seconds before she heard his boots on the steps. She was at the stove and she turned and had the mug ready and he came through the door and stopped when he saw her standing there holding coffee out toward him before he'd made a sound in the house.

He looked at the coffee. Looked at her.

"How long," he said.

"Since Tuesday," she said. "Maybe longer. I'm just noticing it now."

He took the coffee. Drank. Stood at the window looking at the road — clear this morning, no sedan, just the ordinary road doing what roads do. "Is it everything," he said. "Or just people you know."

She thought about that. "People I know. So far."

So far. They both heard it.

He turned from the window. His face was doing the complicated thing she'd catalogued by now — not the fear exactly, more the thing underneath the fear, the thing a person feels when the world turns out to be larger than the map they were given and they're standing at the edge of the unmapped part deciding whether to step forward or back. She watched him decide. Watched him choose forward the way he always chose forward, quietly, without announcement, the way water finds its level.

"Okay," he said.

Just that. She was beginning to understand that *okay* was his most complete sentence.

Thursday she drove to the barn early.

Marcus was there, which she'd expected. David was there too, which she'd also somehow expected, though he hadn't said he would be. He was at the back table with a laptop and three folders spread open and the focused stillness of someone in the middle of something he didn't want interrupted. She got herself tea and sat in one of the circle chairs and waited.

Marcus came and sat beside her. Not across. Beside. The way you sit when what you have to say is for one person and the barn has ears.

"I want to show you something," he said. "Before the others get here."

She waited.

He held out his left hand, palm up, on his knee between them. She looked at it. An ordinary hand. Broad across the palm. The hands of someone who had worked with them.

"Thirty years," he said. "Osteoarthritis. The two middle joints. Some mornings I couldn't make a fist. Drove in winter with my wrist because gripping the wheel was — " He stopped. Flexed the hand slowly, all the way open, all the way closed. Smooth. Complete. "Eighteen months ago it stopped. Not improved. Stopped. Overnight." He looked at the hand. "I've had it looked at. The radiologist showed me the films. The deterioration is still visible in the bone structure. The damage is documented. But the inflammation is gone and the pain is gone and the function is — " He closed the hand into a fist. Opened it again. "The function is better than it was at forty."

Sarah watched his hand.

"Emma," she said.

"Her vision has been deteriorating since her thirties. She's worn correction for twenty-two years. Six weeks ago she left her glasses on her nightstand and drove to work and didn't realize until she got there. She went back for them. Wore them all day. The next morning left them again." He paused. "She had an exam last week. Her optometrist repeated the test three times. She's testing at better than twenty-twenty. He told her the equipment must be malfunctioning."

"The equipment isn't malfunctioning," Sarah said.

"No."

"Who else."

Marcus was quiet for a moment. "Tom Brierly — you haven't met him, he stopped coming six months ago, we think they got to him before he understood what was happening — Tom had a cardiac arrhythmia he'd been managing for eleven years. Medication twice daily. Then didn't need it." He paused again. "Robert, the quiet man in the back corner you may have noticed, the one who hasn't been here for six weeks — Robert had a tremor. Left hand. His neurologist had been tracking it as early-stage Parkinson's. Then the tremor stopped." His voice changed on that last sentence. Flattened slightly. The way a voice flattens when the information it's carrying is heavier than the words.

She heard the weight in it.

"Robert," she said carefully. "James."

"I've been calling him James for simplicity. His name is Robert James Caulfield. He's sixty-one. Retired schoolteacher. Has a daughter in Grand Rapids he calls every Sunday." He stopped. "He hasn't called her in six weeks. She contacted me because she found my number in his address book. She's filed a missing persons report."

The barn sat around them. The afternoon light in the high windows. The kettle on the back table. David across the room not appearing to listen, which meant he was listening carefully.

"They took him," Sarah said.

"I don't know that."

"Yes you do."

Marcus looked at his left hand again. Open. Closed. The hand that had stopped hurting eighteen months ago when something in this group began to change. "I think something is happening to people in this group," he said. "Something physical. Something that doesn't have a category in the literature that I can find. And I think whoever is watching us from the end of your road knows about it. I think it may be a significant part of what they're watching for."

Sarah thought about her phone ringing before it rang. Daniel's boots on the step, the coffee ready, his face in the doorway. The small sure knowledge that had arrived without invitation and without explanation and without any apparent interest in being dismissed.

"How long has it been happening," she said. "In the group."

"I can document eighteen months. But I think longer. I think it was slower at first. Subtle enough that people explained it away." He looked at her. "The way you've been explaining things away."

She met his eyes.

"It started when you came back," he said. "The rate of change. The — acceleration. I've been watching the group for years and what was gradual became rapid around the time you came back from wherever you went last winter."

"I didn't go anywhere," she said. "I was here."

"I know," he said. "I mean wherever you went inside yourself. Whatever happened that changed the way you move through a room."

She didn't know what to say to that. So she said nothing, which was increasingly feeling like the right answer to the things in her life that mattered most.

The others arrived between six and six-thirty.

Rachel, who came through the door with the specific alertness of someone who had checked her mirrors the whole way. Emma, who sat in her usual chair and folded her hands in her lap and looked around the circle with the clear unfocused gaze that saw everything. Daniel, who came in last, found Sarah's eye across the barn, and sat beside her without making a production of it.

Grace arrived with Rachel and took her chair in the circle with a steadiness that was new — less fragile than the first night, less provisional. Like someone remembering how to inhabit themselves.

Marcus sat in the circle. David closed his laptop and pulled his chair in.

They talked about the cars first. David had run the plate Sarah photographed. Registered to a property management company in Chicago that he was fairly certain was a shell. He was working on it. The cars were a coordination effort — not local, not improvised. Someone with resources had organized this and the resources were not small.

Rachel said: "They followed me again. Different car. I almost didn't catch it."

David looked at her. "What made you catch it."

She thought about it. "I just knew," she said. Then, more carefully: "I felt it. Before I checked the mirror. There was a — pressure. Behind my sternum. Like a warning with no words attached."

The circle was quiet.

Emma said: "I've been feeling that."

Grace said, very quietly: "I used to feel that. Before."

Sarah looked at her hands in her lap. Said nothing.

Marcus looked around the circle at all of them. At Emma's eyes that had stopped needing correction. At his own left hand resting on his knee. At Grace, who had been systematically walked backward away from herself by people with credentials and patience and a vested interest in her being manageable, and who was finding her way back one Thursday night at a time.

"I want to say something," he said, "and I want to say it plainly, because I think we're past the point where careful language is more useful than honest language."

The barn listened.

"Something is happening to the people in this room," he said. "I don't have a name for it that I trust. The names I've found in books are either too small or too dramatic or belong to a tradition that doesn't quite fit what I'm watching. So I'm going to describe it instead of naming it." He looked around the circle. "People in this group are healing from things that don't heal. People in this group are perceiving things before the physical evidence arrives. People in this group are — " He paused, choosing. " — becoming more of what they are. More present. More themselves. More capable of things they couldn't do before." Another pause. "And someone outside this barn has a file on this group that I believe documents exactly what I just described, and I believe that file exists because it has happened before, and I believe the cars at the end of our roads are there because the people who keep that file are very motivated to prevent it from continuing."

The circle sat with this.

Daniel said: "What do they do. The people with the file. When they decide to move."

Marcus and David exchanged a look. Brief. The look of two people deciding how much to say.

David said: "They use what's available. Legal pressure where it works. Professional pressure — employers, licensing boards, medical records. For people who can't be reached that way — " He stopped.

"Robert," Sarah said.

The barn was very quiet.

"We don't know that," David said.

"You know it," Sarah said. "You just said we're past careful language."

David looked at her for a long moment. Then, without inflection: "We know it."

Grace had gone very still across the circle. Marcus was watching her with the careful attention of someone monitoring a structure under stress, ready to move if it shifted. But Grace didn't shift. She sat with what David had said and absorbed it with the steadiness of someone who had already been through the worst version of this and survived it and was not going back.

She looked up.

"Then we find him," she said.

Same words as before. Same voice. The circle looked at her.

"We find Robert and we don't stop meeting and we don't make ourselves small because there are cars at the end of our roads." She looked at Marcus. He looked back. "That's what we do."

Marcus said: "Yes."

Nobody disagreed.

Outside the barn the October wind moved through the stripped branches of the tree line and somewhere down the road a car that had been idling for the past thirty minutes with its lights off turned its engine over and pulled slowly away into the dark, and inside the barn seven people sat in a circle of chairs on a Thursday night feeling something that had no adequate word for it — not bravery exactly, not defiance exactly, something older than both of those, something that lived underneath the fear and was not diminished by it — and the barn held them the way it had always held them, the way good spaces hold the people who need them, quietly, without asking for anything in return.

Sarah drove home with Daniel. The road was clear. No sedan.

She lay awake for a while with Daniel's breathing beside her and the dark pressing at the windows and the knowing — the small quiet knowing that had been arriving all week without permission — telling her that the clear road tonight was not an absence of watching.

It was a different kind of message.

We can be there when we choose.

She lay with that for a long time.

Then she thought about Marcus's hand. Emma's eyes. Rachel's pressure behind the sternum. Grace sitting in the circle with the steadiness of someone who had been taken apart and was putting herself back together piece by piece and was not going to be stopped from doing it.

She thought about Robert James Caulfield, sixty-one, retired schoolteacher, daughter in Grand Rapids he called every Sunday.

She thought about the file. The template. The pattern David had seen in four other groups in eleven years.

She thought about what Marcus had said. *Becoming more of what they are.*

She put her hand over the place behind her own sternum where the knowing lived.

It was quiet now. Steady. Present.

Not a warning this time.

Just: *I'm here.*

She closed her eyes.

Slept.

Chapter 11
CHAPTER ELEVEN: TOM

He called on a Friday morning, which was how she knew it wasn't his idea.

Tom was a Saturday caller. Had been for the entirety of their twenty-two year marriage and apparently remained one in whatever version of himself existed after it. Saturday morning, nine-fifteen, the specific time slot of a man who had finished his coffee and his paper and was now performing the items on his list. She had been one of those items for two decades. She had some feelings about that which she had largely finished having.

Friday meant someone had told him to call.

She let it ring twice. Not to be difficult. To give herself two rings worth of steadiness before she answered.

"Tom."

"Sarah." His voice had the particular warmth of someone who had been coached on warmth. She knew his actual warm voice. This wasn't it. This was the voice he used with her parents and his boss and anyone he needed something from. Friendly and slightly formal and calibrated. "How are you doing."

"I'm fine, Tom. You?"

"Good, good. Listen, I was hoping we could get together. Coffee. Just to — check in."

She looked out the kitchen window. The road empty this morning. Grey sky, the last of the leaves finally down, the tree line bare and legible. "Check in on what."

A pause. Brief but there. "On you. On how things are going." Another pause. "There are some people who care about you, Sarah. People who've been a little worried."

People. Plural. Not *I've been worried.* Not *I miss you* or *I'm concerned* — the language of someone speaking for a group that had briefed him.

"What people," she said.

"Just — friends. People who knew you before." He shifted gears with the smoothness of someone who'd rehearsed the shift. "Dr. Hendricks has reached out to me. He's concerned about some of the changes he's been hearing about."

Dr. Hendricks. Her physician for eleven years, who had treated her tension headaches and her annual physical and had once, during the worst year of the marriage, suggested she might benefit from *something to take the edge off* in the manner of someone suggesting aspirin for a sprained ankle. She had declined. He had noted it.

"What changes," she said.

"Just — Sarah, you left your marriage, you moved in with someone you'd known for a short time, you've been spending time with a group of people that — some people find unusual. That's all. Nobody's attacking you. People just want to make sure you're okay."

She heard the architecture of it clearly. The careful language that sounded like concern and carried something else underneath. *Left your marriage* — stated as symptom. *Someone you'd known for a short time* — Daniel reduced to a risk factor. *A group of people that some people find unusual* — the barn, the circle, all of them on a Thursday night, reduced to a red flag in someone's assessment.

"I'm okay, Tom," she said. "I appreciate you calling."

"Sarah — "

"I'm going to let you go. Have a good weekend."

She hung up before he could find the next piece of the script.

Stood at the window for a moment. The bare tree line. The empty road. The grey sky doing what grey skies do in November, which is press down on everything with the patient weight of something that has all the time in the world.

She called David.

They met at a coffee shop twenty minutes from the cabin. Not the one closest to her — David had suggested this one specifically, which told her something about how he thought. He was already there when she arrived, at a corner table with his back to the wall and a clear view of the door, drinking black coffee and reading something on his phone that he put face-down when she sat.

She told him about the call. All of it. Tom's voice, the coached warmth, Hendricks, the specific language. David listened without interrupting, which was one of the things she was coming to appreciate about him — he listened the way people listened when they were actually building something from what they heard rather than just waiting for their turn.

When she finished he was quiet for a moment.

"Hendricks," he said. "He's been your physician how long."

"Eleven years."

"And he has your records."

"Yes."

"Your history. Anything in there that could be characterized as — instability. Anything they could point to."

She thought about it honestly. "He offered me antidepressants once. About four years ago. I declined. It's probably in the file. The offer and the refusal both."

David nodded slowly. "That's what they're looking for. They go backward through your records looking for anything that can be reframed. A declined prescription becomes *patient resistant to treatment.* A difficult period becomes *history of emotional instability.* They build a narrative and then they find the professionals to support it." He picked up his coffee. "It's legal. It's documented. It's very hard to fight because it uses your own history against you and the people doing it have credentials and you don't have — " He stopped.

"I don't have what," she said.

"You don't have proof of what's actually happening to you. You have your experience. Which they will characterize as the problem."

She sat with that. The coffee shop around them doing its ordinary Friday morning business — laptops and conversations and the hiss of the espresso machine and nobody paying attention to the two people in the corner having a conversation that was quietly about whether her mind was going to be used as a weapon against her.

"What do they want," she said. "Ultimately. What's the goal."

"Separation," David said. "From the group. That's always the first goal. Isolated, you're manageable. In the group you're — something else." He paused. "The wellness hold is the tool they prefer at this stage. It's clean. It has medical authority behind it. If they can get two physicians to sign off on an emergency psychiatric evaluation they can hold you for seventy-two hours minimum. During which time the group loses its center and the pressure on the others accelerates and by the time you're released — if you're released in any reasonable timeframe — the group has usually scattered."

Sarah looked at her hands around her coffee cup. "You said *if* I'm released."

"I said in a reasonable timeframe." He looked at her steadily. "Grace was in there for four months."

She thought about Grace in the parking lot at two in the morning. Fragile and blinking at the open sky. *Thank you,* she'd said. Just that.

"So Tom calling is the beginning of building that case," she said.

"Tom calling is the beginning of documenting that people close to you have expressed concern. Which becomes part of the file. Which becomes part of the application for the hold." He set down his coffee. "I want to be clear with you about something. This is not inevitable. They can't move on this quickly and they won't — they need the documentation to be solid or the hold gets challenged and falls apart and they lose the legal avenue. That takes time. We have time." He paused. "What we do with that time matters."

"What do we do with it."

He looked at her in the direct way she had come to understand meant he was deciding how much to say and had decided all of it. "You need someone in your corner with credentials. A therapist you choose, not one they steer you toward. Someone whose notes will reflect what is actually happening to you rather than what Hendricks and whoever is coaching Tom want to be happening to you." He paused. "And you need to be very careful about who you talk to. Tom will report everything. Hendricks will document anything you say to him. Anyone connected to your previous life who has been contacted by these people is a liability right now."

She thought about her sister in Columbus. Her friend Diane from before, who had called twice in the past month with a warmth that had felt slightly effortful, slightly performed. The way Tom's warmth had sounded this morning.

"How many people have they talked to," she said.

"I don't know yet," David said. "I'm working on it."

She looked out the window of the coffee shop at the parking lot. Ordinary Friday morning. A woman loading groceries. Two teenagers on their phones. A black sedan parked at the far end of the lot that she noticed without meaning to notice and looked at for two seconds before looking away.

"Is that one of theirs," she said.

David didn't turn to look. "Silver Camry in the second row was behind me from my apartment," he said. "The black one at the far end I don't know yet."

She appreciated that he didn't say *don't look* or *don't worry* or any of the things people said when they were managing you. He just gave her the information and let her sit with it.

"I'm not going to stop," she said.

"I know."

"I want you to know it's not bravado. I've thought about it." She looked at her coffee. "I spent twenty-two years making myself smaller to fit inside a life that wasn't working. I was very good at it. I know how to do it." She looked up. "I'm not doing it again."

David looked at her for a moment with the expression she couldn't quite read — the one that appeared sometimes when she said something that landed in a place past his professional distance. "Okay," he said.

"That's Daniel's word," she said.

Something shifted in his face. Almost a smile. Not quite. "It's a good word," he said.

She drove home the long way. Not because David had told her to. Because she needed the extra twenty minutes and the moving and the bare November landscape going past the windows to settle something in herself before she walked back into the cabin and looked at Daniel and told him what Tom's call actually was.

He was at the kitchen table with his coffee and the newspaper he still subscribed to in paper form, which she found endearing in a way she'd never told him. He looked up when she came in. Read her face the way he read her face, which was thoroughly and without pretending he wasn't doing it.

"Sit down," he said.

She sat. Told him. All of it — Tom, Hendricks, the wellness hold, David's assessment, the silver Camry, the black sedan in the parking lot she didn't know yet. She watched him take it in piece by piece, the newspaper forgotten, his coffee going cold. His face doing the complicated thing and then settling past it into something simpler and harder.

When she finished he was quiet for a long moment.

"A therapist," he said. "David said you need a therapist you choose."

"Yes."

"I know someone," he said. "She's not — she's not conventional exactly. But she's good and she's solid and she won't be recruited." He paused. "Her name is Patricia Wren. She worked for the county for twelve years. She's private practice now. I've known her a long time."

Sarah looked at him. "How long have you known this might be necessary."

He met her eyes. Held them. "Since I saw the first car," he said. "I didn't say anything because I was hoping I was wrong." He paused. "I wasn't wrong."

"No," she said. "You weren't."

He reached across the table and put his hand over hers. Not squeezing, not performing comfort. Just there. The plain fact of his hand on hers in the kitchen on a Friday morning with the grey sky outside and the bare tree line and the empty road that wasn't really empty, that was full of things they couldn't see from here.

"I'm staying," he said. Unprompted. Unasked.

She turned her hand over under his. Held it properly.

"I know," she said.

Outside, somewhere down the road, a car she couldn't see from the kitchen window idled quietly in the cold November air, its driver doing what the driver always did, which was wait, and watch, and write things down, and wait some more.

Inside the kitchen a woman who had spent twenty-two years making herself small sat at a table holding the hand of a man who had never once asked her to be smaller and felt — beneath the fear, underneath the legal machinery being assembled against her, below the Tom-calls and the Hendricks-files and the documented concerns of people who had been recruited into someone else's agenda — the same steady pressure behind her sternum that had been arriving without invitation all week.

Not a warning.

Not this time.

Something closer to: *you already know what you're made of.*

She did.

She was beginning to.

Chapter 12

CHAPTER TWELVE: RACHEL AND DAVID

Rachel had been good at not wanting things for a long time.

It was a skill she'd developed the practical way you develop skills that keep you functional.

Gradually. Without drama.

Through the simple repetition of wanting something and not getting it until the wanting itself became more trouble than it was worth.

She wanted her marriage to work.

It didn't.

She wanted her ex-husband to be someone other than who he was.

He wasn't.

She wanted the facility where she worked to actually care about the people inside it rather than the billing codes attached to them.

It didn't.

Each of these she had filed under *the world as it is* and adjusted accordingly and kept moving.

Keeping moving was what Rachel did. Had always done. She was good at it and it kept the lights on and the mortgage paid and Grace's medication quietly reduced to a level that allowed Grace to find her way back to herself one Thursday night at a time.

Wanting David Cross was not a complication she had budgeted for.

She'd noticed him the way she noticed everything — catalogued his competence, his careful listening, the way he moved through a room with the unhurried attention of someone who read environments before he read people.

She'd noted his habit of arriving early to the barn.

Noted the way he looked at her when she came through the door. Not the look men gave women they were interested in. Nothing that obvious. Something more restrained and more considered.

The look of someone who had decided to pay close attention to a thing without yet deciding what to do about it.

She had filed all of this under *noted* and kept moving.

Then he'd put his hand over hers at the corner table when she told him how long she had before Hendricks moved.

She had not moved her hand.

Neither had he.

They had both looked at his hand on hers and then at each other and then at the table.

She had kept moving in every sense except the one that mattered — something had shifted in the place behind her sternum where she kept the things she didn't examine too closely.

It had not shifted back.

He called Saturday morning.

Not about the group. Not about the cars or the file or the legal machinery being assembled around Sarah's history.

He called and said: "I was going to get breakfast. Do you want to get breakfast."

Plain as that.

No preamble. No professional framing. Just the question, direct, with the slight quality of someone who had decided to say the thing before the decision reversed itself.

She stood in her kitchen in the stillness of someone whose body has already answered before their mind has caught up.

"Yes," she said.

The place he chose was a diner twenty minutes from her apartment.

Not close to the barn. Not close to the coffee shop where he met Sarah. Not close to anything connected to the group or the opposition or the file or any of it.

A booth in the back. Red vinyl seats. A laminated menu. The specific timeless quality of diners that have been the same since 1987 and intend to stay that way.

She got there first. Took the booth. Ordered coffee.

He came through the door at eight-fifteen exactly.

Not late on purpose. Not early to perform eagerness. Simply there when he said he would be there — consistent, she was discovering, with everything else about him.

He slid into the booth. Picked up the menu. Put it down.

"I already know what I want," he said.

"What do you want," she said.

And heard herself say it.

And did not look away.

He looked at her steadily across the laminated menu and the sugar dispenser and the small artificial flower that had probably been there since 1987.

"Eggs," he said. "Over easy."

She picked up her coffee. "Safe choice."

"I'm not always a safe choice," he said.

She looked at him.

He looked back.

The diner moved around them and neither of them looked away for a moment that was slightly longer than eggs over easy required.

The waitress arrived.

They ordered.

The moment rearranged itself into something more ordinary without disappearing entirely.

"How did you find the group," Rachel said. "Originally."

He picked up his coffee. She understood this was a real question for him — not small talk, not deflection. He was deciding how much of the true answer to give her.

She waited. She was good at waiting.

"I was looking for groups like this one," he said. "It's what I do. I find them before the opposition does, or after, and I try to mitigate."

"Mitigate," she repeated. "What does that mean specifically."

"Different things at different stages." He set down his coffee. "Early — it means helping the group understand what it is and what it's likely to face. Documentation. Legal preparation. Connections." A pause. "Later it means other things."

"What happened to the other groups," she said. "The ones you found."

He looked at her with the expression she had seen at the barn — the one that lived in the gap between what he knew and what he'd decided to say.

"Two of them scattered before the opposition moved. They exist still, separately. Not the worst outcome."

A pause.

"One group in Portland held together. The opposition came at them through the legal route. They'd prepared. They fought it and mostly won."

Another pause. Longer.

"The fourth group I found too late."

Rachel waited.

"Seattle," he said. "Three years ago. By the time I got there they had already moved on two members. Wellness holds, both of them."

He stopped.

Started again.

"The catalyst was a woman named Diane. Fifties. Former teacher. She held the group together for six weeks after that. Then her employer received documentation. She lost her job. Lost her insurance. The prescription she needed for a heart condition became something she couldn't afford."

He looked at his coffee.

"She's fine. She's in Phoenix now. Teaching again. But the group is gone."

Rachel looked at him. "And Robert Caulfield."

"Robert is not fine." Flat. Honest. "I don't know where he is. I know the facility he was most likely taken to. I have someone working on confirming it." A pause. "I'm not going to tell you it's going well because it isn't yet."

"But you're trying."

"I'm trying."

She looked at her coffee. "Why do you do this. What are you."

He turned his cup in his hands. The habit of someone who thought better with something to hold.

"I'm a person who found out what was happening to groups like this one and decided I wasn't going to watch it happen and do nothing." He paused. "I have a background that makes me useful. Connections that make me effective sometimes and ineffective others."

He stopped.

Started differently.

"I had someone I cared about who was in a group like this one. Ten years ago. Before I knew what to look for. Before I had any of the tools I have now."

He looked at his cup.

"She's okay. She got out. But it took two years and it cost her things she didn't get back."

"Who was she," Rachel said.

He looked up.

"My sister."

Rachel nodded once. Filed it in the right place.

Not a curiosity.

A foundation. The thing underneath everything else he did. The reason the competence had a direction.

They ate for a while without talking.

It wasn't uncomfortable. It was the silence of two people who had said enough for now and were content to sit in the same space and let the morning be what it was.

"Grace is doing better," he said eventually.

"Yes."

"That's because of you."

She looked at him. "It's because of Grace."

"It's because of both of you." He picked up his coffee. "What you did — going back into that facility every week, cutting the dose, getting her out — that wasn't a small thing. That was significant personal risk for someone who had no claim on you beyond being a human being who needed help."

Rachel looked out the window at the parking lot.

Ordinary Saturday. Cars. People. The unremarkable November morning.

"She reminded me of someone," she said.

"Who."

She was quiet for a moment.

"Me. Ten years ago. Before I figured out that the people telling me I was too much and too intense and too everything — were wrong."

She paused.

"She had that look. The look of someone who has been told so many times that who they are is the problem that they've started to believe it."

David was looking at her.

She turned from the window and met his eyes and did not perform anything.

Not strength. Not composure. Not the brisk professional competence that got her through her days.

Just sat there in the red vinyl booth and let him look.

"You're not too much," he said.

The words landed in the place behind her sternum where she kept the things she didn't examine too closely.

They landed without fanfare.

With the specific weight of something true said plainly by someone with no reason to say it except that it was true.

"You don't know me well enough to say that," she said.

"No," he said. "But I will."

The diner moved around them.

The cook. The regulars. The coffee being refilled by the waitress who had probably seen ten thousand people sit in this booth and say things that mattered.

Rachel sat across from David Cross with her eggs going cold and the November light coming through the window and the thing behind her sternum that she had kept filed under *noted* for weeks now.

Fully open.

Not going back.

"Okay," she said.

He almost smiled. "That's Daniel's word."

"It's a good word," she said.

She drove home through the grey afternoon and sat in her parked car in front of her building for five minutes.

Doing nothing.

Which was unusual for Rachel, who did not sit in parked cars doing nothing.

She was thinking about want.

About the long disciplined practice of not wanting things likely to cost more than they delivered. About the careful life built around what was reliable, what was manageable, what could be filed under *the world as it is* without destroying anything.

She was thinking about Grace in the parking lot at two in the morning.

Thank you. Just that.

She was thinking about David's hand over hers at the corner table.

She was thinking about *I will* — not *I might*, not *I'd like to*, not the careful conditional language of someone managing expectations.

Just *I will.*

Plain. Without hedge.

She was thinking that the careful life she'd built was good and solid and had served her well.

And had also been built at a certain distance from things that could hurt her.

And that distance was not the same as safety.

Just the appearance of it.

And that appearing safe and being alive were not the same project.

She got out of the car.

Went inside.

Fed her cat, whose name was Gerald and who had no interest in her emotional developments, expressing this through the medium of sitting with his back to her until she opened a can of food.

She stood at the kitchen window while Gerald ate. Looked at the street below. Ordinary Saturday. The neighbors. The parked cars.

None of them black sedans. As far as she could tell.

She thought about calling someone. Her friend Jana. Her sister in Milwaukee. Someone to say *I think I may be developing feelings for a man I work with in a complicated situation* and receive the appropriate response involving wine and reasonable caution.

She didn't call anyone.

She had a bath.

Read forty pages of a novel.

Made soup.

Went to bed at a reasonable hour and lay in the dark listening to Gerald settle at the foot of the bed.

Thought about David Cross saying *I will* across a laminated diner menu on a grey Saturday morning.

Felt — quietly, without permission, without any intention of being filed under *noted* — something she recognized from a long time ago.

Hope.

Actual, inconvenient, unreasonable hope.

She closed her eyes.

Slept better than she had in months

Chapter 13

CHAPTER THIRTEEN: THE PERFORMANCE REVIEW

The meeting request came through on Monday morning.

HR. Conference room B. Tuesday at ten.

No agenda listed.

Sarah looked at it on her screen for a moment.

Then closed her email and went back to work.

She'd learned something in twenty-two years of marriage — the dread you feed grows. The dread you starve sometimes doesn't show up at all.

This one showed up.

Conference room B was the small one at the end of the hall.

Not the main conference room where they held team meetings and quarterly reviews and the birthday gatherings with sheet cake that nobody really wanted but everyone attended.

The small one.

The one with one window facing the parking lot and a round table that seated four and the particular fluorescent hum of a room that was used for things people didn't want overheard.

She'd been in this room once before.

Three years ago when they'd let Dennis Hartley go after seventeen years and two commendations and the specific offense of asking too many questions about the billing discrepancies in the Medicaid accounts.

She had not thought about Dennis Hartley in three years.

She thought about him now.

The HR director was a woman named Carolyn Marsh.

Fifty-something. Reading glasses on a beaded chain. The careful neutral expression of someone professionally trained to deliver bad news in language that couldn't be quoted against the company later.

There was a second person in the room.

A man Sarah didn't recognize. He was introduced as Mr. Gerald Foss, which told her nothing, and described as a *consultant*, which told her everything.

Consultants in conference room B at ten on a Tuesday were not there to consult.

She sat down.

Folded her hands on the table.

Waited.

Carolyn opened a folder.

The folder was thin. Three or four pages. Sarah noted the thinness and understood it — this was the beginning of a file, not the end of one. The beginning of a file looked thin. The end of one looked like a case.

"Sarah," Carolyn said. "Thank you for making time."

"Of course."

"We wanted to check in." A small pause. Practiced. "We've noticed some changes recently and we want to make sure you have the support you need."

Changes.

Sarah kept her hands still on the table.

"What kind of changes," she said.

Carolyn glanced at her papers. "Your engagement with the team has shifted somewhat. There have been a few comments from colleagues about — " Another pause. Slightly longer. "About your demeanor. Your focus."

"Specific comments," Sarah said. "From specific colleagues."

"We're not able to share the specifics — "

"Then I'm not able to respond to them."

Carolyn's neutral expression did not change.

Mr. Gerald Foss, who had not yet spoken, wrote something on his notepad.

Sarah watched him write it.

She thought about David in the coffee shop. *They document everything. They build the narrative from whatever they can find.* She thought about the folder on the table. Three pages now. How many pages later.

"We're not here to create a problem," Carolyn said. "We genuinely want to support you through whatever you may be experiencing."

Whatever you may be experiencing.

The language of someone who had already decided what she was experiencing and was now inviting her to confirm it.

"I'm not experiencing anything that requires support," Sarah said. "My work is current. My numbers are good. If there are specific performance concerns I'm happy to address them specifically."

Foss looked up from his notepad.

He had the eyes of someone paying a particular kind of attention. Not HR attention. Not consultant attention.

The attention of someone who had been briefed on her and was now checking the briefing against the reality and finding the reality more than they'd expected.

She looked back at him steadily.

He looked back down at his notepad.

"We'd like you to consider speaking with someone," Carolyn said. "We have an employee assistance program — "

"I have a therapist," Sarah said.

This was not yet true.

It was going to be true by Thursday.

She had called Patricia Wren on Sunday morning and left a message and received a call back within the hour — Daniel had been right, the woman was good, the twenty-minute conversation had told her that much — and they had an appointment scheduled for Thursday at four.

Carolyn paused. "Oh. That's — that's good. That's a positive step."

"Yes," Sarah said. "It is."

Foss wrote something else on his notepad.

She wondered what he was writing. She wondered who he would call when he left this building. She wondered if the call would be to the same person Tom had talked to before his coached Friday morning phone call, or to someone above that person, or to someone she would never be able to trace no matter how good David's connections were.

She wondered about Robert Caulfield.

Retired schoolteacher. Daughter in Grand Rapids.

She kept her hands still on the table.

"Is there anything else," she said.

There was not anything else.

Or rather — there was a great deal else, visible in the careful language and the thin folder and the notepad and the particular way Carolyn closed the meeting with the specific warmth of someone who wanted the interaction documented as supportive rather than threatening.

But nothing she could point to.

Nothing she could quote.

That was the point.

She walked back to her desk through the open office. Her colleagues at their screens. The ordinary machinery of a workday proceeding without drama. Nobody looking at her directly. One or two looking at her indirectly in the way of people who knew something had happened and were deciding how visible to make their knowing.

She sat down.

Opened her email.

Stared at it without reading it for approximately ninety seconds.

Then she picked up her phone and texted David.

Conference room B. HR plus a consultant named Gerald Foss. They have a file started. They mentioned the EAP. I told them I already have a therapist.

Three dots appeared almost immediately.

Good. Who is Foss?

Don't know. Introduced as consultant. Not HR. Took notes the whole time.

A pause. Longer than the first.

I'll find out. You okay?

She looked at the question.

Thought about conference room B and the thin folder and the practiced neutral expression and the notepad and the specific sensation of sitting across a table from people who had decided what story they were telling about her and were now collecting evidence to support it.

She thought about Dennis Hartley. Seventeen years. Two commendations.

She thought about the barn on Thursday nights. The circle. Marcus's left hand. Grace's eyes coming back from wherever they'd been. Rachel's laugh — the real one — in the diner with David.

Yes, she typed. *I'm okay.*

She put her phone down.

Went back to work.

She told Daniel that evening.

He listened without interrupting. Sitting across the kitchen table with his coffee and the particular stillness he brought to things that mattered, which was the same stillness he brought to everything, which was one of the reasons she was still learning him after all these months and suspected she had a long way to go.

When she finished he said: "Foss."

"You know him."

"I know the name." He looked at his coffee. "He's not a corporate consultant. He consults for — " He paused. "He consults for organizations that manage risk. Human risk specifically."

"What does that mean."

"It means when a company or an institution has a person who is generating what they consider to be an unacceptable level of disruption, they bring in someone like Foss to assess the situation and recommend a course of action."

Sarah looked at him. "A company brought him in. Or someone brought him in through the company."

Daniel met her eyes.

"Someone brought him in through the company," he said.

She sat with that.

The kitchen around them. The ordinary evening. The smell of the soup she'd made earlier still in the air. Outside, somewhere down the road, probably, a car that may or may not have been there.

"They're using my employer," she said.

"Your employer probably doesn't know they're being used," Daniel said. "Someone in HR received a call from someone they trusted — a colleague, a professional contact, someone with credibility — expressing concern about an employee. Framed correctly, that's a liability issue. HR responds to liability issues. They brought in Foss as due diligence."

"And Foss reports back to — "

"Whoever called HR in the first place."

She looked at her hands on the table.

The ordinary hands of a woman sitting in a kitchen on a Monday evening while the machinery of something organized and patient and not local quietly assembled itself around her life.

"Patricia Wren," she said. "Thursday at four."

"Good."

"David is looking into Foss."

"Also good."

She looked at him. "You're not going to tell me to be careful."

"Would it help."

"No."

"Then I won't." He reached across and put his hand over hers. "I'm going to tell you something else instead."

She waited.

"They brought in a consultant," he said. "Which means the car at the end of the road and Tom's phone call and Hendricks expressing concern weren't enough. They needed to escalate." He looked at her steadily. "You know what escalation means."

She thought about it.

"It means the first approach didn't work," she said slowly.

"It means you didn't scare." He paused. "That frightens them more than the group does. A frightened catalyst scatters. An unfrightened one — " He stopped.

"An unfrightened one what."

He looked at her with the look she was still learning. The one that lived underneath the fear and was not diminished by it.

"Becomes something they don't have a protocol for," he said.

She drove past the river road on the way to work Tuesday morning.

Her hands slowed on the wheel the way they always did.

She didn't stop.

Not yet.

But she felt it — the pull of the water, the particular patience of it, the sense of something there that had been there before her and would be there after and was entirely unbothered by Gerald Foss and his notepad and conference room B and the thin folder getting thicker.

She felt it and she filed it.

Not under nothing.

Under *later.*

Under *soon.*

Under *when the time is right I'm going to need that.*

She drove to work.

Sat at her desk.

Did her job.

Kept moving.

Thursday she sat across from Patricia Wren in a small office on the second floor of a converted Victorian on the west side of town.

Plants in the windows. Two chairs angled toward each other. No desk between them — Sarah noticed this immediately and appreciated it. No clipboard. No folder. No notepad visible.

Patricia Wren was sixty, or close to it. Silver hair cut short. The kind of face that had earned its lines. She sat in her chair with the relaxed uprightness of someone comfortable in their own body and in no hurry whatsoever.

She had let Sarah talk for twenty minutes without interrupting.

Now she said: "What do you want from this."

Not — *how are you feeling.* Not — *tell me about your childhood.* Not — *I'm hearing that you're experiencing significant stress.*

Just: *what do you want from this.*

Sarah looked at her.

"I want documentation," she said. "I want someone with credentials who has seen me and assessed me and can say clearly and on record that I am a functional, coherent, grounded adult making deliberate choices about my own life."

Patricia nodded once. "That's the practical answer. What's the other answer."

Sarah paused.

"I want someone to talk to who isn't in the middle of it," she said. "Everyone I trust is inside the situation. I need someone outside it."

"Also practical." Patricia tilted her head slightly. "Is there a third answer."

Sarah looked at her hands in her lap.

At the plants in the windows. The afternoon light coming through them green and filtered and quiet.

Thought about the river. The current around her ankles. The edge of herself becoming less insistent. The thing she couldn't name that arrived without invitation and stayed without permission and was, she was increasingly certain, the most real thing that had ever happened to her.

"I want to understand what's happening to me," she said. "Not have it explained away. Not have it managed. Understand it."

Patricia Wren looked at her for a long moment.

"Good," she said.

Just that.

Sarah felt something in her chest release that she hadn't known she was holding.

"Good," she said.

She drove home through the early dark of November.

No sedan at the end of the road tonight.

She went inside. Made tea. Stood at the kitchen window looking at the empty road and the bare tree line and the sky going from grey to black above it.

Daniel came in from the back porch with an armful of wood.

She told him about Patricia Wren.

He listened. Set down the wood. Came and stood beside her at the window.

"Good," he said.

She leaned into him slightly.

Outside the bare trees stood in the dark exactly as they had stood for years before any of this and would stand for years after, patient and indifferent and tall, and the road was empty and the night was cold and inside the kitchen it was warm and smelled like tea and woodsmoke and the ordinary extraordinary fact of two people choosing to be in the same place at the end of a hard day.

She felt the thing behind her sternum.

Steady.

Quiet.

Still here.

She knew.

Chapter 14

CHAPTER FOURTEEN: GRACE REMEMBERS

It came back in pieces.

Not the way she'd hoped — all at once, a door opening, herself stepping through it back into who she'd been before. That was the version she'd imagined during the worst months at the facility, lying in the narrow bed in the narrow room listening to the specific silence of a place that managed everything including the silence.

She had imagined a door.

There was no door.

There were fragments.

A word arriving in the middle of a sentence that she hadn't been able to find for months. The taste of coffee the way it used to taste before the medication flattened everything into a grey approximate version of itself. The ability to read three pages of a book without losing the thread.

Small things.

To anyone watching — small things.

To Grace, who had been without them — everything.

She had been staying with Rachel.

Rachel had offered the second bedroom the night of the parking lot and Grace had said yes without deliberating because deliberating required energy she didn't have yet and Rachel's second bedroom had a window that faced east and the morning light came through it without asking anything of her and that was, at that particular moment, exactly what she needed.

A window.

Morning light.

Nothing asking anything.

Rachel moved through her apartment with the brisk competent energy of someone who had decided a thing and was executing it without drama. She cooked real food and left it in the refrigerator with small notes — *eat this, it's good* — and did not hover and did not check in with the performed casualness of someone checking in and did not treat Grace like something that might break if handled incorrectly.

She treated her like a person who was tired.

Which was what she was.

Just a person who was very, very tired and needed a window and morning light and food in the refrigerator with notes that said *eat this, it's good.*

Grace ate the food.

Slept ten hours a night.

Sat in the morning light.

Began, slowly, to find the edges of herself again.

The barn helped.

The first Thursday she'd sat in the circle and mostly listened and watched and said almost nothing and gone home and slept for eleven hours.

The second Thursday she'd said three sentences and meant all of them.

The third Thursday Marcus had been at the back table when she arrived and he'd looked up and said *tea* and she'd sat down and they'd been quiet together in the way that was becoming, she realized, its own kind of language between them.

A language without performance.

Without the managed warmth of people who needed her to be better so they could feel good about helping.

Just — *tea* and the barn and the afternoon light in the high windows and the particular patience of a man who apparently had nowhere else he needed to be and no investment in what she did with the time except that she spent it however she actually needed to spend it.

She was not accustomed to that.

It was taking some getting used to.

Four weeks after the parking lot she sat in the barn with Sarah.

Rachel had brought them together deliberately — Grace understood this and did not mind. Rachel was a person who identified what was needed and arranged for it with the minimum of ceremony and the maximum of effectiveness. It was one of the things Grace had come to love about her.

Sarah arrived with two coffees from somewhere good.

Handed one to Grace without asking how she took it.

It was made exactly right.

Grace looked at her.

Sarah smiled. "Lucky guess."

Grace thought it probably wasn't a guess.

She was beginning to notice things like that about the people in this group. The small knowings. The coffee made right. The phone answered before it rang. She'd had that once. Before.

She was starting to remember what before felt like.

They sat in two of the circle chairs angled toward each other.

The barn quiet around them.

Outside the November wind moved through the tree line and the light through the high windows was the thin pale light of a season running out of itself.

Sarah didn't open with a question.

Didn't say *how are you doing* or *you seem better* or any of the things people opened with when they wanted information framed as care.

She just sat.

Drank her coffee.

Let the barn be the barn.

After a while Grace said: "I keep trying to remember when it started."

Sarah waited.

"The changing. Whatever this is." Grace looked at her coffee. "I know I felt it before the facility. I know it was there — the sense of something larger than my ordinary life pressing at the edges of it. A frequency I could almost hear." She paused. "I thought I was developing a problem. That's what I thought at first. That something was wrong with me."

She stopped.

"That's what they counted on," Sarah said quietly.

"Yes." Grace looked at her hands. "By the time I understood it wasn't a problem — that it was actually the most real thing that had ever happened to me — I had already told enough people about it that the machinery was in motion."

"What machinery."

"Dr. Hendricks," Grace said. "He was my physician too."

Sarah went still.

"For six years," Grace said. "I trusted him. I told him what I was experiencing because he asked the right questions in the right order and I thought — " She stopped. "I thought he was trying to help me understand it."

"He was documenting it," Sarah said.

"He was documenting it." Grace's voice was steady. The steadiness of someone who had moved through the anger and the grief of it and come out the other side into something cleaner and colder. "Three months after I first told him — the facility. Voluntary at first. Then not voluntary."

Sarah looked at her.

"They have a system," Grace said. "It's elegant if you don't mind it being monstrous. Voluntary entry creates a record of consent. The record of consent is used to establish a pattern of instability. The pattern of instability becomes the justification for involuntary hold when the voluntary period ends." She paused. "By the time I understood what I'd walked into I had signed enough forms and attended enough sessions and been observed by enough credentialed people that my own signature was being used against me."

The barn held this.

The wind outside.

The pale November light.

Sarah said: "How long."

"Four months." Grace looked at the high windows. "They're very good at the medication. They don't want you gone — gone is obvious and obvious creates problems. They want you present enough to function and absent enough not to matter." She paused. "They want you to look fine. They want everyone around you to see you looking fine and conclude that you are fine and that whatever you said before — whatever you described, whatever you felt, whatever was real — was the problem, not the solution."

She looked back at Sarah.

"The medication does that very well," she said. "It makes you look fine."

Sarah said nothing.

Grace appreciated this.

People who said *I'm so sorry* in this moment — she understood the impulse and she was done with it. She didn't want sorry. Sorry was for things that were over.

This was not over.

"What do you remember," Sarah said. "From before. What it felt like."

Grace considered the question seriously.

Not the therapeutic version of it. Not the version she'd been asked forty times by people with clipboards who wanted her to describe symptoms in language they could classify.

The real version.

"Expansion," she said. "That's the closest word. Like the container I'd been living inside my whole life was — not breaking, not dissolving, just becoming optional." She paused. "Like finding out the room you've always lived in has a door you didn't know about and opening it and discovering it doesn't lead to another room."

"What does it lead to," Sarah said.

Grace looked at her.

"Everything else," she said.

Sarah's expression did something Grace recognized.

Not surprise.

Recognition.

The specific look of someone hearing a thing described that they have experienced and not yet put words to.

"Yes," Sarah said quietly. To herself as much as to Grace.

Grace looked at her steadily. "You're further along than you know," she said.

Sarah looked up. "What do you mean."

"I mean — " Grace paused. Chose carefully. "I mean the thing you're feeling, whatever you're calling it or not calling it, is not in its early stages. It may feel uncertain to you. It may feel like something that comes and goes." She paused. "It doesn't come and go. It deepens. What feels uncertain now is the last of the uncertainty." She looked at her coffee. "I know because I remember what that stage felt like. From before they interrupted it."

Sarah was quiet for a moment.

"Does it come back," she said. "After what they did to you. Does it come back fully."

Grace looked at her hands.

The hands that were hers again.

The hands that had learned to hold a mug of tea in a barn on Thursday nights with a man who said *tea* and meant something larger than tea.

"Yes," she said. "It comes back."

She paused.

"It comes back angry," she said. "Which I didn't expect. I expected it to come back gentle — the way it arrived the first time, slow and quiet and patient." She almost smiled. "It came back like water that's been held back. Not violent. Just — insistent. Like it had somewhere to be and had been kept waiting and was done waiting."

Sarah looked at her for a long moment.

"That doesn't frighten you," Sarah said.

"No," Grace said.

"It frightens me," Sarah said. "Sometimes. The insistence of it."

"I know." Grace looked at her steadily. "It frightened me too. Before I understood what it was insisting on."

"What was it insisting on."

Grace considered this the way she considered everything now — slowly, from all sides, without the medicated smoothing that had once removed the texture from her thinking.

"That I stop being partially here," she said finally. "That I stop living at half the volume I was capable of." She paused. "It was insisting on me. The full version. Not the managed version. Not the version that fit inside other people's comfort."

She looked at Sarah directly.

"It was insisting on exactly what they were afraid of," she said.

Marcus came into the barn an hour later.

He stopped when he saw them.

Not surprise — he'd known Grace was coming. Something else. The expression of a man walking into a room and finding it changed from when he left it and understanding that the change is good without yet knowing how good.

He looked at Grace.

She looked back.

There was a moment.

Sarah picked up both empty coffee cups and stood.

"I'm going to get more coffee," she said.

She went to the back table and busied herself with the kettle and studied the middle distance with the focused attention of someone absolutely not listening to the two people behind her.

She heard nothing because nothing was said.

But when she turned around with the two fresh cups Marcus was sitting in the chair she'd vacated and Grace was looking at him with the expression Sarah was beginning to recognize — the one that appeared on Grace's face when she was seeing something clearly for the first time after a long time of not being able to see clearly.

She set the cups down between them.

"I'll be outside," she said.

Neither of them appeared to hear her.

She went outside and stood in the cold barn lot and looked at the bare tree line and the pale sky and the road that was empty today, no black sedans, no idling engines.

Just the road.

Just the cold.

Just the sound of the wind through the stripped branches.

She felt the thing behind her sternum.

Quiet and steady and present.

Thought about what Grace had said.

It was insisting on me. The full version.

She stood in the cold for a long time.

The full version.

She was beginning to understand what that meant.

She was beginning to understand that the cars at the end of the road and the thin folder in conference room B and Gerald Foss and his notepad all added up to the same thing — a very organized, very patient, very well-resourced effort to prevent exactly that.

The full version.

Of her.

Of all of them.

She looked at the road.

Empty.

For now.

She went back inside.

Chapter 15

CHAPTER FIFTEEN: THE SECOND LOVE SCENE

She didn't tell Daniel about the conversation with Grace that day. Not because she was keeping it from him.

Because some things need to settle before you pour them into language.

Like coffee grounds.

Like river silt.

Like the particular thing Grace had said that had been sitting in the place behind her sternum all afternoon, quiet and insistent and not yet ready to be words.

It was insisting on me. The full version.

She drove home through the early dark and made dinner and they ate and talked about ordinary things — Daniel's work, the woodpile getting low, whether the weather would turn hard before December — and she was present for all of it and also slightly elsewhere, which Daniel noticed and did not mention, because Daniel was a man who understood the difference between somewhere a person needed to come back from on their own and somewhere they needed help getting back from.

He was good at that distinction.

It was one of the things she was still learning to receive.

After dinner he built a fire.

She sat on the couch with her feet tucked under her and watched him do it — the unhurried competence of someone who had built ten thousand fires and found neither pride nor tedium in it anymore, just the thing itself, just the work.

The fire caught.

He sat beside her.

Not close enough to be deliberate. Close enough to be chosen.

The fire did what fires do — filled the room with the smell of woodsmoke and the sound of itself and the particular quality of light that makes everything look like it's been there for a long time and intends to stay.

She leaned into him.

He put his arm around her without adjusting or shifting or making a production of it.

Just — there.

They sat.

After a while she said: "Grace told me something today."

"What did she say."

Sarah looked at the fire.

"She said it comes back. After what they did to her. The — whatever it is. The thing." She paused. "She said it comes back fully."

Daniel was quiet.

"She said it came back insisting," Sarah said. "Like water that's been held back. She said it was insisting on her. The full version of her."

The fire popped once.

Settled.

Daniel said: "What did that do to you. Hearing that."

She thought about it honestly.

"It frightened me," she said. "And it — opened something." She paused. "Both at the same time."

"What did it open."

She turned to look at him.

His face in the firelight. The face she had been learning for months and was nowhere near finished learning. The face of a man who asked real questions and waited for real answers and did not flinch from either.

"I think I've been experiencing this thing — whatever it is — at a distance," she said. "Like standing at the edge of water and feeling the cold of it without going in." She paused. "I think I've been managing it. Keeping it at a level I could explain to myself."

"And now."

"And now I'm not sure I can keep doing that."

He looked at her.

"Do you want to," he said.

She held his gaze.

"No," she said.

Something moved through his expression.

Not the complicated thing — not the fear and the staying and the both-and.

Something simpler than that.

Something that looked, she thought, like relief.

"Good," he said.

She kissed him.

Not the way she sometimes kissed him — carefully, with the residual habit of a woman who had learned to monitor the temperature of a room before she did anything that might change it.

Without monitoring.

Without the half-second of calculation she hadn't even known she was performing until she stopped performing it.

He felt the difference immediately.

She knew he felt it because he went still for a moment — the stillness of someone recalibrating, updating, recognizing — and then he kissed her back differently too.

More present.

More himself.

Like two people who had been having a very good approximation of a conversation and had just discovered the real one.

They moved to the bedroom without hurrying.

The fire still going in the other room. The cold pressing at the windows. The dark outside complete and ordinary and entirely indifferent to what was happening inside.

She was aware of herself differently.

Not performing. Not monitoring. Not the small background management of a woman making sure she was acceptable, making sure she wasn't too much, making sure the experience she was having aligned with the experience she was supposed to be having.

Just — here.

Her hands on his shoulders.

His face above her in the dim room.

The full version.

She thought of Grace saying it and then stopped thinking about Grace because Daniel's hands were doing something that made thinking about anything else briefly impossible and she let it make thinking impossible because she was done with managing the temperature of rooms.

She was done with that entirely.

Afterward they lay in the dark.

His hand moving slowly up and down her arm in the absent way of someone whose body is content and whose mind is quiet.

The fire sound from the other room.

The wind outside.

She lay looking at the ceiling in the particular stillness of someone who has arrived somewhere they didn't know they were going.

Not the ceiling.

Through the ceiling.

The sky beyond it. The dark beyond that. The —

She stopped.

Breathed.

Let it be what it was without reaching for it.

It was there anyway.

Quiet and vast and entirely unbothered by her reaching or not reaching.

Like the river.

Like the current around her ankles.

Like the thing Grace had said — *not breaking, not dissolving, just becoming optional.* The container becoming optional.

She lay in the dark and felt the edges of herself go soft and unhurried and present.

Not frightening.

Not tonight.

Tonight it felt like the most natural thing that had ever happened to her. Like something that had been waiting with the patience of something that had no concept of being tired of waiting.

She breathed.

In.

Out.

The dark room.

Daniel's hand.

The fire.

The wind.

Something underneath all of it that had no name and needed none.

"You're somewhere," he said.

Not accusation. Not even a question.

Just — noticing.

She turned her head to look at him in the dark.

"I'm here," she said.

"You're here and somewhere else."

She considered this.

"Yes," she said.

He was quiet for a moment.

"Is it the thing," he said. "The thing that's been — "

"Yes."

"Is it okay."

She thought about it honestly.

Took the full measure of what was happening in her chest and her skin and the soft undefended place behind her sternum where it lived when it came.

"It's more than okay," she said.

He absorbed this.

Lay still beside her.

She waited for the complicated thing — the fear, the both-and, the hands that memorized her like something that might be taken away.

It didn't come.

"Good," he said.

Simple as that.

Good.

She felt something shift in the room.

Not dramatically. Not with ceremony.

Just — a settling. Like a structure finding its right load. Like two people arriving at the same place from different directions and recognizing each other when they got there.

She reached for his hand under the blanket.

He turned it over and held hers properly.

She lay awake after he slept.

Not anxiously.

With the clear-eyed, slightly amazed wakefulness of someone to whom something has happened and who wants to be present for the aftermath rather than sleep through it.

She thought about the twenty-two years.

The long practice of smallness. The monitoring. The calculation. The half-second before every action in which she checked whether the action was acceptable, whether it was too much, whether it fit inside the space she had been allocated.

She thought about conference room B and Carolyn Marsh's neutral expression and Gerald Foss's notepad.

Whatever you may be experiencing.

Whatever she may be experiencing.

She looked at the dark ceiling.

What she was experiencing was this — a woman lying in a warm bed next to a man who had never once asked her to be smaller, feeling the edges of herself expand past the old boundaries without apology and without drama and without the permission of anyone.

What she was experiencing was herself.

The full version.

She almost laughed.

She didn't, because Daniel was sleeping and he'd earned his sleep. But the almost-laugh was real and it was the laugh of someone who has seen something clearly for the first time and found it both completely obvious and completely astonishing.

They were afraid of this.

All of it — the cars and the file and the thin folder in conference room B and Gerald Foss flying in from wherever Gerald Foss came from — all of it was afraid of this.

A woman in a warm bed feeling the full measure of herself.

She thought about Robert Caulfield.

Sixty-one. Retired schoolteacher. Daughter in Grand Rapids.

She thought about the Oregon group. Two car accidents six months apart.

She thought about Diane in Portland who had lost her job and her insurance and her heart medication.

She thought about Grace in the narrow bed in the narrow room listening to the managed silence.

She held all of it.

The warmth of the bed and the cold outside and Daniel sleeping and the thing in her chest that was expanding without apology.

She held all of it at once.

And found — to her own quiet astonishment — that she was large enough.

In the morning she stood at the kitchen window with her coffee.

The road empty.

The bare tree line.

The sky just beginning to go from black to grey.

Daniel came in behind her. Put his hands on her shoulders. Stood looking out the window with her.

"No car," he said.

"Not this morning."

He was quiet for a moment.

"Sarah."

She turned to look at him.

His face in the early grey light. The face she was still learning.

"Last night," he said. "You were different."

She waited.

"Not different wrong," he said. "Different — " He paused. Looking for the right word with the seriousness of someone for whom the right word mattered. "Different arrived," he said finally.

She looked at him.

"Yes," she said. "I was."

He nodded slowly.

Poured himself coffee.

Stood beside her at the window.

They looked at the empty road together.

The bare tree line.

The sky going from grey to pale.

The ordinary extraordinary morning.

"She said it comes back fully," Daniel said.

"Yes."

"Grace."

"Yes."

He drank his coffee. Said nothing for a moment.

Then: "I want you to know something."

She waited.

"Whatever fully looks like," he said. "I'm not going to ask you to be less of it."

She looked at him.

The morning light on his face.

The man who had never once asked her to be smaller standing in her kitchen on a cold November morning telling her he didn't intend to start.

She felt the thing behind her sternum.

Not quiet this time.

Not the steady undercurrent she'd grown accustomed to.

Something warmer.

Something that moved through her chest like the first real heat of a fire catching — the moment after the kindling and before the log, the brief brilliant moment when you know it's going to hold.

"I know," she said.

She did know.

She had known for a while.

She was just, she realized, finally allowing herself to know it without managing the knowing.

The full version of knowing.

The full version of everything.

She leaned into him.

Outside the pale sky continued its slow business of becoming morning and the bare tree line stood in the cold exactly as it had always stood and the road was empty and the world was large and she was — for the first time in a very long time — exactly the right size for it.

Chapter 16

CHAPTER SIXTEEN: DAVID'S BACKGROUND

David Cross had learned to read rooms before he learned to read people.

Rooms first.

The temperature of a space. The arrangement of furniture. Where the exits were and whether they were being watched. The quality of silence — whether it was empty silence or occupied silence, whether it was the silence of nothing happening or the silence of something about to.

He'd learned this at eleven years old in a house in rural Ohio where the difference between those two silences was the difference between an ordinary evening and one that wasn't.

He didn't talk about the house in Ohio.

He talked about almost nothing from before he was nineteen, which was the age he left and did not go back, which was also the age a man named Carver Ellison found him sleeping in a bus station in Columbus and bought him breakfast and asked him three questions and then offered him a job.

The job was not what it appeared to be.

Most things worth doing weren't.

Rachel asked him about it on a Wednesday.

Not at the barn. Not at the diner.

She'd called and said she was making dinner and there was too much of it and he could come or not. Plain as that. The Rachel version of an invitation, which left no room for performance and required no response except yes or no.

He said yes.

Her apartment was on the third floor of a building that was older than it looked and better maintained than its age suggested. She buzzed him up without using the intercom, which meant she'd heard his car, which meant she'd been listening for it, which she would not have admitted to and he did not intend to mention.

The apartment smelled like garlic and something with wine in it.

Gerald the cat assessed him from the couch with the expression of an entity that had reached conclusions and was not interested in revising them.

"He doesn't like anyone," Rachel said from the kitchen.

"I'm not trying to make him like me."

"That's probably why he's only looked at you twice. Usually it's a sustained stare."

David looked at the cat.

The cat looked back.

Then looked away.

He took off his coat and hung it by the door and went into the kitchen.

She cooked the way she did everything else.

Without wasted motion. Without consulting the recipe she'd clearly made enough times to not need. Without performing competence or inviting observation.

Just — cooking. The thing itself.

He sat at the kitchen counter and watched her and felt the particular ease of being in a space where nothing was being managed on his behalf.

He was not accustomed to that.

Most spaces managed something on his behalf. His apartment managed solitude. The barn managed purpose. The coffee shop where he met Sarah managed information. Even the diner managed the specific comfortable neutrality of a place with no personal investment in either of them.

Rachel's kitchen managed nothing.

It was just a kitchen.

He was just a person in it.

He found this unexpectedly difficult to sit with and sat with it anyway.

They ate at the small table by the window.

The city outside doing its Wednesday evening business. The apartment warm. Gerald relocating from the couch to a position near the radiator from which he could observe both of them without appearing to.

Rachel poured wine.

They talked about the group first because the group was always first — the cars, Foss, Sarah's appointment with Patricia Wren, the slow progress on Robert Caulfield's location.

Then they didn't talk about the group.

They talked about other things.

She asked about the work — not the current work, the earlier work, the thing before the groups and the files and the careful navigation of spaces between what was documented and what was real.

He told her about Carver Ellison.

The bus station in Columbus. The breakfast. The three questions.

"What were the questions," she said.

He picked up his wine. "What do you see when you look at a room full of people. What do you do when someone lies to you. What would you do if you found out something was wrong and doing something about it would cost you everything you had."

Rachel considered these.

"What did you say."

"I said I saw who was afraid of who. I said I waited. I said I didn't know yet but I thought I'd do something."

"And he hired you based on that."

"He hired me based on the fact that I didn't lie on any of the three." He set down his wine. "He said most people lie on at least one. They say they see dynamics but they mean they see status. They say they confront liars but they mean they avoid conflict. They say they'd do something but they mean they'd do something safe."

Rachel looked at him.

"What did he want you to do," she said.

"Watch," David said. "At first. He was building a picture of something he'd been tracking for years. Organizations — some of them companies, some of them government adjacent, some of them harder to categorize — that had a consistent pattern of behavior toward certain kinds of people."

"What kinds of people."

"People who were changing in ways the organizations found threatening. People who were gathering together in ways that suggested they were becoming more than the sum of their parts." He paused. "People like the ones in Marcus's barn."

Rachel was quiet for a moment.

"Carver Ellison knew about groups like this one."

"He'd been documenting them for eleven years when he found me." David looked at his glass. "He'd seen fourteen groups. Watched eight of them get dismantled. Managed to help three of them survive in some form." He paused. "He died six years ago. Heart attack. Genuine — I had people check."

"You had people check if his heart attack was genuine."

"Yes."

Rachel looked at him steadily.

He met her eyes.

"You live in a world where that's a necessary thing to check," she said.

"Yes."

"And you've been living in that world since you were nineteen."

"Yes."

She picked up her wine.

Drank.

Set it down.

"That's a long time to be careful," she said.

He looked at her.

Nobody had ever said it quite like that before.

Not — *that must be exhausting* or *that sounds lonely* or the various therapeutic framings he'd received over the years from the two therapists he'd seen and largely not talked to.

Just — *that's a long time to be careful.*

Like she saw the specific weight of it without needing him to describe it.

"Yes," he said.

"Is it — " She paused. Chose. "Is it something you chose. Or something that chose you."

He thought about the house in Ohio.

About eleven years old and the two kinds of silence and the learning to read rooms before he read people because rooms told you what was coming and people sometimes lied.

About the bus station and Carver and the three questions.

About fourteen years of watching and documenting and trying to be useful to people who were becoming something larger than the world they'd been assigned and paying the cost of it.

"Both," he said. "In that order."

She nodded.

Not sympathetically.

With the understanding of someone who recognized the distinction because she lived it herself.

It chose me and then I chose it back.

He didn't say that part.

She seemed to hear it anyway.

After dinner he helped with the dishes.

She washed. He dried.

The domestic simplicity of it was not lost on either of them. Two people who operated in complicated spaces standing at a kitchen sink in the ordinary way of people who had been doing this together for years, which they hadn't, which somehow didn't matter.

Gerald relocated again. Closer this time.

David looked down at the cat.

The cat looked up at him with the expression of an entity revising its conclusions.

"He's never done that," Rachel said without looking up from the dishes.

"What."

"Moved toward someone he doesn't know."

David looked at Gerald.

Gerald looked back.

Then, with the air of an entity that had made a decision and intended to live with it, sat down on David's left foot.

Rachel turned and looked at the cat on David's foot.

Looked at David.

Something shifted in her face.

Not a smile exactly.

The thing that lived in the same neighborhood as a smile and was sometimes more honest than one.

"He decided," she said.

"Apparently."

"He takes a long time to decide."

David looked at her.

"I know the feeling," he said.

They moved to the couch with their wine.

The city outside going from evening to night. The radiator ticking. Gerald establishing himself between them with the territorial confidence of a cat who had made a decision and was now enforcing it.

"Your sister," Rachel said.

Not a question. Not a prompt. Just — placing the subject in the room and leaving it there for him to do what he wanted with.

He looked at his wine.

Her name was Caroline.

She was four years younger than him and had been, for most of their childhood in Ohio, the person he was reading rooms for. Not for himself. For her. The calculation of each evening's particular silence had been in service of getting them both through it intact, and mostly it had worked, and the mostly was something he had made a certain peace with and occasionally had not.

She was in Denver now.

Taught elementary school.

Had two kids and a husband who was, by all available evidence, exactly what he appeared to be, which David had verified once and felt both relieved and ashamed about verifying.

She called on Sundays.

He always answered.

"She found a group," he said. "In Denver, ten years ago. Before I knew what to look for. Before I had any framework for it." He paused. "She called me and tried to describe what was happening to her. The changes. The — expansion." He looked at his glass. "I didn't understand what she was describing. I thought she was — I thought something was wrong. I thought Carver's work had made me see patterns where there weren't any."

Rachel waited.

"By the time I understood what was actually happening they had already moved on her. Employer first. Then her landlord received a letter — anonymous, documented concerns about a tenant. Then her physician, who was Hendricks in everything but name, filed a report suggesting she was a danger to herself." He stopped. "She wasn't held. She was — managed. Her life made small enough that the group scattered and she had nowhere to go back to."

"How long," Rachel said.

"Eight months." He set down his wine. "She's fine now. Better than fine. The group is gone but what happened to her didn't go anywhere. She carries it. She always will." He paused. "I carry the eight months."

"It wasn't your fault," Rachel said.

"I know that."

"But you carry it anyway."

"Yes."

She looked at him.

"That's why you do this," she said. "Not just because of what happened to her. Because of the eight months you didn't understand what you were looking at."

He looked at her.

The apartment around them. Gerald between them on the couch with the satisfied air of a successful negotiator. The city outside. The ordinary Wednesday night.

"Yes," he said.

She reached across Gerald — who registered this with a flattened ear but did not move — and put her hand over his on the couch cushion.

Not squeezing. Not performing comfort.

Just there.

The plain fact of her hand.

He looked at it.

Turned his hand over and held hers properly.

Gerald looked up at both of them with the expression of an entity whose work here was done.

He left at ten-thirty.

At the door he put on his coat and she leaned against the doorframe with her arms crossed and the expression that wasn't quite a smile.

"Your cat decided," he said.

"He did."

"Does that mean anything."

She looked at him.

"It means he's a good judge," she said.

He held her gaze for a moment.

Then he said: "Friday."

Not a question.

She understood.

"Friday," she said.

He went down the stairs.

She stood in the doorway until she heard the building door close below.

Then she went back inside and sat on the couch and Gerald climbed immediately into her lap with the confidence of an animal that had accomplished something and expected to be acknowledged for it.

She put her hand on his back.

Sat in the quiet apartment.

Thought about David at nineteen in a bus station in Columbus.

Thought about Caroline in Denver teaching elementary school.

Thought about eight months and the weight a person carries when they understand something too late and choose to carry the understanding instead of setting it down.

She thought about want.

About the careful life and the managed distance and the things filed under *the world as it is.*

She thought about Friday.

She was not afraid of Friday.

She was — and she sat with this the way she sat with everything, directly and without flinching — she was glad of Friday.

Actual, uncomplicated, unreasonable gladness.

Gerald purred.

She sat in the warm apartment while the Wednesday night continued its business outside and felt the thing behind her sternum that had been open since the diner and showed no signs of closing.

Good.

She was done with closing.

Chapter 17

CHAPTER SEVENTEEN: FOLLOWED

She noticed it on a Tuesday.

Not the barn road. Not the road past the cabin.

The grocery store parking lot on Maple Street at ten in the morning in plain November daylight with other people's carts and other people's ordinary Tuesdays moving around her.

She'd come out with two bags and was loading them into the back seat when she felt it.

Not saw.

Felt.

The specific pressure behind her sternum that had become, over the past weeks, her most reliable instrument.

She straightened.

Looked around the parking lot without making it obvious she was looking.

Minivan. Pickup. Older Honda. Woman with a stroller. Man loading lumber.

Black sedan. Far end of the lot. Backed in.

Facing her.

She loaded the second bag.

Closed the back door.

Got in.

Sat for a moment with her hands in her lap before she started the engine.

Test it.

David's voice in her head from two weeks ago, sitting in the coffee shop.

If you think you're being followed, test it. Two unnecessary turns minimum. If it stays with you both times it's not coincidence.

She started the engine.

Pulled out of the lot heading north.

The sedan pulled out behind her.

Three car lengths back.

She drove two blocks. Signal left. Turned.

Drove one block. Signal right. Turned.

Checked the mirror.

Three car lengths back.

Her hands were steady on the wheel.

Her heart was not particularly steady but it was functional and she allowed it to be functional without adding the layer of being frightened of being frightened, which she had found was the thing that actually made it worse.

One more turn.

The sedan stayed with her.

She pulled into a gas station.

Parked at the far pump even though she didn't need gas.

Got out.

The sedan drove past the entrance without turning in. She watched it go without watching it, the peripheral trick David had shown her.

It turned left at the light.

Gone.

She stood at the pump for a moment.

Then she took out her phone and called David.

He was there in twelve minutes.

She was inside the gas station with a coffee she didn't want when he came through the door.

He looked at her face.

"You okay."

"Yes." She was. Surprisingly. "Maple Street Kroger. Black sedan. Backed into the far end of the lot facing my car. Followed me through three turns. Left when I pulled in here."

He sat down across from her.

"Did you get the plate."

"Partial. Ohio. Starts with FKR. I couldn't get the rest without making it obvious."

He took out his phone. Made a note. "That's enough to start with." He looked at her. "How did you know. Before you saw it."

She looked at her coffee.

"The thing," she said. "The pressure. It was there before I looked up."

He nodded slowly. Not surprised. Not performing unsurprise. Just — filing it in the right place with the seriousness it deserved.

"It's getting more reliable," she said.

"I know."

"Does that — " She paused. "Does that matter. For the file. For what Foss is building."

He looked at her steadily. "It matters for you," he said. "For Foss — what Foss is building doesn't depend on what's actually happening to you. It depends on the narrative. Those are two different projects."

She looked at her coffee.

"Right," she said.

"Sarah."

She looked up.

"The fact that it's getting more reliable is a good thing," he said. "Whatever else is happening — that's a good thing. Don't let them make it the thing that frightens you."

She held his gaze.

He was right.

She knew he was right.

The pressure behind her sternum had told her about the sedan before her eyes had. It had been accurate and it had been useful and the only frightening thing about it was the framework other people were trying to build around it.

"Okay," she said.

"Okay," he said.

She almost smiled. "It is a good word."

"Apparently contagious," he said.

She didn't tell Daniel that night.

Not because she was keeping it from him.

Because she wanted one evening without the weight of it. One evening of the fire and the dinner and the ordinary conversation and his hand finding hers on the couch without it being about any of this.

She had it.

It was good.

She told him in the morning over coffee.

He listened without interrupting. His face doing the complicated thing and then settling past it.

"Three turns," he said.

"Three."

"And the pressure told you before you looked."

"Yes."

He drank his coffee. Looked at the window. The road empty this morning, bare tree line, grey sky pressing down on the last of November.

"I want to show you something," he said.

He took her out to the barn lot behind the cabin.

Not Marcus's barn. Their barn — the smaller outbuilding at the back of the property that stored the kayaks in winter and smelled like old wood and river water and the particular dry cold of a space that didn't get heated.

She hadn't been in it since September.

He moved the kayaks to one side. Cleared a space in the middle of the floor.

She watched him do this with the expression of a woman who has learned that when Daniel moves kayaks without explanation the explanation is usually worth waiting for.

He stood in the cleared space.

"Come here," he said.

She went.

He positioned her in front of him. Turned her so her back was to him.

His hands on her shoulders.

"Close your eyes," he said.

She closed them.

"Now." His voice quiet in the cold barn. "Tell me when I'm about to move."

"Daniel — "

"Just try."

She stood in the dark behind her eyelids.

The cold of the barn. The smell of river water and old wood. His hands on her shoulders, still and warm.

She breathed.

Let the thinking settle.

Let the pressure behind her sternum come forward the way it came when she let it — not reaching for it, not demanding it, just making room.

She stood there for a moment.

Then —

"Now," she said.

He moved.

She felt it a half second before he did. Before his weight shifted. Before his hands changed pressure. Something that was not sound and not movement and not any of the ordinary things you might explain it as.

Just — *now.*

He stopped.

She opened her eyes.

Turned around.

He was looking at her with the expression she was still learning.

Not the complicated one.

Not even the arrived one from the morning after Grace.

Something new.

The expression of a man who has suspected something for a long time and has just watched it confirmed in a cold barn on a November morning and is not afraid of what he's seen.

Is, in fact, looking at her like she is the most extraordinary thing he has ever been standing near.

"Again," she said.

They did it again.

And again.

Five times.

Five times she said *now* before he moved.

Five times she was right.

They stood in the cold barn afterward.

Not talking.

The kayaks against the wall. The smell of old wood. The grey light coming through the one small window.

"How long," he said.

"The phone. The footsteps. Those started weeks ago." She paused. "The sedan today was different. That was — further out. More specific."

He nodded.

"Patricia Wren should know about this," he said.

"Yes."

"And David."

"I already told David."

He looked at her. "You told David before me."

She met his eyes. Held them.

"I needed one evening," she said. "I needed one evening where it wasn't this. Where it was just us."

He was quiet for a moment.

Something moved through his face.

"Okay," he said.

She watched him decide it was okay. Watched him choose it genuinely rather than performing it. Watched the choice settle in him until it was real.

It took about four seconds.

She loved him for those four seconds.

She didn't say that.

But she thought it clearly and without the managing of it and let the thought be the full size it was.

Patricia Wren listened to the whole thing.

Thursday at four. The small office. The plants in the windows. The two chairs angled toward each other.

Sarah told her about the sedan. The three turns. The pressure before the seeing. The barn with Daniel. The five times.

Patricia listened without expression.

When Sarah finished she said: "How does it feel. The pressure. Describe it physically."

Sarah thought about it.

"Behind the sternum," she said. "Like a weight that isn't heavy. Like something pressing gently from the inside." She paused. "It's warm. It's always warm."

"And when it comes before something external — before the phone rings, before the car — does it feel different from when it comes in other contexts."

Sarah considered this carefully.

"It has a direction," she said slowly. "The other times — the fire, lying in the dark, the river — it's diffuse. Everywhere at once. When it's about something external it has a — " She paused. "A pointing. Like a compass that's just slightly warmer on one side."

Patricia nodded.

Made a note.

Not a clinical note. Sarah had learned to read the difference. This was a note of someone recording something they found genuinely interesting.

"Has it ever been wrong," Patricia said.

Sarah thought about it honestly.

"No," she said.

Patricia looked up.

"In my experience," she said carefully, choosing her words with the precision Sarah had come to expect from her, "people who develop this kind of perceptual accuracy — and I want to be clear that I'm describing something I've observed clinically, not something I can explain — people who develop it typically report the same thing." She paused. "It is not wrong. It is occasionally incomplete. Those are different things."

Sarah looked at her.

"You've seen this before," she said.

Patricia held her gaze.

"I've seen things I couldn't explain using the frameworks I was trained in," she said carefully. "Which is why I stopped using only those frameworks."

Sarah sat with this.

The plants in the windows. The afternoon light. The sound of the street outside, ordinary and indifferent.

"Is it in your notes," Sarah said. "What I just told you."

"It's in my notes as a patient describing subjective perceptual experiences that are consistent with heightened intuitive function," Patricia said. "Which is both accurate and entirely defensible."

Sarah almost smiled.

"You've done this before," she said. "Protected people this way."

Patricia looked at her with the direct gaze of someone who answered real questions with real answers.

"Yes," she said.

She drove home through the early dark.

Turned onto the cabin road.

Slowed.

The sedan was there.

Same position. End of the road. Facing the cabin.

Different car entirely. Same message.

She pulled into the driveway.

Sat for a moment.

Looked at the car in her rearview mirror.

It sat looking back.

She got out.

Went inside.

Daniel was in the kitchen. He looked at her face.

"End of the road," she said.

He looked at the window.

She put her bag down.

"Patricia said it's not wrong," she said. "The pressure. She said it's occasionally incomplete but it's not wrong."

He turned back from the window.

"Okay," he said.

"She's documented people like me before. She knows what she's doing."

"Good."

She looked at him.

"We have a good team," she said.

He considered this.

"We do," he agreed.

She went to the window and looked at the road.

The sedan sitting in the dark at the end of it.

Patient and present and entirely certain of its own authority.

She looked at it for a long moment.

Then she turned away and went to help Daniel with dinner.

Let it watch.

Let it sit there in the cold with its engine off and its driver doing whatever the driver did.

She was in a warm kitchen with a man who had stood in a cold barn and watched her say *now* five times and looked at her afterward like she was the most extraordinary thing he'd ever been standing near.

She was not afraid of the car.

She was not afraid of the car at all.

Chapter 18

CHAPTER EIGHTEEN: EMMA'S STORY

Emma Hartfield had been grey for eleven years.

Not her hair.

Her hair was coming back dark at the roots now, which still startled her sometimes in the bathroom mirror in the morning — the dark line advancing slowly down from the scalp like a tide coming in, reclaiming something.

Not her hair.

Everything else.

The grey had arrived the way it always arrived in the people she'd come to recognize in the barn — not dramatically, not with a single identifiable event, but gradually, the way light leaves a room in the evening. Slowly enough that you almost don't notice until you look up and realize you've been sitting in the dark for a while and can't say exactly when the last of the light went.

For Emma it had started at thirty-four.

A Tuesday. She remembered it was a Tuesday because she'd been at her desk at the architecture firm where she'd worked for nine years and she'd been designing a staircase and she'd looked at the drawing and felt — nothing. Not dissatisfaction. Not frustration. Nothing. The drawing was good and she could see that it was good and she felt nothing about it being good.

She had filed this under tired.

She was always tired.

She had been tired for so long that tired had become indistinguishable from her baseline.

The grey deepened over the following two years.

She still functioned. That was the thing about the grey — it didn't prevent functioning. It prevented the other thing. The thing underneath functioning that made functioning worth doing.

She still designed buildings.

She still attended meetings and answered emails and had lunch with colleagues and went to her sister's house for holidays and did all the things that constituted a life from the outside.

From the inside she was doing them from a slight distance.

Like watching herself through glass.

Not unhappy. Not depressed in the clinical sense — she'd been assessed twice and both times the clinician had said the same thing, variations on *you seem to be managing well* said with the slight puzzlement of someone who had expected to find more and hadn't.

She was managing well.

She was managing herself right out of herself and nobody could find the problem because the problem wasn't something you could measure.

She'd found the barn by accident.

Which was, she'd come to understand, the way most of them found it.

A colleague of a colleague had mentioned Marcus in a conversation Emma hadn't been fully present for — she was rarely fully present for conversations during the grey years — and something had snagged. Not the words. Something underneath the words. A frequency she almost recognized.

She had written down Marcus's name on a Post-it and put it in her coat pocket and found it three weeks later and called the number.

Marcus had answered on the second ring.

He had said very little.

But what he said had the quality of something true said plainly by someone with no investment in what she did with it.

She had gone to the barn on a Thursday night.

Sat in the circle.

Said nothing.

Driven home and sat in her parked car for ten minutes doing nothing.

Gone back the following Thursday.

The grey had started lifting eight months after she found the barn.

Slowly at first. The way it had arrived — gradually, in no hurry, without announcing itself.

She'd been at her desk designing a pedestrian bridge and she'd looked at the drawing and felt something.

Not nothing.

Something.

Small. Quiet. The distant relative of the thing she'd felt about drawings at twenty-five, before the grey — but related. The same family.

She'd sat very still at her desk for a moment.

Then she'd gone back to the drawing.

The vision was the last thing to change.

Or the first thing she noticed changing.

She'd left her glasses on her nightstand one morning and driven to work and arrived and reached for them on the desk and found she didn't have them and then found she didn't need them.

She'd gone to the optometrist.

He'd repeated the test three times.

On the third repetition he'd said, with the careful voice of a man unwilling to commit to what his own instrument was telling him: "You're testing significantly better than your last examination."

"How significantly," she'd said.

A pause.

"You're testing better than twenty-twenty."

She had looked at him.

He had looked at his equipment.

"I'll need to recalibrate," he'd said.

She had not told him it wasn't the equipment.

She told Sarah all of this on a Thursday afternoon.

Not planned. Not arranged.

They'd both arrived early to the barn — Sarah coming from Patricia Wren's office, Emma coming from the architecture firm where she was currently designing a community center that was, for the first time in eleven years, genuinely exciting to her — and they'd fallen into it the way conversations fell into things in the barn.

Naturally. Without ceremony.

Emma talked and Sarah listened in the particular way Sarah listened, which was with her whole attention and without the performance of it.

The barn quiet around them.

The winter light flat and thin in the high windows.

"The kitchen sink," Sarah said.

Emma looked at her.

"You mentioned it once before," Sarah said. "Briefly. You said the water felt like your own blood for thirty seconds."

Emma considered this.

"That was about six months into the barn," she said. "Before the vision changed. Before the hair." She looked at her hands. "I was washing a dish and the water was running over my hands and for thirty seconds — exactly thirty seconds, I know because I counted after, when I was trying to understand it — the water felt like it was mine. Not foreign. Not external. Part of the same system."

Sarah was very still.

"Like the boundary between you and it became optional," she said quietly.

Emma looked at her sharply.

"Yes," she said. "Exactly that. How did you — "

"Grace said something like it," Sarah said. "The container becoming optional."

Emma was quiet for a moment.

"It frightened me," she said. "At the time. I thought — " She stopped. "I thought I was having a neurological event. I thought something was wrong with my brain." She paused. "I almost called my doctor."

"Almost."

"Something stopped me." Emma looked at the high windows. "I don't know what. Just — a sense that calling my doctor was the wrong direction. That whatever this was, a medical framework was not the right container for it."

She looked back at Sarah.

"Was that right," she said. Not rhetorically. Actually asking.

"Yes," Sarah said. "It was right."

Emma nodded slowly.

"How do you know," she said. "You're further behind me in this — not behind, that's not the right word — you're at an earlier — "

"I know because I've felt it too," Sarah said. "And I know that the second I try to put a medical framework around it it becomes smaller than it is and starts to look like something it isn't."

Emma looked at her for a long moment.

"What does it look like to you," she said. "When you don't put a framework around it."

Sarah thought about this carefully.

The barn around them. The winter light. The particular smell of the place. The circle of empty chairs waiting for Thursday night.

"Like finding out you're larger than you thought," she said finally. "Not metaphorically. Literally. Like the self you've been operating as is a room and you've found out the room has windows."

Emma was quiet.

Then she said: "That's exactly it."

She said it the way you say something when you've been trying to find the words for years and someone else just found them.

"That's exactly it," she said again. More quietly. To herself.

They were quiet for a while.

The barn holding them.

Emma turned her mug in her hands.

She was thinking about the grey years.

About thirty-four and the staircase drawing and the nothing where the something used to be.

About the distance. The glass. The managing.

"I wasted eleven years," she said.

Sarah looked at her.

"You didn't know," Sarah said.

"No." Emma looked at her coffee. "But they did. Whoever they are. The people with the files and the cars. They knew something was there worth suppressing. They built a system for suppressing it." She paused. "The grey wasn't an accident."

Sarah went still.

Emma looked up.

"I've been thinking about this," Emma said. Her voice was steady. The steadiness of someone who had thought something through to the end and was now reporting the view from there. "The grey arrived the way it arrived in everyone I've talked to in this group. Gradually. Indistinguishably from tiredness, from aging, from the ordinary diminishment people accept as normal." She paused. "What if it isn't ordinary. What if the ordinaries of it is the point."

Sarah said: "You think it's manufactured."

"I think some of it is environmental," Emma said carefully. "I think some of it is the cumulative effect of living inside systems designed for a different kind of person than we are. The work. The consumption. The noise." She paused. "And I think some of it — in specific cases, in people like the ones in this barn — is assisted."

The word sat in the air between them.

Assisted.

Sarah thought about Tom's phone call.

About conference room B and Gerald Foss.

About Hendricks asking the right questions in the right order.

About Grace in the narrow bed in the narrow room with the medication that made you look fine.

"They don't wait until you're a threat," Sarah said slowly. "They start before that."

"Before you know you could be," Emma said. "Before you know what you are."

The barn was very quiet.

Outside the winter wind moved through the bare tree line with the sound of a season that had finished its work and wasn't pretending otherwise.

Sarah looked at her hands.

Thought about thirty-four.

Her own thirty-four — the marriage already calcifying, the smallness already setting in, the slow grey that she had called unhappiness and her doctor had called low-grade depression and nobody had called what it actually was.

Assisted.

"How do you come back from eleven years of that," she said. Not despair. Genuine question.

Emma looked at her.

She was fifty-one years old and her roots were coming in dark and her eyes were better than twenty-twenty and she was designing a community center that genuinely excited her and she was sitting in a barn on a Thursday afternoon with the particular quality of aliveness that the grey years had been specifically designed to prevent.

"You already know," Emma said. "You've been doing it."

Sarah looked at her.

"One Thursday night at a time," Emma said.

The others arrived at six.

The circle filling.

Rachel and David coming in together without making anything of it, which made something of it. Grace and Marcus from different directions, ending up in adjacent chairs, which they had been ending up in for three weeks running. Daniel coming in last, finding Sarah's eyes across the barn, sitting beside her.

Emma watched all of them settle.

The frequency of the room doing the thing it did on Thursday nights when they were all in it — the settling, the completion, the barn becoming the most honest space any of them occupied all week.

She thought about thirty-four.

About the grey.

About the assisted diminishment of something that the people with the files apparently considered dangerous enough to spend considerable resources preventing.

She thought about what that meant.

If you were dangerous to a system it was because you threatened the system.

If what you were threatened the system it was because the system depended on you being something less.

She sat in the circle in the barn on a Thursday night and looked around at the people in it and felt — warm and certain and completely without apology — the full measure of what they were to each other and to whatever came next.

Dangerous.

Good.

After the gathering she stayed to help stack chairs.

Marcus was at the back table. She brought him the last two chairs.

He looked at her face.

"You had a good conversation today," he said.

Not a question.

"Yes," she said.

He nodded.

Started folding the table.

She picked up the other end.

They carried it to the back wall together.

Set it down.

"Marcus," she said.

He looked at her.

"The grey," she said. "Was yours assisted. Do you think."

He was quiet for a long moment.

His left hand resting against the wall.

The hand that had stopped hurting.

"Yes," he said.

"How long did it last."

"Fourteen years."

She looked at him.

He looked back.

Two people who had lost a combined twenty-five years to something that had been specifically designed to take those years from them, standing in a barn on a Thursday night on the other side of it.

"We're getting them back," she said.

He looked at his hand.

"Yes," he said.

"However many we have left."

He looked at her.

Something in his face that she recognized.

Not grief.

Not anger.

Something older and steadier than either.

"However many we have left," he agreed.

She drove home through the dark.

No sedan tonight.

She parked. Went inside. Fed her cat — a large orange animal named Sullivan who had been with her through the grey years and had apparently found her adequate company regardless.

She stood at the kitchen sink.

Ran the water over her hands.

Warm.

She stood there for a moment.

Let it come.

The boundary becoming optional.

The water and her hands and the small warm knowing that she was not separate from the thing running over her skin.

Not thirty seconds this time.

Longer.

She stood at the sink in her kitchen in the dark house and felt herself expand past the old boundaries with the particular unhurried confidence of something that had been here all along and was done waiting to be acknowledged.

Sullivan wound around her ankles.

She turned off the water.

Dried her hands.

Looked out the kitchen window at the dark street.

Empty.

She was not afraid of the empty street.

She was not afraid of much anymore.

She went to bed.

Slept the deep unmanaged sleep of someone who has found their way back to themselves after a long time away and is no longer interested in the managed version.

Sullivan settled at her feet.

The dark house held them both.

Outside the winter night continued its cold indifferent business.

Inside Emma Hartfield — fifty-one, architect, eleven grey years behind her — lay in the dark and felt, without drama and without apology, the full size of herself.

It was considerable.

It had always been considerable.

She was done pretending otherwise.

Chapter 19

CHAPTER NINETEEN: THE FILE

David called on a Friday morning.

Not a text. A call.

She knew before she answered that it wasn't good news. Not the pressure — just the logic of it. David texted for logistics. David called when he needed her to hear his voice while he said the thing.

She answered on the second ring.

"I found Foss," he said.

"And."

"He's not a corporate consultant."

She waited.

"He works for an organization called Meridian Group. Private. Incorporated in Delaware, offices in Chicago and Washington. Their public profile describes them as a crisis management and organizational resilience firm." He paused. "Their actual work is different."

"How different."

"They specialize in the identification and management of what they internally call anomalous cohesion events."

She sat down.

"What does that mean," she said.

"It means groups of people who are changing in ways that Meridian's clients consider destabilizing." Another pause. "They have a taxonomy. Categories of threat level. Documentation protocols. A team of what they call integration specialists — which is what Foss is — who are deployed when a group reaches a certain threshold."

"What threshold."

"When the group produces what they call a confirmed catalyst."

The kitchen around her.

The ordinary Friday morning.

The bare tree line through the window.

"Me," she said.

"You," he said.

She called Marcus.

He came to the cabin within the hour.

Sat across the kitchen table from her with his coffee and the particular stillness he brought to things that required stillness.

She told him everything David had said.

He listened without interrupting.

When she finished he was quiet for a long moment.

"Meridian," he said.

"You've heard of them."

"Not by name." He looked at his left hand. "But I've seen their work." He paused. "The group before this one. Eight years ago. Three people I knew — good people, clear-eyed people — all had their lives systematically dismantled over fourteen months. Jobs. Relationships. Medical records suddenly full of concerns that hadn't been concerns before." He looked up. "I never knew who was behind it. I assumed it was local. Opportunistic."

"It wasn't local," Sarah said.

"No." He drank his coffee. "It wasn't."

She looked at him.

"How many groups have they done this to," she said.

"David doesn't know the full number. He has documentation on nine. He thinks the actual number is significantly higher."

Marcus was quiet.

"The taxonomy," he said. "The categories. What are they."

She had written them down.

She looked at her notepad.

"Level one — emerging cohesion. A group beginning to form. Low priority monitoring." She paused. "Level two — active cohesion. The group meeting regularly, members showing early signs of change. Increased monitoring. Local assets deployed."

She paused.

"Level three," she said. "Catalyst present. Full integration protocol initiated."

The kitchen was very quiet.

"We're level three," Marcus said.

"Yes."

He looked at his coffee.

She watched him absorb it.

Not with fear. With the expression of a man recalibrating, updating the map to match the territory, deciding what to do with accurate information.

"What's the integration protocol," he said.

"David is still building the picture. What he has so far — employer pressure, medical documentation, legal instruments where available." She paused. "And removal of the catalyst."

Marcus looked at her.

"Define removal," he said.

"He doesn't know yet." She held his gaze. "He's working on it."

She didn't tell Daniel until that evening.

Same reason as before — she needed the day to carry it first. To turn it over and find its edges and understand what she actually felt about it before she brought it into the space between them.

What she felt was clearer than she expected.

Not fear.

Not the paralysis of someone who has been told the thing they feared has a name and an office in Chicago and a taxonomy.

Something colder and more useful than fear.

Clarity.

She felt the full shape of it clearly for the first time — not the local pressure of cars at the end of roads and coached ex-husbands and HR meetings, but the organized patient architecture underneath all of it. The system. The history of it. The nine documented groups and the unknown number above nine.

She felt the full shape of it and found that knowing the full shape was better than not knowing.

You couldn't navigate around a thing you couldn't see.

Now she could see it.

Daniel listened.

All of it.

Meridian. The taxonomy. Level three. The integration protocol. Removal of the catalyst.

He sat across the kitchen table with his coffee going cold and his face doing something she hadn't seen before.

Not the complicated thing.

Not even the arrived thing.

Something harder than both.

The expression of a man who has been patient and measured and steady and has just heard the word *removal* applied to someone he loves and is deciding what to do with that.

She watched him decide.

It took longer than usual.

"Removal," he said.

"David doesn't know what it means specifically yet."

"It means Grace," Daniel said. "It means four months in a facility. It means Robert Caulfield, sixty-one, retired schoolteacher, daughter in Grand Rapids, hasn't called her in six weeks."

She held his gaze.

"Yes," she said.

He was quiet.

"They're not going to do that," he said.

Not a declaration. Not bravado.

The flat statement of someone who has made a decision and is informing the room of it.

She looked at him.

"No," she said. "They're not."

Friday night she called the group.

Not a meeting. A call — Rachel, David, Marcus, Grace, Emma. Each of them separately, each conversation five minutes, each one ending the same way.

Thursday. Barn. Early. Come ready to talk.

Each of them said the same thing back.

I'll be there.

She couldn't sleep.

Two in the morning.

Daniel sleeping beside her, his breathing the slow steady rhythm of someone who had made his decision and was at peace with it.

She lay in the dark.

Thought about Meridian.

About the taxonomy. Level one, two, three. The clinical language of people who had been doing this long enough to build categories for it. Long enough to have integration specialists with business cards. Long enough to have a protocol for removal.

She thought about nine documented groups.

About the unknown number above nine.

About all the people who had sat in circles in barns and community rooms and kitchen tables and felt the thing she felt — the expansion, the warmth behind the sternum, the edges becoming optional — and had been systematically walked backward away from it by people with credentials and patience and the specific confidence of an organization that had never failed to complete its protocol.

She lay in the dark and felt something move through her chest.

Not the warm diffuse thing.

Not the compass pointing.

Something larger than both.

The immensity Grace had described.

The insistence.

The full version.

It moved through her chest like the tide coming in — not violent, not dramatic, just the vast unstoppable patience of something that had been doing this since before Meridian existed and would be doing it long after.

She lay very still.

Let it come.

Didn't manage it.

Didn't reach for the edges of it or try to assess its dimensions or file it under anything.

Just — let it.

It was large.

Larger than the bedroom. Larger than the cabin. Larger than the road with its black sedans and the thin folder in conference room B and the nine documented groups and the unknown number above nine.

Larger than Meridian.

She lay in it like floating.

Like the river.

Like Daniel's hands under the water feeling something that wasn't there before.

She thought about what Grace had said.

It came back insisting. Like water that's been held back.

She thought about what Emma had said.

Dangerous. Good.

She thought about Marcus's hand.

About Emma's eyes.

About Grace in the parking lot at two in the morning blinking at open sky.

About Rachel sleeping better than she had in months.

About David Cross at nineteen in a bus station in Columbus, being found by a man who asked three questions and hired him because he didn't lie on any of them.

About all of them.

All of them in the barn on Thursday nights.

The frequency of it.

The thing the taxonomy had a category for.

Anomalous cohesion.

She lay in the dark and the immensity moved through her chest and she thought —

You named it wrong.

Not anomalous.

Not a deviation from what was normal.

The most normal thing.

The thing that had been trying to happen since before the systems were built to prevent it.

The most natural thing in the world.

Just — people finding each other.

Finding what they were.

Blooming.

She fell asleep somewhere after three.

Deeply.

Without the managed half-wakefulness.

Without monitoring.

In the morning she stood at the kitchen window with her coffee.

The road.

The bare tree line.

The black sedan at the end of it.

She looked at it.

It looked back.

She thought about Meridian in their Chicago office.

About the file with her name on it.

About the template David had seen in nine other groups.

They've never let one reach full term.

She drank her coffee.

Looked at the sedan.

Felt the thing in her chest.

Steady.

Warm.

Unhurried.

I'm not the same as the others in your file.

Not arrogance.

Just — the clean knowing.

The compass without a direction this time.

Just pointing at her.

Just saying: *here.*

Here is what they haven't encountered before.

She turned from the window.

Made more coffee.

Daniel came in.

Read her face.

"You figured something out," he said.

She looked at him.

"Yes," she said.

"What."

She thought about how to say it.

About the immensity that had moved through her chest at two in the morning like a tide coming in. About the taxonomy and the nine groups and the template David had seen in all of them. About what made this group different. About what made her different.

Not the knowing.

Not the pressure behind the sternum.

Not the eyes better than twenty-twenty or the hand that stopped hurting or the grey lifting or any of the specific things Meridian documented in their categories.

Something underneath all of those.

Something they hadn't put in the file because they couldn't see it.

Couldn't measure it.

Couldn't name it.

"I think they've always moved on groups like this one before the group understood what it was," she said. "Before it understood the full size of it."

Daniel looked at her.

"And we understand," he said.

"We're starting to," she said. "That's the difference." She paused. "They have a protocol for groups that don't know what they are. They move before the knowing arrives." She looked at the window. At the sedan. "They're too late."

Daniel was quiet for a moment.

Then: "Does David know this."

"He will Thursday," she said.

Daniel looked at the window.

At the sedan sitting patient and certain at the end of their road.

Then back at her.

"Okay," he said.

She picked up her coffee.

"Okay," she said.

Saturday afternoon she drove to the river road.

Parked.

Sat for a moment.

Got out.

Walked the path behind the cabin.

The root that caught the toe.

The place where the light changed.

The path narrower. The grass dead and flat now. The willows stripped and bare and still somehow leaning toward her in the grey December air.

She waded in to her knees.

The cold of it moved up through her.

She stood in the current.

The water low and clear and moving with the patient indifference of something that had been doing this since before she was born and would be doing it long after she was gone.

She stood in it.

Let the edges of herself become optional.

Let the current and the cold and the bare willows and the grey sky all be part of the same thing she was part of.

Let the immensity come.

It came.

Not the whisper.

Not the thirty seconds.

She stood in the December river and let it come fully and it came fully and she stood in it the way you stand in something vast — not fighting it, not performing it, not managing the size of it down to something explicable.

Just — stood in it.

The ripple and the river.

The water and the thing that knew it was water.

She stood there for a long time.

Walked back.

Made coffee.

Sat at the kitchen table with her notepad.

Wrote one sentence.

They are too late.

Looked at it.

Crossed it out.
Wrote instead:
We are just in time.
Closed the notepad.
Drank her coffee.
Waited for Thursday.

Chapter 20

HAPTER TWENTY: THE BARN — FULL FREQUENCY

They came early.

All of them.

No one had said come early. Sarah had said Thursday, barn, ready to talk, and somehow they all arrived before six-thirty, before the light was gone, before the December dark had fully settled on the bare fields and the stripped tree line and the road that ran past the barn with its patient black sedan.

Two sedans tonight.

Rachel had counted them pulling in.

She didn't say anything about it until they were all inside.

Marcus had the fire going in the small iron stove in the corner.

The barn held the heat imperfectly — cold coming through the old boards, the high windows, the gaps that no amount of weatherproofing fully addressed — but the stove put out enough to make the circle warm.

Emma was already there when Rachel arrived.

Then David.

Then Grace, who came with Marcus from the direction of the small table where they'd apparently been sitting together for some time, talking quietly, stopping when the others arrived in the natural way of two people who have a conversation that belongs to them and know how to set it aside without closing it.

Daniel and Sarah came last.

Together.

Sarah carrying the folder David had sent her on Wednesday.

She set it on the small table.

Nobody opened it yet.

They made tea.

Moved the chairs closer to the stove.

Sat.

The barn doing its thing — the settling, the completion, the frequency of the place changing quality when all of them were in it together.

Sarah looked around the circle.

Marcus with his hands around his mug, left hand easy and unhurried. Emma with her clear eyes that the optometrist still hadn't found an explanation for. Grace sitting with the uprightness of someone who had found their spine again after a long time of being without it. Rachel with the particular alertness that was her baseline but softer tonight, the edges of it less defended. David beside her — not quite touching, not quite not touching, the two of them occupying adjacent space with the ease of people who had made a decision and were living quietly inside it.

Daniel beside Sarah.

His hand finding hers under her chair in the way it always did.

She let herself feel the room.

All of them.

Not reaching for it. Not performing it.

Just — letting the circle be what it was.

It was considerable.

She told them about Meridian.

Plainly. Without drama. The way David had told her.

The taxonomy. The levels. The integration protocol.

She watched them take it in.

Emma went very still.

Rachel's jaw tightened once and released.

Grace looked at Marcus. He looked back. Something passed between them that Sarah couldn't read and didn't need to.

David had heard it already but sat with the same seriousness as the others because hearing it in the group was different from hearing it alone and he understood that.

Marcus said nothing for a long time.

When he spoke his voice was level.

"Nine documented groups," he said.

"Nine confirmed," David said. "The actual number is higher. I'm working on establishing how much higher."

"And we're level three."

"Confirmed catalyst. Yes."

Marcus looked at Sarah.

She met his eyes.

"Tell them the rest," he said.

She looked around the circle.

"I think they moved on those other groups before the groups understood what they were," she said. "The taxonomy assumes a certain stage of — unknowing. The protocol is built for people who are changing without understanding the change." She paused. "I don't think it's built for what we are now."

The barn held this.

"Which is what," Emma said.

Sarah thought about the river on Saturday. The December cold. The immensity coming fully without management.

"People who know," she said. "People who understand the full size of what's happening and have chosen it anyway." She looked around the circle. "They've never encountered that. David's documentation on the nine groups shows the same pattern in all of them — the protocol moved before the group reached this stage." She paused. "We're past the stage they have a protocol for."

The fire in the stove.

The cold coming through the boards.

The circle of them in the warm.

Grace said quietly: "They'll adapt the protocol."

"Yes," Sarah said. "They will."

"So we don't have long."

"No. We don't have long."

David opened the folder.

Laid three pages on the table in the center of the circle.

Not the full file — the summary. What they knew. What they didn't. What was coming and in what order based on the pattern of the nine documented groups.

They went through it methodically.

Employer pressure — already in motion for Sarah, building for Rachel. Emma's firm had not yet been contacted but David expected it within two weeks.

Medical documentation — Hendricks active. Patricia Wren counter-documenting. The balance there was uncertain.

Legal instruments — no wellness hold application filed yet. Could move quickly when it moved.

Physical pressure — the sedans escalating. The night passes. Sarah run off the road. The pattern suggested the next escalation would be more direct.

More direct.

Nobody asked him to define it.

They all knew what more direct meant.

Robert Caulfield had been more direct.

Rachel said: "What about Robert."

David looked at her.

"I have a location," he said.

The barn went very quiet.

"Where," Marcus said.

"A facility in central Indiana. Private. Not on any list I can access through normal channels." He paused. "I have someone inside. Former colleague. She confirmed a John Doe intake six weeks ago matching Robert's description."

"John Doe," Grace said.

Her voice was steady.

The steadiness of someone who knew exactly what John Doe intake at a private facility meant.

"They stripped his identity on entry," she said.

"That's what the evidence suggests," David said.

Grace looked at her hands.

Marcus put his hand over hers on the arm of her chair.

She turned hers over and held his.

Neither of them looked at each other.

Both of them looking at David.

"Can we get him out," Grace said.

"I'm working on it," David said.

"That's not an answer."

"No," he said. "It isn't." He looked at her directly. "I don't know yet. I'm trying to build the legal instrument that makes his continued detention untenable. That requires establishing his identity, which requires documentation they've made deliberately hard to access, which requires time I'm not certain we have."

Grace was quiet for a moment.

"He has a daughter," she said.

"In Grand Rapids," David said. "I've been in contact with her. She's filed the missing persons report. I'm helping her build a parallel legal case."

"Does she know what her father is," Emma said.

A pause.

"She knows her father is someone worth finding," David said. "That's enough for now."

They sat with all of it.

The fire.

The cold through the boards.

The folder on the table between them.

The two sedans at the end of the road.

Sarah looked around the circle and felt the particular weight of a room full of people who have been given the full honest picture and are deciding what to do with it.

Not scattered.

Not panicked.

Present.

All of them present.

Marcus said: "What do we need."

David said: "Time. Documentation. And for everyone in this circle to be very careful about what they say to anyone outside it."

"What else," Marcus said.

David looked at him.

"I need the group to stay intact," he said. "That's the primary target of the protocol. Not any individual. The group. If we scatter they win. If we stay together and stay visible and stay — " He paused.

"Blooming," Grace said quietly.

He looked at her.

"Yes," he said. "If we stay blooming — then the protocol has no entry point. Everything they're doing is designed to create an entry point. Isolation. Fear. The performance of madness forced on people who aren't mad." He looked around the circle. "Don't give them the entry point."

Nobody said anything.

Because nobody needed to.

After the practical conversation ended they sat for a while without talking.

The fire.

The barn.

The December dark outside.

And then something happened that none of them would describe the same way afterward and all of them would agree on the fact of.

Sarah felt it first.

The warmth behind her sternum — not the compass, not the pointing, the other one. The diffuse one. The one that came at the river and in the dark after Daniel slept and sometimes in the barn on Thursdays when the circle was complete.

It came.

Fuller than before.

She didn't say anything.

She felt it come and she let it come and she sat in the circle and breathed.

And then —

Emma made a small sound.

Involuntary. Surprised.

Sarah looked at her.

Emma was looking at her hands.

Then Rachel said quietly: "Does anyone else feel that."

The circle went still.

Not the stillness of nothing happening.

The stillness of everything happening at once.

David — practical, documented, eleven years of careful navigation between what was real and what could be proven — sat very still in his chair with an expression Sarah had never seen on him before.

The expression of a man whose framework has just become insufficient and is watching it become insufficient in real time and is not, she realized, afraid of that.

Is in fact leaning toward it.

Grace had her eyes closed.

Her face was the face of someone who has been somewhere very far away and is back.

All the way back.

Fully.

Marcus was looking at Grace.

He was not performing stillness.

He simply was still.

The particular stillness of a man in the presence of something he has waited for without knowing he was waiting for it.

Sarah sat in the middle of it.

The ripple and the current.

Both at once.

She could feel each of them.

Not metaphorically.

Each of them distinct and warm and present behind her sternum like knowing where all her fingers were at once.

Rachel.

David.

Emma.

Grace.

Marcus.

Daniel.

She could feel each of them.

All of them together.

The frequency the taxonomy had a category for.

Anomalous cohesion.

She sat in it.

Let it be the full size it was.

It was large.

Larger than the barn.

Larger than the road with its two sedans and the folder on the table and the nine documented groups and Meridian in their Chicago office with their integration specialists and their level three protocol.

It was very large.

And it was very quiet.

And it was very completely unbothered by any of it.

It lasted twenty seconds.

Maybe thirty.

Then the fire popped.

Grace opened her eyes.

Daniel exhaled.

Emma looked up from her hands.

The barn was just the barn again.

The circle was just people in chairs near a stove in December.

Nobody said anything for a long time.

Then Marcus, in the voice he used for things that were true and didn't need decoration:

"That's what they're afraid of."

Nobody disagreed.

They left in ones and twos.

Emma first, with a look on her face Sarah had not seen before.

The look of an architect who has just seen a structure she didn't know was possible and is already thinking about how it was built.

Rachel and David together, not discussing it, not performing the not-discussing of it.

Just — together. Leaving the barn together into the December night.

Grace last, with Marcus.

They stood in the barn doorway while Sarah and Daniel stacked the final chairs.

Grace turned to look at Sarah across the barn.

She didn't say anything.

She didn't need to.

She looked at Sarah with the eyes that had come back from very far away and were fully present now and fully hers and the look said everything the words would have gotten in the way of.

Sarah looked back.

The same.

Marcus put his hand at the small of Grace's back.

Not a gesture of guidance.

Not proprietary.

Just — there. The plain fact of his hand saying *I'm here* in the language they'd been building since the first cup of tea in the September barn.

Grace leaned into it slightly.

They went out into the dark.

Sarah and Daniel walked to their car.

She stopped.

Looked back at the barn.

The light in the high windows.

The stovepipe sending a thin line of smoke into the December sky.

The two sedans at the end of the road watching all of it with the patient certainty of something that had done this many times before and expected to do it again.

She looked at the sedans.

Felt the immensity.

Still there.

Quieter now.

The way a river is quiet — not still, not absent, just doing its work without announcing it.

We are just in time.

She had written it Saturday.

She believed it now with the full weight of what had just happened in the barn.

Not the managed version of believing.

The full version.

Daniel stood beside her.

Looking at the sedans.

"They felt it," she said. "All of them."

"Yes."

"That's never happened before. All of them at once."

"No."

She looked at the barn.

At the smoke from the stovepipe.

At the December sky above it, clear and cold and full of stars indifferent to Meridian and their protocols and their file and their nine documented groups.

"It's going to be harder for them now," she said. "After that."

Daniel looked at her.

"Why."

She thought about how to say it.

About the frequency in the barn.

About all of them feeling it simultaneously.

About what that meant for a group that an organization had spent considerable resources trying to isolate and fracture and dismantle one person at a time.

"Because they're trying to separate things that just found out they're the same thing," she said.

Daniel was quiet for a moment.

Then he took her hand.

They walked to the car.

The sedans watched them go.

The barn stood in the December dark sending its thin line of smoke into the stars.

Inside the iron stove the fire continued its patient work.
Burning.
Warm.
Not going anywhere.

Chapter 21

CHAPTER TWENTY-ONE: TOM AGAIN

He called on a Monday.

Same time as before. Same coached warmth. Same Friday-that-wasn't-his-idea energy except now it was Monday which meant the timeline had accelerated and someone above Tom had decided the Friday approach hadn't produced results and had told him to try again sooner.

She let it ring three times.

Answered.

"Tom."

"Sarah." The warmth. Calibrated. "I was hoping we could talk."

"We're talking."

A small pause. He hadn't expected that. The previous calls she'd been civil and brief and gotten off the line quickly. Civil and brief was manageable. Civil and present was harder.

"I'd like to see you," he said. "In person. Just coffee."

"What would we talk about."

"I'm concerned about you."

"You said that last time."

"I'm still concerned."

She looked out the kitchen window. The road empty this morning. The bare December tree line. The sky the flat white of a day that couldn't decide whether to snow.

"Tom," she said. "I want to ask you something and I want you to answer me honestly. Not the coached version. The actual answer."

A pause.

Longer than the previous ones.

"Okay," he said. Carefully.

"Who told you to call me."

Silence.

Not the silence of someone formulating an answer.

The silence of someone who has been asked the one question they were specifically told not to answer and is now experiencing the collision between the instruction and the person they used to be before the instruction.

She waited.

"Sarah — "

"Tom."

Another silence.

She heard him breathe.

She heard, underneath the breath, something she hadn't expected.

Not calculation.

Not the coached patience of someone executing a script.

Something older than the script.

Something that had been there through twenty-two years of marriage and had not entirely gone away just because the marriage had.

Shame.

He was ashamed.

She sat with this discovery.

It changed the shape of things slightly.

Not enough to change what was happening.

Enough to change how she felt about Tom specifically.

"I can't tell you that," he said finally.

"Can't or won't."

A long pause.

"Can't," he said.

She understood the distinction.

Can't meant there were consequences attached to telling her.

Can't meant someone had made it worth his while to make these calls and the worth-his-while came with conditions.

Can't meant Tom was also, in his own diminished way, caught in something he didn't fully understand.

"Are you okay," she said.

The question surprised him.

She heard it surprise him — the small intake of breath, the recalibration, the script becoming suddenly inadequate because the script hadn't prepared him for her asking about him.

"I'm — yes," he said. "I'm fine."

"You don't sound fine."

"Sarah — "

"I'm not saying that to be unkind," she said. "I'm saying it because I spent twenty-two years with you and I know what you sound like when you're fine and this isn't it."

Another long silence.

She waited.

She was not doing this for Tom.

She was doing it because Patricia Wren had said something in their last session that had stayed with her.

The people they use are rarely villains. They're people with pressure points. Finding the pressure point tells you something about the organization using it.

What was Tom's pressure point.

She was starting to understand.

"There were some business problems," Tom said finally.

His voice had changed.

The coached warmth gone.

Just Tom.

The Tom she'd known before the marriage calcified, back when he was someone she'd actually chosen, actually seen something in, actually believed in the possibility of.

That Tom. Tired. A little lost.

"What kind of business problems," she said.

"The firm. We had a contract fall through. A significant one." A pause. "Someone helped me salvage it. Made a call. The right call to the right person." Another pause. "And then some time later they asked me to make a call of my own."

"To me."

"To you."

She sat with this.

The kitchen. The flat white sky outside. The bare tree line.

"Tom," she said. "Do you understand what you're involved in."

"I'm making phone calls," he said. "Checking on my ex-wife."

"You're building a documented record of concern that will be used to support a legal instrument designed to have me involuntarily held for psychiatric evaluation," she said.

Silence.

Complete silence.

The kind that meant she'd said something he hadn't known and the not-knowing of it was rewriting things in real time.

"That's not — " He stopped. "That's not what they told me this was."

"What did they tell you it was."

"They said you were — that people were worried. That there were signs of — instability. That reaching out was the kind thing. The right thing." His voice was doing something now. Something she hadn't heard in years. The voice of a man discovering he's been the instrument of something he wouldn't have agreed to had he known what it was. "They said they were trying to help you."

"They're trying to remove me," she said. "From a group of people they consider a threat. The calls you've been making are part of the legal architecture they're building to do that."

Silence.

"Tom."

"I didn't know," he said.

She believed him.

She wasn't sure that made it better.

"I know you didn't," she said.

"Sarah — "

"I need you to stop making the calls," she said. "I need you to understand that every conversation we've had since this started has been documented and is being used as evidence of my instability by people you don't know who are working toward an end you didn't agree to."

A very long silence.

"Okay," he said.

His voice scraped at the word.

Like a man picking up something heavy.

"Okay," he said again. More settled this time. The decision arriving and being made.

"Thank you," she said.

She meant it.

She hung up.

Sat for a moment at the kitchen table.

Thought about twenty-two years.

About the way a person could be used by something larger than themselves without understanding they were being used.

About Tom's shame.

About the pressure point.

The failing business. The contract. The person who had made the right call at the right moment and then collected on it.

She called David.

David listened to all of it.

When she finished he was quiet for a moment.

"He told you about the business," he said.

"He didn't give me details. Enough."

"Enough is enough." She heard him writing. "This is useful. If they used a business rescue to recruit Tom it means they have commercial connections. That's a different network than the one I've been mapping."

"Is that good or bad."

"It's information," he said. "Information is always good." A pause. "How did he sound."

"Ashamed," she said. "And I think genuinely surprised. I don't think he knew what he was building toward."

"He probably didn't. They compartmentalize. The people they use rarely see the whole picture. They see their piece and it looks reasonable from where they're standing." He paused. "Tom saw a concerned professional network worried about a woman behaving erratically. That's a reasonable thing to participate in if you believe it."

"He believed it," she said.

"Until just now."

"Until just now."

A pause.

"Sarah," David said.

"Yes."

"He could go back to them. Tell them you confronted him. They'll know the approach failed and they'll adjust."

She had thought about this.

"I know," she said.

"Are you okay with that risk."

She thought about Tom's voice when the coached warmth left it. The tired, slightly lost voice.

The shame.

"Yes," she said. "I think so."

"Why."

She looked out the window at the flat white sky.

"Because he's not a bad person," she said. "He's a person who got used and didn't know it and now he knows it. Those people usually don't go back." She paused. "And because treating him like an enemy when he's actually a casualty seemed wrong."

David was quiet for a moment.

"Patricia Wren is good for you," he said.

She almost smiled.

"Tell her that," she said. "She'll find it professionally appropriate."

She told Daniel over dinner.

He listened. Ate. Listened more.

When she finished he said: "The business rescue."

"Yes."

"They recruited him through a financial favor."

"That's what it sounds like."

He ate for a moment. "That's a significant operation. That's not a local effort. You don't rescue a failing business contract on short notice without connections that go — " He paused. "That go well above cars at the end of roads and HR consultants."

"I know," she said.

"Meridian has those connections."

"David thinks so too."

He was quiet.

She watched him sit with the expanding size of it.

Not the local pressure — Tom and Foss and Hendricks and the sedans. The architecture beneath that. The organization with commercial connections and political adjacency and the operational capacity to reshape a person's business circumstances as a recruitment tool.

The full size.

She watched him find the edges of it.

Watched him decide.

"Okay," he said.

She looked at him.

"That's it," she said. "You hear this and you say okay."

He met her eyes.

"What would you prefer."

She thought about it honestly.

"Nothing," she said. "Okay is right."

He reached across the table.

She gave him her hand.

"They recruited Tom through his fear," Daniel said. "His fear about the business. His fear about failing." He looked at her. "Fear is the entry point. It's always the entry point."

She thought about the taxonomy.

The levels. The protocol.

The nine groups that had scattered.

"They found the fear in each of those groups," she said slowly. "And used it."

"Yes."

She thought about the barn on Thursday night.

The circle.

The twenty seconds.

Maybe thirty.

The frequency moving through all of them at once.

She thought about what Marcus had said afterward.

That's what they're afraid of.

She looked at Daniel.

"We're afraid too," she said. "All of us. There's real fear in that circle."

"Yes," he said.

"But there's something bigger than the fear."

"Yes."

She held his gaze.

"That's the difference," she said. "That's what they don't have in their protocol." She paused. "The other nine groups had fear and didn't have the other thing yet. Or didn't know they had it." She paused again. "We have both. And we know we have both."

Daniel looked at her steadily.

"Both-and," he said.

She felt the thing behind her sternum.

Warm.

Steady.

Pointing nowhere.

Just present.

Just: *here.*

"Both-and," she said.

Wednesday she ran into Tom.

Not arranged.

The hardware store on Fifth Street at two in the afternoon.

He was in the paint aisle.

She was looking for weatherstripping.

They nearly walked into each other at the end cap.

He went still.

She went still.

They looked at each other in the way of people who have known each other for twenty-two years and are currently in the middle of something complicated and are standing in a hardware store on a Wednesday afternoon in the paint aisle which is not where either of them would have chosen for this.

"Sarah," he said.

"Tom."

He looked different than he had the last time she'd seen him in person.

Smaller. Not physically. Something else. The specific smallness of a person carrying something they haven't put down yet.

She felt his fear.

The way she'd felt it on the phone. Except closer now.

Warmer. More specific.

Not the compass.

Just — his fear. Present in the air between them like a temperature she was the only one registering.

She didn't perform not-feeling it.

She felt it and stood with it and looked at him steadily.

"I haven't called them," he said.

"I know," she said.

He looked at her. "How do you know."

She held his gaze.

"I just do," she said.

He looked at her for a long moment.

Something moved through his face.

Not shame this time.

Something adjacent to wonder.

The expression of a person realizing for the first time that the thing other people told him was the problem with his ex-wife might actually be something else entirely.

"Are you okay," he said. Genuinely. Not coached.

"Yes," she said. "Are you."

He looked at the paint cans.

"I'm working on it," he said.

She nodded.

She believed that too.

They stood in the paint aisle for a moment longer.

Then she said: "Take care of yourself, Tom."

He looked at her.

"You too," he said.

She went to find her weatherstripping.

He stayed in the paint aisle.

She didn't look back.

But she felt him standing there as she walked away — his fear, his shame, his working-on-it — felt it the way she felt the group on Thursday nights, distinct and warm and present.

Not behind her sternum this time.

More like alongside.

The way things are when they're neither threat nor belonging.

Just — there.

Just human.

Just the hardware store on a Wednesday.

She found the weatherstripping.

Paid.

Drove home.

The road clear.

No sedan today.

She parked in front of the cabin and sat for a moment and thought about twenty-two years and the person you become inside a life that doesn't fit and the person you become when you leave it and how both of those people are still you and the leaving doesn't erase the before, it just adds the after.

She thought about Tom in the paint aisle.

Working on it.

She hoped he meant it.

She thought he did.

She went inside.

Put the kettle on.

Waited for Daniel to come home.

Chapter 22

CHAPTER TWENTY-TWO: THE BARN — FULL FREQUENCY

The Thursday before Christmas the snow came.

Not the tentative first snow of November that arrives and apologizes and disappears by morning.

The real one.

The one that means it.

Six inches by noon. Eight by the time the group arrived at the barn, coming through the white dark in ones and twos, stamping their boots at the door, bringing the cold in with them and the particular aliveness of people who have driven through bad weather to be somewhere they chose to be.

Nobody canceled.

Sarah had half-expected someone to cancel.

Nobody did.

Marcus had the stove going since four.

The barn was warm when they arrived. Warmer than usual. The snow against the boards outside making the inside feel more itself—the contrast of the storm and the stove and the circle of chairs in the amber light doing something to the atmosphere that Sarah felt when she walked through the door.

Like the barn had been waiting.

Like it had known.

She stamped her boots. Unwound her scarf.

Looked around.

Emma already in her chair with her hands around a mug, looking at the high windows where the snow was coming down past the glass in steady diagonals.

Grace at the small table with Marcus.

Not talking.

Just — there. The language they'd built between them that didn't require words. His left hand on the table between them. Her hand beside his. Not touching. Almost.

Rachel came in behind Sarah with David close enough behind her that the cold came in once for both of them.

Daniel last.

He closed the barn door against the weather and the sound of the storm dropped by half and the barn enclosed them completely.

The circle.

All of them.

The snow outside.

The stove inside.

The particular completion of it.

They talked first.

That was always how it went — the practical business of the group before the other thing, whatever the other thing was, which none of them had named accurately yet and all of them had felt.

David had updates.

Robert Caulfield first.

He laid it out without preamble.

"His daughter filed a civil suit Friday," he said. "Wrongful detention. I helped her find the attorney. The facility in Indiana received the filing Monday." He paused. "They haven't responded yet. But the filing establishes his identity on the legal record. They can no longer hold a John Doe because there is no John Doe. There is Robert James Caulfield, sixty-one, retired schoolteacher, and his daughter is looking for him and has an attorney and a case number."

Grace was very still.

"Is he okay," she said.

"I don't know," David said. "I know he exists in that facility. I know he's alive. Beyond that — " He stopped. "Beyond that I'm working on it."

Grace nodded once.

The nod of someone accepting an honest answer they don't like.

Marcus's hand moved slightly on the table.

Grace's moved slightly toward it.

Still not touching.

Almost.

"Tom," David said. Looked at Sarah.

"He's out," she said. "He hasn't contacted them since Monday. I saw him Wednesday. He's — " She thought about the paint aisle. The working-on-it. "He's out."

"Foss filed a supplementary report to Meridian last Thursday," David said. "Before the barn meeting. The report recommends accelerating the timeline."

The barn absorbed this.

"What does accelerating mean specifically," Emma said.

"It means the wellness hold application is being prepared. They need one more signature. Hendricks has signed. They're looking for a second physician."

"Who," Rachel said.

"I don't know yet."

"How long do we have."

"A week. Maybe two. After the second signature they can move at any time." He looked at Sarah. "Patricia Wren is preparing counter-documentation. She's also contacted two colleagues who have agreed to provide supporting assessments. That will slow any hold attempt and give us grounds to challenge it." He paused. "It's not a guarantee."

"What is a guarantee," Rachel said.

"Nothing," David said. "Right now nothing is a guarantee."

The snow against the boards.

The stove.

The circle.

Nobody pretending that was a comfortable answer.

Nobody needing it to be.

Rachel said: "My termination hearing is January fourth."

She said it the way she said things that mattered.

Plainly. Without performance of either worry or bravado.

"Hendricks filed the report to the licensing board last week," she said. "Unprofessional conduct. Compromising patient care." She looked at her hands. "The irony being that compromising patient care is exactly what I was preventing." She looked up. "David has the documentation. The dose records. The timeline of Grace's improvement after I started reducing the medication."

"It's solid," David said. "The documentation is solid. The question is whether the board will look at it honestly or whether Meridian has reach inside the board."

"Do they," Rachel said.

David met her eyes.

"I don't know yet," he said.

Rachel nodded.

Once.

The nod of a woman who has been carrying this since October and has not put it down and does not intend to.

Grace looked at her from across the circle.

Something passed between them.

Not words.

The specific look of two people who have been through something together that most people haven't and are on the other side of it changed and still changing and not done with each other.

"Whatever happens January fourth," Grace said.

Rachel looked at her.

"You didn't do anything wrong," Grace said.

Rachel was quiet for a moment.

"I know," she said.

"I want you to know I know," Grace said.

Rachel looked at her hands.

Back up at Grace.

"Thank you," she said.

Quietly.

The way you say something when the words are too small for the thing and you say them anyway because they're what you have.

David covered the rest.

Emma's firm had received a letter. Not termination — a concern letter. The kind of letter that preceded termination the way clouds preceded weather.

Emma listened with the expression of a woman who had been grey for eleven years and had come back from it and was not going back.

"Let them," she said.

David looked at her.

"I'm a licensed architect with twenty-six years of experience and a reputation that takes more than an anonymous concern letter to damage," she said. "Let them send the letter. I'll have my attorney respond." She paused. "I'm not afraid of them."

She said it without heat.

Just — fact.

The fact of a woman who had found her spine after eleven grey years and was not misplacing it again.

David nodded.

Made a note.

After the practical business they sat.

The snow.

The stove.

The circle.

Sarah looked around at all of them.

Marcus and Grace with their hands almost touching on the table and then — she watched it happen, the small movement, the decision made quietly without announcement — touching.

Grace's hand turning over.

Marcus's closing around it.

Neither of them looking at the other.

Both of them looking at the circle.

But the hands.

The hands were the whole story.

Rachel and David side by side with the ease of people who had stopped pretending they were just colleagues and had not yet needed to define what they were instead.

Emma with her clear eyes looking at the high windows where the snow came down past the glass.

Daniel beside Sarah.

His hand finding hers.

Always finding hers.

The barn warm and full of them and the snow outside doing its indifferent patient work of covering everything equally — the road, the fields, the sedans that she was fairly certain were out there somewhere even in this, even in the snow, because Meridian did not take snow days.

She felt the circle.

Not reaching for it.

Not performing.

Just — sitting in the chair beside Daniel with her hand in his and letting the circle be what it was.

It was what it had been last week.

Fuller.

More certain of itself.

The frequency higher.

She sat in it.

And then Grace spoke.

Not planned.

Not announced.

She simply — began.

Her voice quiet enough that they all leaned slightly forward without knowing they were doing it.

She talked about the facility.

Not the way she'd talked about it before — carefully, in pieces, with the protective distance of someone reporting events they've processed enough to describe.

All the way in.

The narrow room.

The narrow bed.

The specific management of consciousness she'd experienced — the medication that didn't knock you out but moved you to one side of yourself and kept you there. Present enough to sign the forms they needed signed. Absent enough to not understand what you were signing.

The orderly who was kind.

The orderly who wasn't.

The window that faced a wall.

The Thursday nights she'd spent lying in the narrow bed knowing there was a barn somewhere with a circle of chairs and a stove and people who were becoming something larger than themselves and she was not there and each Thursday was a Thursday she didn't get back.

She talked about what it cost.

Not dramatically.

The way things cost that are real — specifically, precisely, without exaggeration because exaggeration would make it smaller than it was.

What it cost her professionally.

What it cost her personally.

What it cost her in the place behind the sternum where the thing lived, the thing that was now fully back and insisting and done waiting but had been during those months receding, receding, the medication walking it backward away from her like the tide going out and taking the color of everything with it.

She talked about Rachel in the parking lot.

Two in the morning.

The cold air.

The open sky.

Thank you.

She looked at Rachel when she said it.

Rachel was not crying.

Rachel did not cry in public, Sarah had come to understand.

But she was the color of someone who might.

And she was looking at Grace with the expression of a woman who has done something at significant personal cost and is looking at the evidence that it was worth it and finding the evidence considerable.

Grace talked about the barn.

The first Thursday.

Sitting in the circle and saying almost nothing and going home and sleeping eleven hours.

The second Thursday.

The third.

Marcus and the tea.

His left hand.

The silence that wasn't awkward.

The way the barn had felt like the first honest space she'd been in in a very long time.

The way honest space was, she'd discovered, medicinal.

The way it undid what the narrow room had done.

Slowly. Steadily. Thursday by Thursday.

She talked about what was coming back.

The expansion.

The container becoming optional.

The room finding its windows.

She talked about it without borrowed language and without apology and without performing either strength or vulnerability.

Just — true.

Everything she said was just true.

The barn held it.

The circle held it.

Sarah felt the warmth behind her sternum begin.

Not the pointing.

The other one.

The diffuse one.

Rising.

When Grace finished nobody spoke for a long time.

The snow.

The stove.

The circle.

Then Marcus said — in the voice he used for things that were true and didn't need decoration:

"That's why we're here."

Nobody disagreed.

And then —

Sarah felt it arrive.

The same way it had arrived last week.

Fuller.

More certain.

The warmth spreading past the sternum past the chest past the ordinary boundaries of a woman sitting in a chair in a barn in December.

She didn't say anything.

She sat in it.

Let it come fully.

Emma made the small sound again.

Involuntary.

Recognized.

Rachel said quietly: "There it is."

David Cross — eleven years of careful navigation, documented groups, the gap between what was real and what could be proven — sat with his eyes closed and his face the face of a man who has just stepped from one world into a larger one and is standing at the threshold deciding and then — deciding.

Stepping through.

Grace had her eyes open this time.

Looking at the high windows.

The snow coming down past the glass.

Her face the face of someone home.

All the way home.

The way she'd looked in the parking lot at two in the morning was the before.

This was the after.

Marcus was looking at her.

He was not performing anything.

He was simply present.

Fully.

The particular fullness of a man who has waited without knowing he was waiting and is now here in the thing he was waiting for and is not wasting a second of it by being anywhere else.

His hand tightened slightly around Grace's.

She didn't look at him.

She didn't need to.

She knew.

Sarah felt each of them.

Distinct.

Warm.

Present.

Rachel — the contained brightness of her, the careful fire of someone who had spent years keeping herself useful and was only now learning to let herself be large.

David — the precise careful intelligence of him, the eleven years of documentation and careful navigation, and underneath all of that something that had been waiting to be let out into the larger room and was now — tentatively, then less tentatively — out.

Emma — the architectural mind of her, the pattern-recognition, the eleven grey years burned away and what remained underneath clear and strong and considerably larger than the grey had allowed.

Grace — the fullness of her. The full version. The thing the narrow room had tried to manage into absence and had failed to manage because it was too fundamental to be managed, only delayed. And now not delayed. Now entirely present. Now enormous.

Marcus — the steadiness of him. The patience. The hand that had stopped hurting. The fourteen grey years behind him and the barn in front of him and the woman beside him and the full quiet power of a man who has found what he was building toward without knowing he was building.

Daniel —

Sarah felt Daniel and felt herself feel him and felt the specific quality of what was between them — not separate, not merged, something more accurate than either.

Two people who had each become more fully themselves and found that the more themselves they became the more completely they fit together.

Not despite.

Because of.

She held his hand.

He held hers.

The current moving through all of them.

Thirty seconds.

Maybe forty.

Then Emma exhaled.

A long breath.

The kind that empties completely and refills differently.

Grace came back from the high windows.

David opened his eyes.

The barn was just the barn again.

The circle was just people in chairs.

The snow outside.

The stove.

The amber light.

Nobody spoke for a long while.

Then Rachel said — dry, precise, the voice of a woman who had felt something undeniable and was Rachel about it:

"I'd like to see Meridian's protocol for that."

The barn laughed.

Not polite laughter.

Real laughter.

The kind that arrives when something releases and the release needs a sound.

The kind that fills a barn on a Thursday night in December while the snow comes down outside and the stove does its steady work and the circle sits in the aftermath of something none of them have adequate language for and all of them know was real.

Real and large and completely unbothered by Gerald Foss and his notepad.

They stayed late.

Nobody wanted to leave.

The snow still coming down past the high windows.

The stove still going.

They talked about ordinary things eventually.

Christmas. Emma's community center project. Rachel's cat. David's terrible coffee maker that he refused to replace on the grounds that it still functioned technically. Marcus's woodpile. Grace's first week back at her old job, which had welcomed her return with the specific warmth of colleagues who had been told she was ill and were now presented with evidence to the contrary.

Ordinary things.

Life things.

The things that were the point — not the opposition, not the protocol, not Meridian — the actual point.

The lives they were living.

The lives they were choosing.

The full versions.

They left in ones and twos.

Into the snow.

Emma first, with her coat and her clear eyes and the expression of a woman designing something in her head that nobody had asked her to design yet.

Rachel and David together, their shoulders almost touching, the snow covering the parking lot white and clean and equal over everything.

Grace and Marcus at the barn door.

She had her coat on.

He had his hands in his pockets.

They stood in the doorway looking at the snow.

"I'll walk you to Rachel's car," he said.

She looked at him.

Not at the snow.

At him.

In the direct complete way she had developed over the Thursday nights of looking at things clearly now that the medication was fully gone and her eyes were fully hers again.

"Marcus," she said.

"Yes."

She stepped forward.

Kissed him.

Brief.

Warm.

The barn doorway. The snow outside. His hands coming out of his pockets. Her hand finding the front of his coat.

Not a long kiss.

Not a dramatic one.

Just — the thing being said that had been building since September and the tea and the left hand and the silence that wasn't awkward.

Said.

She stepped back.

He looked at her.

His face the face of a man who has been given something he'd stopped expecting and is discovering that it fits exactly where he'd been keeping the space for it without knowing that's what the space was for.

"Okay," he said.

His voice slightly different than usual.

She smiled.

It arrived fully this time.

Not the almost-smile of the first Thursday.

The real one.

The full version.

"Come on," she said.

They walked out into the snow together.

Sarah and Daniel were last.

She turned off the barn light.

Stood in the dark for a moment.

The stove ticking as it cooled.

The snow sound against the boards.

The empty chairs.

The circle gone home.

She stood in the dark barn and felt the residue of the evening — the warmth of it, the frequency of it, Grace's telling, Rachel's laugh, Marcus and Grace in the doorway, all of it — and felt it settle in her the way good things settle.

Deeply.

Without drama.

Into the place where they become part of you permanently.

She went out into the snow.

Daniel was waiting by the car.

She stopped.

Looked up.

The snow coming down through the dark in the particular silence of heavy snowfall — the world muffled, the ordinary sounds of the road and the fields gone, just the snow and the cold and the dark sky and the barn behind her and the man in front of her and the two sedans at the end of the road barely visible through the white.

She looked at the sedans.

Felt nothing from them tonight.

Not the compass.

Not the pointing.

Just — cars in the snow.

Just — men doing a job in the cold.

She almost felt sorry for them.

Almost.

She got in the car.

Daniel drove.

She looked out the window at the snow-covered road.

"Grace kissed Marcus," she said.

Daniel drove for a moment.

"In the doorway," he said.

"You saw."

"I saw."

She looked at the white fields going past.

"It's been coming since September," she said.

"Yes," he said.

"The tea," she said. "The left hand."

"Yes."

She settled into the seat.

The heater doing its work.

The snow-covered road unspooling in the headlights.

"Rachel laughed," she said.

"She did."

"The real one."

"Yes."

She was quiet for a moment.

"David stepped through," she said.

Daniel glanced at her.

"You felt it."

"I felt all of them," she said. "Individually. All at once." She paused. "It lasted longer this time."

He was quiet.

"Is that — " He paused. "Is that frightening."

She thought about it honestly.

The full honest answer.

"No," she said.

"What is it."

She looked out at the snow.

At the white fields.

At the dark sky sending down its patient indifferent cover over everything.

She thought about the ripple and the ocean.

The water and the thing that knew it was water.

The room finding its windows.

She thought about all of them in the circle.

Each of them distinct and warm and present behind her sternum like fingers she knew without looking.

She thought about what it meant that she could feel them.

What it meant that they could feel each other.

What it meant that Meridian had a protocol for groups that didn't know what they were and did not have a protocol for this.

For people who knew.

For the full versions.

"It feels like the right size," she said.

Daniel drove through the snow.

Didn't say anything for a moment.

Then: "For what."

She looked at him.

At the profile of him in the dark car.

The man who had never asked her to be smaller.

Who had said *okay* and meant it.

Who had stood in a cold barn and watched her say *now* five times and looked at her afterward like she was the most extraordinary thing he had ever been standing near.

"For whatever comes next," she said.

He reached across.

Found her hand.

Held it.

The snow came down.

The road went on.

The barn behind them in the white dark sending no smoke now from the stovepipe — the stove cooling, the fire doing its last quiet work.

Ahead of them the cabin.

The warm kitchen.

The ordinary night.

The life they were choosing.

The full version.

Both of them.

Both-and.

Always both-and.

Chapter 23

CHAPTER TWENTY-THREE: THE TRUCK

The knowing arrived on a Tuesday morning like weather.

Not dramatic.

Not the sharp pointing of the compass.

More like pressure dropping.

The way your ears know a storm is coming before the sky shows you anything.

She was driving to work.

The usual route.. The county road that ran through the flat December fields, the stripped corn stubble coming through the snow on both sides, the sky the low grey of a week that intended to stay grey.

Radio on.

Thinking about the January fourth hearing.

About Rachel sitting across from the licensing board with David's documentation and the specific uprightness of a woman who had done the right thing and knew it and was prepared to say so clearly and at length to anyone who asked.

Thinking about Robert Caulfield.

The civil suit.

The facility in Indiana that was now holding a man with a name and a case number and a daughter who was looking for him with an attorney.

Thinking about Meridian and the second signature and the timeline David had said was a week maybe two and that had been eight days ago.

Thinking about all of it.

And underneath the thinking —

The pressure.

She noticed it without reaching for it.

Let it be what it was.

Turned down the radio.

Drove.

The county road straight and flat and empty at seven forty-five on a Tuesday morning.

Nobody behind her.

Nobody ahead.

Just the road and the grey sky and the snow-covered fields and the pressure behind her sternum that was not the diffuse warmth and not the compass pointing at something external.

Something else.

Both at once.

Diffuse and pointing simultaneously.

She had not felt that combination before.

She drove.

Paid attention.

The truck appeared on the horizon ten minutes later.

Coming toward her.

Ordinary enough.

Farm truck. Dark. The kind of vehicle that belonged on a county road in December in this part of the state without explanation.

She watched it come.

The pressure increased.

Not dramatically.

Like a volume being turned up by one.

She watched the truck.

Her hands on the wheel.

Her heart doing what hearts do when the body knows something the mind is still catching up to.

The truck was in its lane.

Coming toward her at the ordinary speed of a vehicle on a county road.

Nothing wrong.

Nothing she could point to.

Except the pressure.

Except the both-and quality of it.

Except her hands which were — she noticed this with the slight remove of someone watching themselves from a short distance — already adjusting.

Not dramatically.

Moving toward the shoulder by one, maybe two feet.

Giving room she didn't rationally need to give.

The truck came on.

She watched the driver through the windshield as it closed the distance.

Far away.

Then less far.

Then close enough to see the face.

The face was wrong.

She couldn't have said what wrong meant precisely.

Not monstrous. Not overtly threatening.

Wrong the way a room is wrong when something in it has been moved and you can't identify what.

Wrong the way Tom's coached warmth had been wrong.

Wrong in the specific way of a person who is present in their body but absent from their eyes.

Vacant.

The particular vacancy of someone executing an instruction.

The truck was in its lane.

Coming at her at the ordinary speed.

And then —

It wasn't.

It moved.

A deliberate drift.

Not a swerve. Not sudden. Deliberate. The slow certain movement of a vehicle whose driver has decided something and is executing the decision.

Crossing the center line.

Coming into her lane.

Her hands moved before the decision arrived.

Full shoulder.

The gravel loud under the tires.

The ditch coming up fast on the right.

She steered into the skid the way Daniel had shown her in the barn lot after the first truck, practicing in the snow, her hands learning the correction before her mind could think it.

The truck passed.

Three feet from her driver's side door.

Maybe two.

She felt the displacement of air.

She felt the wake of it.

She did not feel afraid.

She felt — and this surprised her — clear.

The absolute clarity of a body that has just done exactly what it needed to do and knows it.

She brought the car back onto the road.

Stopped.

Engine running.

Hands on the wheel.

The county road empty in both directions.

The truck gone around a curve a quarter mile back.

The grey sky pressing down.

The snow-covered fields on both sides saying nothing.

She sat.

Breathed.

Her hands steady on the wheel.

She thought about the driver's face.

The vacancy.

The instruction being executed.

She thought about the first truck.

The daylight. The corn. The deer she'd told Daniel she'd swerved for.

This was not that.

This was not a warning.

This was not an attempt to frighten her.

She understood the difference clearly and coldly in the way you understand things in the aftermath of something that almost wasn't an aftermath.

The first truck was a message.

This was an attempt.

She sat on the county road for four minutes.

She knew it was four because she counted.

Not to calm herself.

Because she wanted to know how long it took her to be ready to move again.

Four minutes.

She filed that.

Then she pulled back onto the road and drove.

Not home.

Not to work.

To David.

He opened the door before she knocked.

Looked at her face.

Stood back.

She came in.

Sat at his kitchen table.

Told him.

All of it.

The pressure on the drive. The both-and quality she hadn't felt before. The truck and the face and the two feet of air and the four minutes on the county road.

He sat across from her and listened with the complete stillness of someone for whom what he was hearing was simultaneously expected and not expected.

Expected because the pattern said it was coming.

Not expected because knowing a pattern doesn't fully prepare you for the moment it arrives.

When she finished he said: "The face."

"Vacant," she said. "Executing an instruction."

"You're sure it was deliberate."

She looked at him.

He held up a hand.

"I believe you," he said. "I need to know if you're sure."

"I'm sure," she said.

He nodded.

Made notes.

"The pressure before," he said. "The both-and. You said you hadn't felt that combination before."

"No."

"What do you think it was."

She thought about it.

"Warning and something else simultaneously," she said slowly. "The compass and the — the other thing. The large thing." She paused. "Like the knowing came from two directions at once and met in the middle."

He looked at her.

"You were ready before it happened," he said.

"My hands were ready," she said. "Before I decided anything."

He was quiet for a moment.

Not the quiet of someone processing information.

The quiet of someone sitting with something that his eleven years of documentation had not given him a category for.

"You're not shaking," he said.

She looked at her hands on the table.

Steady.

"No," she said.

"The others," he said. "In the groups I documented. After a physical approach — the car accidents, the road incidents — they shook for days. Some of them didn't drive alone again." He paused. "I've been watching for the fear. For the entry point." He looked at her. "Where is it."

She thought about this honestly.

Looked inside for the fear the way you check a room for something you expect to find.

Found something.

But not what he was looking for.

"There's fear," she said. "It's there. I'd be lying if I said it wasn't." She paused. "But it's — underneath something. Like it's present but it's not the load-bearing thing." She looked at him. "Does that make sense."

"Yes," he said.

"What's load-bearing," she said. "In the others. When the fear becomes the entry point."

"Isolation," he said. "The fear creates the impulse to withdraw. To protect. To stop being visible." He paused. "And once someone withdraws from the group the group loses coherence. And once the group loses coherence — "

"The frequency drops," she said.

"Yes."

She looked at her hands.

Thought about Thursday night.

Grace kissing Marcus in the barn doorway.

Rachel's laugh.

David stepping through.

The thirty seconds. Maybe forty.

The full frequency.

All of them.

"They're trying to frighten me away from the barn," she said.

"Yes."

"It won't work."

He looked at her.

Not the assessment look.

Something else.

"I know," he said.

She called Daniel from David's kitchen.

He answered on the first ring.

She told him.

Heard him be very still on the other end.

Not silent. Still. The specific quality of someone holding themselves together around something they want to respond to differently than they're going to allow themselves to respond to.

"Are you hurt," he said.

"No."

"Where are you."

"David's."

"Stay there," he said. "I'm coming."

"Daniel — "

"Stay there," he said again.

Not a demand.

The voice of someone who needed to see her with his own eyes before the stillness could become something other than what it currently was.

She understood.

"Okay," she said.

He arrived in twenty minutes.

Came through David's door and looked at her sitting at the table and his face did several things in quick succession that he didn't try to control or manage.

She stood up.

He crossed the room.

Held her.

Not gently.

The way you hold someone when the alternative to holding them was a thing you don't want to think about.

She let him hold her.

Held him back.

His heart against her ear going faster than his voice had been on the phone.

She felt the fear she'd filed under *present but not load-bearing* arrive more fully with his arms around her.

The body knowing what the mind had been managing.

The almost of it.

The two feet.

She breathed into his shoulder.

He breathed into her hair.

David sat at the kitchen table and looked at his notes and gave them the room.

After a while Daniel stepped back.

Held her face in his hands.

Looked at her the way he looked at her.

"You're okay," he said.

"I'm okay."

"The car."

"The car is fine."

He looked at her for another moment.

Then released her.

Turned to David.

"The plate," he said.

"She got a partial," David said. "I'm working on it."

"The face she described."

"I know who to ask," David said. "There's a contractor Meridian has used before for physical approaches. The description is consistent."

Daniel was quiet.

The quiet of a man doing what men did when someone they loved had been put in danger and they were deciding what to do with the feeling that produced.

"What do we do," he said.

"Documentation," David said. "I'm filing an incident report with the county sheriff's office. Not because I expect action but because it creates a public record. It establishes a pattern. If they try again — and they will try again — we have this on record as the precedent."

"And Sarah."

David looked at her.

"She doesn't drive the county road alone," he said. "Until we've resolved this."

She started to speak.

"Sarah," David said.

She stopped.

"One concession," he said. "Not isolation. Not withdrawal. One operational concession. Different route or not alone. That's all I'm asking."

She looked at him.

At Daniel.

At her hands that had moved without deciding.

That had known before she knew.

"Different route," she said.

David nodded.

Daniel nodded.

"And Thursday," she said. "I'm at the barn Thursday."

Neither of them said anything.

Because neither of them had expected anything different.

She drove home with Daniel.

He drove.

She sat in the passenger seat and watched the December fields go past and thought about the driver's face.

The vacancy.

The instruction being executed.

She thought about what it took to make a person vacant like that.

What it took to take a human being and use them as an instrument so completely that the eyes went empty.

She thought about Tom in the paint aisle.

Working on it.

She thought about the difference.

Tom recruited through fear and shame and a failing business.

Still — Tom.

Still the person underneath the recruitment.

Still capable of shame which meant still capable of choosing differently.

The driver this morning had not been choosing.

Had been chosen.
Had been made into a thing that executed instructions.
She sat with the difference.
It was not a comfortable difference.
But it was important.
Not everyone on the other side of this was the same.
Some of them were Tom.
Some of them were the driver.
Understanding the difference mattered.
She filed it.
Not under nothing.
Under: *the world as it actually is.*
That evening she sat at the kitchen table with her notepad.
Daniel making dinner.
The smell of it.
The warm kitchen.
The ordinary evening that was also not ordinary at all.
She wrote:
They escalated.
Which means the barn on Thursday frightened them.
Which means the frequency frightened them.
Which means we're past the stage they have a protocol for.
Which means we are just in time.
She looked at what she'd written.
Crossed out the last line.
Wrote instead:
Which means we are exactly on time.
Closed the notepad.
Looked at Daniel at the stove.
His back to her.
The ordinary extraordinary fact of him.
"Daniel," she said.

He turned.

She looked at him.

"Thank you," she said.

He looked back.

"For what."

She thought about the barn lot in the snow. The five times. The cold. His face afterward.

About *okay* said and meant in all its forms.

About the both-and of a man who was terrified and staying.

Always staying.

"For staying," she said.

He looked at her for a moment.

Then turned back to the stove.

"There's nowhere else," he said.

Simple as that.

Just — true.

She opened her notepad again.

Added one more line.

There is nowhere else.

Closed it.

The kitchen warm.

The snow outside.

The ordinary night.

The full version.

Hers.

Chapter 24

CHAPTER TWENTY-FOUR: DAVID'S FULL HAND

He called Thursday morning.

Not a text.

A call.

She knew before she answered.

"Come in," he said. "Before the barn. Bring Daniel."

His apartment was on the second floor of a building that was older than it looked and quieter than its location suggested.

She had been here twice before.

Both times for information she hadn't wanted but needed.

This felt like a third time.

Daniel drove.

She sat in the passenger seat watching the December streets go past and feeling the pressure behind her sternum — not the compass, not the warmth, something in between.

The both-and again.

Not as sharp as Tuesday.

Present.

She let it be present.

Didn't manage it down.

David opened the door before they knocked.

Gerald assessed them from the couch.

Allowed Daniel's presence with the mild interest of a cat whose standards had been revised recently.

Rachel was already there.

Sitting at the kitchen table with both hands around a mug and the expression of a woman who had arrived early because she'd needed to arrive early and was not going to explain that to anyone.

David poured coffee.

They sat.

He put a folder on the table.

Thicker than the last one.

Sarah looked at it.

Didn't reach for it yet.

"I found the second signature," David said.

No preamble.

The voice he used when what he had to say required no decoration.

"Who," Rachel said.

"A psychiatrist named Warren Cobb. Private practice. Downtown." He paused. "He's examined Sarah twice."

Sarah looked at him.

"I've never met a Warren Cobb," she said.

"No," David said. "You haven't." He opened the folder. "He submitted documentation to the county court last Tuesday claiming to have conducted two evaluations of you. One in October. One in November." He turned the pages toward her. "Both documenting significant concerns about your mental state. Both recommending involuntary evaluation."

Sarah looked at the pages.

Her name.

Her address.

Her date of birth.

Two dates in the fall.

She looked at October fourteenth.

She had been at the barn on October fourteenth.

She knew this because she kept her Thursday calendar in her phone and Thursday October fourteenth had been the night Marcus told them about James.

She had been in the barn.

Not in Warren Cobb's office.

She looked at November eleventh.

The day after the hardware store.

The day after Tom in the paint aisle.

She had been at Patricia Wren's office in the afternoon.

She had driven home.

Made soup.

She had not been in Warren Cobb's office.

She had never been in Warren Cobb's office.

"He fabricated the evaluations," she said.

"Yes."

"That's fraud," Daniel said.

"Yes," David said.

"Then we take it to — "

"I know where to take it," David said. He looked at Daniel steadily. "I need you to understand something first."

Daniel was quiet.

David looked around the table.

At Sarah.

At Rachel.

At Daniel.

"Meridian has filed the wellness hold application," he said. "Both signatures are on it. Hendricks and Cobb. The application was submitted to the county court yesterday afternoon." He paused. "A judge will review it today or tomorrow. If the judge signs it the hold can be executed at any time."

The kitchen was very quiet.

Gerald walked off the couch and sat on the kitchen floor in the particular way of a cat who has decided the situation requires his floor-level presence.

"How long do we have," Sarah said.

"I don't know," David said. "Once the judge signs it — hours. Maybe less."

"Patricia's documentation," Daniel said.

"Is good," David said. "It's solid. It will matter when we challenge the hold." He paused. "It won't prevent the hold from being executed. The challenge comes after."

"After meaning after she's already inside," Daniel said.

"Yes."

The word sat on the table between them.

After.

After meaning the facility.

After meaning the narrow room.

After meaning what Grace had described in the barn two Thursdays ago — the managed absence, the forms signed under medication, the specific patient dismantling of a person by people with credentials and time and no investment in her being herself.

Sarah looked at her hands.

Her hands that had moved before she decided anything on the county road on Tuesday morning.

That had known.

She breathed.

Let the pressure be what it was.

Felt underneath it for the other thing.

The large thing.

It was there.

Quieter than the barn on Thursday night.

Quieter than the river.

But there.

Steady.

"What do we do," she said.

David had been waiting for that question.

She could tell from the way he reached into the folder without hesitation.

He had been building toward this.

He laid four documents on the table.

"First," he said. "Cobb's fraud."

He put a single page in front of her.

"I have documentation placing you at the barn on October fourteenth and at Patricia Wren's office on November eleventh. Timestamped. Witnessed. Irrefutable." He paused. "I also have documentation that Warren Cobb has submitted fabricated evaluations in two previous cases. Both connected to Meridian. Both in support of wellness hold applications."

Sarah looked at the page.

"You've been building this for a while," she said.

"I suspected Cobb when I identified the Meridian connection," David said. "He's their preferred second signature in this region. I started looking the day I found his name."

"Can we get this to the judge before she signs," Daniel said.

"I'm filing an emergency motion this morning," David said. "My attorney is already at the courthouse." He paused. "It may not stop the signing. Judges receive motions. They don't always read them before they act." He looked at Sarah. "It may not be enough today. It will be enough to get you out quickly if they move on the hold."

Sarah nodded.

"Second," David said.

Another page.

"The facility in Indiana."

The table went still.

"Robert," Rachel said.

"The civil suit created enough legal exposure that the facility's attorneys contacted me Tuesday." He paused. "They're willing to discuss terms."

"Terms," Daniel said.

"His release in exchange for the daughter's agreement to limit the scope of the suit." He looked at Rachel. "I need to be clear — this is not justice. This is a transaction. They release Robert and the suit is narrowed to documented damages rather than the full institutional exposure they're facing." He paused. "Robert comes home. They walk away largely intact."

Rachel looked at him.

"Will he be okay," she said.

"He'll need time," David said. "What was done to him takes time to undo. But he'll be — he'll be Robert. He'll be able to call his daughter. He'll be out of that room." He paused. "Grace was four months. Robert has been six weeks. The shorter the time the less the damage."

Rachel was quiet for a moment.

Looking at the table.

At her hands.

At the two years of Thursday nights and the group and Grace in the parking lot and everything that had been built in the barn one evening at a time.

"Take the terms," she said.

David nodded.

"Third," he said.

Third page.

"Foss."

He turned the page toward Sarah.

She looked at it.

A photograph at the top.

Gerald Foss in what appeared to be a corporate lobby.

Younger than she remembered.

The expression the same.

The specific attention of someone who assessed everything and showed nothing.

"Gerald Foss has been a Meridian integration specialist for seven years," David said. "Before Meridian he worked for two similar organizations under different names." He paused. "He has been the integration specialist on six of the nine documented groups I've mapped."

"Six," Sarah said.

"Six."

"All dismantled."

"All dismantled."

She looked at Foss's photograph.

The lobby behind him. Clean. Corporate. The architecture of something legitimate.

"What's the fourth document," she said.

David looked at her.

A long moment.

The look she had learned to read as someone deciding not how much to say but how to say the full amount.

"The fourth document is what I haven't shown anyone yet," he said. "Including Marcus."

He put the last page on the table.

She looked at it.

A list.

Names.

Fourteen of them.

She recognized none of them.

"Who are these people," Daniel said.

"They're former members of groups Meridian dismantled," David said. "People who were catalysts. People who were at the same stage

Sarah is at now." He paused. "People who went through the full integration protocol."

Sarah looked at the list.

Fourteen names.

"What happened to them," she said.

David was quiet for a moment.

"Three of them are in facilities currently," he said. "Long-term. The documentation around them is solid enough that getting them out would take years of legal work." He paused. "Four of them are out but significantly diminished. The protocol ran long enough that — what was in them, what was happening to them — it didn't come back. Or hasn't yet." He paused again. "Four of them scattered. Changed their lives completely. New cities, new identities, essentially. Functioning but — gone from anything like what they were building."

"That's eleven," Daniel said.

"Yes," David said.

"The other three," Sarah said.

David looked at her.

"The other three refused the full protocol," he said. "Challenged the hold legally. Fought it from inside the facility or from outside when they could." He paused. "It took between eight months and two years. It cost them significantly. Jobs, relationships, financial stability." He paused again. "But they're — intact. What was happening to them continued. They're still — " He searched for the word.

"Blooming," Sarah said.

"Yes," he said. "They're still blooming."

The kitchen.

Gerald on the floor.

The December light in the window.

The folder on the table.

Sarah looked at the list of fourteen names.

Thought about three of them in facilities.

Four diminished.

Four scattered.

Three fighting.

Still blooming.

She thought about the barn on Thursday night.

The full frequency.

Thirty seconds. Maybe forty.

The largest it had ever been.

She thought about Grace's telling.

About Rachel's laugh.

About Marcus and Grace in the doorway in the snow.

She thought about the river on Saturday.

The December cold.

The immensity coming fully for the first time.

Standing in it.

Not managing it.

Not managing it at all.

She thought about what it had felt like to stand in the full size of it without apology and without permission and without the managed version.

She looked at David.

"I'm not going to be the fourth category," she said.

He held her gaze.

"No," he said. "I don't think you are."

"I need you to tell me everything," she said. "Not the managed version. Not what you think I can handle. Everything."

He looked at her for a long moment.

Then he picked up the folder.

And told her everything.

It took an hour.

Daniel sat beside her and said almost nothing.

Rachel sat across from her and said almost nothing.

Both of them letting her hear it without the interference of their reactions to it.

She was grateful for this.

She needed the information clean.

The full picture of Meridian.

Not just the integration protocol.

The organization itself.

Its origins — twenty-three years ago, a private intelligence firm contracted by a coalition of interests that David described carefully as entities with significant investment in the maintenance of existing systems.

Its funding — diffuse, layered, deliberately obscured through a series of holding companies and nonprofits and consultancies.

Its reach — not just the nine groups David had documented. He believed the number was closer to forty. Possibly more.

Forty groups.

Forty circles of people becoming more themselves.

Forty barns.

Forty frequencies.

Managed back into silence.

She sat with forty.

She sat with the full size of what forty meant.

All those people.

All that blooming interrupted.

All those narrow rooms.

And beneath the forty — beneath the documented history of it — something David described carefully and without drama as: a consistent and organized effort spanning decades to prevent a specific kind of human development from reaching critical mass.

"Critical mass," she said.

"Their word," David said. "It's in the internal documents I obtained. They track what they call critical mass indicators. When a group begins to show multiple indicators simultaneously — "

"Level three," she said.

"Yes. Level three is when the indicators suggest critical mass is approaching." He paused. "They've never allowed a group to reach it."

She looked at the folder.

At the list of fourteen names.

"What happens," she said. "If a group reaches critical mass. In their documentation. What do they say happens."

David was quiet for a moment.

"They don't say," he said. "The documentation stops at the threshold. Everything is about preventing the approach." He paused. "They don't have data on what happens after because they've always intervened before after."

She looked at him.

"Until now," she said.

He held her gaze.

"Until now," he said.

She was quiet for a long time after he finished.

Daniel's hand on hers under the table.

Rachel with her coffee.

Gerald relocating to the windowsill with the air of a cat who had heard enough and required sky.

She looked at the folder.

At the photograph of Foss in the corporate lobby.

At the list of fourteen names.

At the documents that laid out the full architecture of something that had been operating for twenty-three years before she walked into a barn on a Thursday night and sat in a circle of chairs and felt the first whisper of something she didn't have a name for.

She thought about the river.

The December cold.

We are exactly on time.

She had written it.

She believed it.

But now she held the full weight of what *exactly on time* meant.

Not just for herself.

Not just for the group.

For the forty barns.

For the fourteen names.

For the three who were still blooming.

For the people in the groups Meridian hadn't found yet who were sitting in circles somewhere not knowing what was coming.

For all of them.

She sat with this for a long time.

Let it be the full size it was.

Then she looked up at David.

"What do you need from me," she said.

He looked at her steadily.

"I need you to stay intact," he said. "I need the group to stay intact. I need Thursday to happen and the frequency to do what it does and — " He paused. "I need you to understand that what happens in that barn on Thursday nights is not incidental to this. It's the whole thing."

She looked at him.

"You felt it," she said. "Two weeks ago. You stepped through."

He was quiet for a moment.

The careful man. The eleven years. The documentation.

"Yes," he said.

"And."

Another moment.

"And I understand now why they're afraid of it," he said. "In a way I didn't before." He paused. "I understood it intellectually. The documentation. The pattern. The forty groups." He looked at his hands. "Thursday I understood it the other way."

She nodded.

"Then you know," she said.

"Yes," he said. "I know."

"Then you know we can't stop," she said.

"I know," he said.

"Whatever they do," she said. "Whatever the judge signs. Whatever the hold looks like. Whatever comes after." She paused. "We don't stop."

He looked at her.

Rachel looked at her.

Daniel's hand tightened around hers.

"We don't stop," David said.

They left at noon.

She and Daniel walking to the car through the December cold.

She stopped on the sidewalk.

Looked up.

The sky the same flat grey it had been all week.

The city around them doing its ordinary business.

People. Cars. The unremarkable Thursday morning.

She felt the pressure behind her sternum.

The both-and.

She stood in it.

The folder in David's apartment with the fourteen names.

The hold application on a judge's desk somewhere in this city.

The facility in Indiana and Robert Caulfield coming home.

The barn tonight.

The circle.

The frequency.

The full size of what they were building and what was trying to prevent it and why and what it meant that they were exactly on time.

All of it.

She held all of it.

Found she was large enough.

She had known she was large enough.

She was done being surprised by it.

"Tonight," Daniel said beside her.

"Tonight," she said.

They got in the car.

The Thursday morning continued its unremarkable business around them.

The December city going about its life.

Indifferent and ordinary and full of people who didn't know about Meridian or the forty barns or the fourteen names or the frequency in a barn on Thursday nights that an organization with twenty-three years of operational history and significant reach had apparently decided was the most dangerous thing they had encountered.

She thought about that.

About ordinary people in an ordinary city living ordinary lives while something moved underneath the ordinary like a current moving under ice.

Not frightening.

The opposite.

She thought about what it would mean when the ice thinned.

When the current came through.

When enough people sat in enough circles on enough Thursday nights and felt the thing she felt and understood what it was.

She thought about critical mass.

About the threshold Meridian had never allowed a group to cross.

About what happened after.

About the fact that they didn't have data on after.

About the fact that she was going to be the data.
They were all going to be the data.
She smiled.
Small.
Private.
She wasn't a woman who smiled at nothing.
This was not nothing.
Daniel glanced at her.
"What," he said.
She looked at him.
"We're going to find out what happens after," she said.
He looked at the road.
A pause.
"Yes," he said.
"Nobody knows," she said. "Not Meridian. Not David. Nobody."
"No," he said.
"Just us."
He drove.
The grey sky.
The December city.
The Thursday morning going toward Thursday night.
"Just us," he said.
She settled into the seat.
Felt the pressure behind her sternum.
Steady.
Warm.
Patient as the river.
Just in time.
Exactly on time.
Time to find out.

Chapter 25

CHAPTER TWENTY-FIVE: THE RIVER — SARAH ALONE

She went before dawn.

Daniel still sleeping.

She dressed in the dark. Quietly. The specific quiet of someone who has made a decision and is executing it before the thinking catches up and complicates things.

She didn't leave a note.

She would be back before he woke.

And if she wasn't — he would know where she was.

He always knew where she was.

The path behind the cabin was frozen.

Her breath coming in small clouds.

The December dark complete and close and smelling of cold and bare earth and the particular mineral smell of a landscape that had put everything away for the season and was resting in the deep unsentimental way of things that understood cycles.

She knew the path without seeing it.

The root that caught the toe.

The place where the light changed in daylight — in the dark just a feeling, a slight opening, the trees stepping back.

The grass dead and flat under her boots.

The willows ahead.

Bare now.

Their stripped branches hanging in the dark like something patient.

Something that had been waiting since September without minding the wait.

She stopped at the bank.

Looked at the river.

Low and dark and moving.

The surface catching no light because there was no light yet.

Just the river doing its work in the dark the way it did its work in the light — without audience, without adjustment, without any particular interest in being observed.

She took off her boots.

Her socks.

Set them on the bank.

The frozen ground under her feet.

She stood there for a moment.

Feeling the cold of it.

The specific sharp honesty of frozen ground in December before dawn.

Then she waded in.

The cold moved through her like a hand pressing at the center of her chest.

Not gentle.

Not cruel.

Just — present.

The current around her ankles.

Low this time of year.

Patient.

She stood in it.

Her feet on the river bottom.

The stones beneath her feet smooth and cold and real.

She breathed.

In.

Out.

The dark around her.

The bare willows.

The sound of the water moving past her and continuing.

Always continuing.

She thought about the folder on David's table.

The fourteen names.

The forty barns.

The hold application on a judge's desk somewhere in the city.

She let herself think about it fully.

Not managing the fear.

Not filing it under useful categories.

Just — feeling the full weight of it.

The organization that had been doing this for twenty-three years.

The patience of it.

The resources of it.

The specific cold intelligence of something that had identified a thing it feared and built a system to prevent it and refined that system across forty attempts and had never once failed to complete its protocol.

Until now.

Maybe.

She stood in the December river and felt the full weight of all of it and did not look away from any of it.

The fear was real.

She let it be real.

And then she let the other thing come.

Not instead of the fear.

Alongside it.

The both-and.

She stood in the current and breathed and let the edges of herself become what they became when she stopped insisting on them.

It was different this time.

Every time was different.

The first time — the surprise of it. The thirty seconds. The cloud passing.

The barn the first time — the whisper of it. Dismissed as wine.

The kitchen sink at Emma's — thirty seconds counted. The water and her hands.

The barn at full frequency — all of them simultaneously. The ripple and the river.

The river in December alone before dawn —

She stood in it and let it come and it came the way Grace had described.

Not gentle.

Not the slow quiet arrival of the early times.

Like water that had been held back.

The insistence of it.

The full version.

Not a whisper.

Not thirty seconds.

Not the edge of it.

All of it.

She was the woman standing in the river.

She was also the river.

Not metaphor.

Not poetry.

Not the borrowed language of traditions that had tried to describe this and gotten it approximately right and worn the words smooth through repetition.

Just — true.

The current moving around her ankles and through her and she was the thing being moved around and she was the moving.

Both.

Simultaneously.

Without contradiction.

The container not broken.

Optional.

She stood in the full size of it.

The December dark around her.

The bare willows.

The cold.

The stones under her feet.

All of it real.

All of it hers.

All of it also something larger than hers.

The ripple and the ocean.

She had written that once.

Sitting at the kitchen table after a conversation that had gone somewhere neither of them had planned.

She understood it now from the inside.

Not as description.

As fact.

She thought about the fourteen names.

From inside this.

From the full size of this.

She thought about the narrow rooms.

About what it would take to walk backward away from this.

About the medication that moved you to one side of yourself and kept you there.

About the grey.

About Emma's eleven years.

About Marcus's fourteen.

About Grace in the facility dreaming of Thursday nights in a barn she couldn't get to.

She stood in the river and thought about all of it from inside the full size of herself and understood something she had not understood before.

Not intellectually.

The other way.

The way you understand the temperature of water by standing in it.

This was what they were afraid of.

Not the group specifically.

Not the barn.

Not the frequency on Thursday nights.

This.

A person standing in the full size of themselves.

Completely.

Without apology.

Without management.

Without the performance of being less than this so that something built on the premise of human smallness could continue to function.

This was the threat.

Not political.

Not ideological.

Not any of the categories that could be argued about in rooms with fluorescent lights.

Just — this.

A woman in a river before dawn.

The full version.

Knowing what she was.

Choosing it.

Unable to be talked out of it.

Unable to be frightened out of it.

Unable to be medicated out of it once it had arrived fully.

Once you had stood in this there was no protocol for walking you backward out of it.

Grace had said it.

It came back insisting.

Not because Grace was special.

Not because any of them were special.

Because this was what people were when the systems built to prevent it failed.

This was what people were underneath.

The full version.

All along.

The sky was beginning to change.

Barely.

The specific imperceptible shift of the dark before it commits to becoming dawn.

She stood in the river.

Felt the cold.

The current.

The immensity.

All three simultaneously.

All three real.

She thought about David saying: *they don't have data on what happens after.*

She thought about standing in this.

About all of them standing in this.

About the barn on Thursday nights and what it built Thursday by Thursday — not just in each of them individually but between them, among them, the frequency that was more than any one of them and was also made of all of them.

She thought about critical mass.

About the threshold Meridian had never allowed.

She thought about what tipped a threshold.

Not one person standing in a river before dawn.

Many people.

Many rivers.

Many Thursday nights.

Many barns.

Many circles.

The current moving through all of them.

Not insisting on itself.

Not announcing itself.

Just — present.

Doing its work.

The way the river did its work in the dark.

Without audience.

Without adjustment.

Patient as something that understood cycles.

She waded out.

Stood on the bank.

Her feet on the frozen ground.

The cold sharp and honest after the water.

She picked up her socks.

Her boots.

Sat on the bank and dried her feet as best she could with the hem of her coat.

Put her boots on.

Stood.

The sky definitively changing now.

The dark becoming dark-grey becoming grey.

The bare willows visible.

The river visible.

Moving.

Always moving.

She stood on the bank and looked at it for a moment.

She had come here to find something.

Or to confirm something.

She wasn't sure which.

Both.

The both-and.

She had found it.

Confirmed it.

She walked back up the path.

The root.

The place where the trees stepped back.

The cabin.

She came through the back door into the kitchen.

Put the kettle on.

Stood at the window while it heated.

The sky outside going from grey to pale.

The bare tree line.

The road.

Empty this morning.

No sedan.

She looked at the empty road.

Thought about the judge.

The hold application.

The timeline David had said was hours maybe less once the signature arrived.

She felt the fear.

Real.

Present.

Underneath the immensity.

Not gone.

Not managed away.

Just — underneath.

The way the river bottom was underneath the current.

Still there.

Still real.

Still the ground of things.

But not the whole thing.

Not even most of the thing.

The kettle boiled.

She made coffee.

Daniel came into the kitchen at seven.

Hair unorderly.

The particular expression of someone who had woken and reached across and found the other side of the bed empty and had done the calculation and had arrived at an answer and was now confirming the answer.

He looked at her.

At her coffee.

At her hair still slightly damp at the ends from the December air.

At her face.

He looked at her face for a long moment.

She let him look.

Let him read whatever he read there.

He went to the counter.

Poured himself coffee.

Came and stood beside her at the window.

They looked at the empty road together.

"The river," he said.

"Yes."

"Before dawn."

"Yes."

He drank his coffee.

She drank hers.

The pale morning outside.

The tree line.

The road.

"How was it," he said.

She thought about standing in the December water in the full dark.

The cold.

The current.

The immensity coming fully.

The full version.

No management.

No apology.

No thirty-second limit.

Just — all of it.

All at once.

The ripple and the river.

Both.

"It was the full size," she said.

He was quiet for a moment.

"You're ready," he said.

Not a question.

The statement of a man who had been watching her become something and was now looking at the completed thing.

Or not completed.

Arrived.

The thing that had been arriving since the first Thursday night in the barn.

Arrived.

"Yes," she said.

He nodded.

Drank his coffee.

Looked at the road.

"Whatever today brings," he said.

"Whatever today brings," she said.

His hand found hers at the window.

She turned hers over.

Held it properly.

The pale December morning continuing its slow work of becoming day.

The road empty.

The tree line bare and honest.

The river behind the cabin doing what it had always done.

Moving.

Patient.

Indifferent to judges and hold applications and Meridian and all of it.

Just — moving.

The way things moved that understood they were larger than anything trying to stop them.

She stood at the window with her coffee and Daniel's hand in hers and felt the full size of the morning.

The full size of herself in it.

The full size of what was coming.

All three at once.

The both-and-and.

She was ready.

Her phone rang at eight-fifteen.

David.

She answered.

"The judge signed it," he said.

His voice level.

The voice he used for information that required her to be level in return.

"When," she said.

"Forty minutes ago. My attorney just called."

Daniel turned from the window.

Read her face.

She held his eyes while she listened.

"What does that mean for tonight," she said.

"It means they can move at any time," David said. "It means tonight at the barn we need to be prepared for — "

"We're going to the barn," she said.

"I know," he said. "I'll be there. I've spoken to Patricia. She's filing the emergency challenge this morning. It won't stop them tonight but it establishes the legal record." He paused. "Sarah."

"Yes."

"I need you to know — the challenge is solid. The Cobb fraud alone is enough to get the hold overturned. If they execute it tonight it will not hold. Days. A week at most."

She thought about Grace.

Four months.

"Days," she said.

"Days," he said. "You have my word."

She looked at Daniel.

At the window.

At the empty road.

"I'll see you tonight," she said.

She hung up.

The kitchen.

The morning.

Daniel in front of her.

"They signed it," he said.

"Yes."

He was very still.

The stillness she knew now.

The both-and of a man who was terrified and staying.

Always staying.

"Tonight," he said.

"Tonight," she said.

She picked up her coffee.

It had gone slightly cold.

She drank it anyway.

The full version of a cold cup of coffee on a December morning while the thing she had been building toward and the thing that had been building against her moved toward each other.

The river behind the cabin moving in the pale morning light.

Patient.

Indifferent.

Certain.

She was all three.

She was ready.

Chapter 26

CHAPTER TWENTY-SIX: WHAT THEY'RE PROTECTING

Marcus called at nine.

She had been expecting David to call again.

Or Rachel.

Not Marcus.

Marcus texted. Texted in the economical way of someone who considered each word a commitment and didn't make commitments casually.

A call from Marcus meant something that couldn't be texted.

She answered.

"Come to the barn," he said.

"The barn isn't until tonight."

"I know," he said. "Come now."

Daniel drove.

The December morning pale and still.

The roads clear.

No sedan behind them.

No sedan ahead.

She watched the mirrors anyway.

The habit of it now as natural as checking the weather.

The barn came up on the left through the bare fields.

Marcus's truck in the lot.

One other vehicle she didn't recognize.

She looked at it.

Old. Dark blue. Michigan plates.

Daniel pulled in.

They sat for a moment.

"Do you know that car," she said.

"No," he said.

She felt the pressure behind her sternum.

Not the compass.

Not the warning.

Something warmer.

Something that felt like — anticipation.

The good kind.

She got out.

The barn was warm.

Stove going.

The amber light.

The smell of the place.

Marcus at the small table.

Grace beside him.

Their hands not quite touching in the way that meant they were about to.

And across the circle —

A man she had never seen.

Sixty-one. Maybe sixty-two.

Thin in the way of someone who had been thin against their will and was in the early stages of undoing that.

Grey at the temples.

The eyes of someone who had been somewhere very far away.

Coming back.

Not all the way back yet.

But coming.

She knew those eyes.

She had seen them in the parking lot at two in the morning.

She had seen them in Grace's face on the first Thursday.

She had seen them in the mirror once, briefly, during the worst year of the marriage.

The eyes of someone the world had tried to make absent and had not quite succeeded.

Marcus stood.

"Sarah," he said.

He said it in the voice he used for things that mattered.

"This is Robert," he said.

She crossed the barn.

Sat in the chair across from him.

He looked at her with the careful attention of someone relearning how to look at people.

How to be in a room with them.

How to trust that the room was safe.

She let him look.

Didn't perform anything.

Didn't rush to fill the space.

The barn held them.

After a moment he said: "David told me about you."

His voice was careful.

Slightly unsteady at the edges.

The voice of someone whose instrument had been out of use and was warming up.

"Good things I hope," she said.

Something moved through his face.

Not quite a smile.

The shape of one.

The memory of how smiling worked.

"He said you didn't scare," Robert said.

She looked at him.

"I scare," she said. "I just don't stop."

He looked at her for a long moment.

The eyes that had been somewhere far away.

Coming closer.

"That's what he meant," Robert said.

Daniel sat beside her.

Grace poured tea.

Marcus sat across from Robert with the patient stillness of a man who understood that what this person needed most right now was a room that didn't ask anything of him and was prepared to provide exactly that for as long as it took.

She watched Marcus do this.

The art of it.

The specific gift of a person who could be fully present without exerting pressure.

A room that was also a person.

Robert wrapped both hands around his mug.

She recognized the gesture.

Grace's gesture on the first Thursday.

The need for something solid.

Something real.

Something that didn't move or lie or get replaced by something else when you stopped paying attention.

A mug.

Warm.

Solid.

Here.

He talked in pieces.

She didn't push for a narrative.

Neither did Marcus.

Neither did Grace, who sat beside Marcus with her shoulder almost touching his and her eyes on Robert with the specific quality of someone who had been where he was and was not going to perform having forgotten what it was like.

The facility.

He described it in fragments.

The intake.

The forms.

The specific managed quality of every interaction — the nurses, the doctors, the orderlies — all of them consistent, all of them careful, all of them speaking in the practiced language of people whose job was to make you believe the problem was you.

The medication.

He described the medication the way Grace had described it.

One side of yourself.

The other side inaccessible.

Present enough to sign.

Absent enough not to understand.

He described the particular loneliness of it.

Not the loneliness of being alone.

The loneliness of being present in a room full of people and feeling yourself at a remove from your own presence.

Watching yourself from slightly outside.

Going through the motions of existing.

He stopped.

Looked at his tea.

"My daughter," he said.

His voice changed on those two words.

The way a voice changes when it arrives at the thing underneath everything else.

"She didn't stop," he said.

He said it with the specific quality of a person who had been in a room where stopping seemed like the only option and had found out from the other side that someone hadn't stopped.

"She called every week," he said. "They told her I didn't want visitors. They told her I was making progress and contact would be disruptive." He paused. "She called anyway. Left messages I wasn't given." He paused again. "And then one week someone made a mistake. Put the message through."

He looked up.

"Her voice," he said.

Just that.

Her voice.

The two words carrying everything they were carrying — the six weeks, the narrow room, the medication, the forms, the managed absence — all of it and on the other side of all of it his daughter's voice coming through a phone in a room where everything was designed to convince him the world outside had moved on without him.

It hadn't.

She hadn't.

"David found her," Grace said quietly.

"Yes," Robert said. He looked at Grace. "He said you helped."

"He did the work," Grace said.

"He said you told him to find me," Robert said. "That first night. At the barn."

Grace looked at her hands.

"Yes," she said.

"Why," he said. "You didn't know me."

Grace looked at him directly.

"I knew what you were," she said. "I knew what they'd done." She paused. "You don't leave people in rooms like that."

Robert looked at her for a long moment.

His eyes not far away right now.

Present.

Fully.

Something in them that was the beginning of the thing she recognized.

The room finding its windows.

Not yet.

Beginning.

"No," he said. "You don't."

After a while the talking fell away.

Not uncomfortably.

The barn doing what it did.

Holding the quiet without requiring anything of it.

Sarah sat in the circle and felt the particular quality of the morning.

Five people in a barn on a December Thursday.

Not the full group.

Not the Thursday night gathering.

Something smaller.

Something that didn't have a name yet.

She thought about what David had said.

The group needs to stay intact.

She thought about intact.

About what it meant.

Not just the people in the circle on Thursday nights.

The people who had been in circles before them.

The fourteen names.

The forty barns.

Robert across from her with his mug and his thin hands and his eyes coming back from somewhere far away.

Grace beside Marcus whose hand was now fully holding hers without either of them appearing to notice they'd crossed the almost.

Intact meant this.

Not just surviving the protocol.

Finding each other on the other side of it.

Robert at the table.

Grace in the barn.

The three names on David's list who were still blooming.

All of them intact in the way that mattered.

The way that couldn't be medicated away once it had fully arrived.

She felt the thing behind her sternum.

Warm.

Steady.

Looking at Robert Caulfield, sixty-one, retired schoolteacher, daughter in Grand Rapids, six weeks in a facility that had tried to make him absent and had not succeeded.

Not quite succeeded.

They took his name, David had said.

John Doe.

She looked at him.

At the eyes coming back.

At the hands on the mug.

At the man underneath the six weeks who was still there.

Still Robert.

Still the quiet man in the back corner of the circle who had a tremor that had stopped and a daughter he called on Sundays and a fundamental quality that Meridian had a protocol for and had not managed to erase.

"Robert," she said.

He looked at her.

"Thursday nights," she said. "You should come."

He looked around the barn.

At the circle of empty chairs waiting for evening.

At Marcus and Grace.

At Daniel beside her.

At the high windows with their thin December light.

At the stove doing its steady work.

At the space of the place.

The specific honest space of it.

Something moved through his face.

The shape of the smile arriving more fully this time.

Not complete.

Coming.

"Yes," he said.

Just that.

Yes.

The word of someone finding their way back to themselves one syllable at a time.

They stayed until noon.

Nobody in a hurry.

The barn around them.

The stove.

The quiet.

Robert talking in pieces.

Marcus listening.

Grace listening.

The particular quality of a space where nothing was being managed and everything was being held.

She sat in it and thought about tonight.

About the hold application with its judge's signature.

About David's emergency challenge.

About Meridian and the integration protocol and the timeline that was hours maybe less.

She thought about all of it and felt the fear and felt the immensity underneath the fear and felt the barn around her and the people in it.

Robert with his mug.

Grace with Marcus's hand.

Daniel beside her.

All of them intact.

All of them here.

All of them choosing this on a Thursday morning in December when the choosing cost something real.

This was what they were protecting.

Not the frequency specifically.

Not the barn.

Not any single person or any single Thursday night.

This.

The choosing.

The continued choosing in the face of real cost.

The refusal to be managed back into absence.

The insistence.

The full version.

This was what Meridian spent twenty-three years and forty barns and fourteen names trying to prevent.

Not because it was dangerous in the way dangerous usually meant.

Because it was contagious.

One person standing in the full size of themselves was remarkable.

Two was a conversation.

Seven was a frequency.

Forty barns was a current.

And a current, once it reached a certain depth and speed and coherence —

Couldn't be held back.

Couldn't be managed.

Couldn't be walked backward away from itself.

Could only move.

The way rivers moved.

The way tides moved.

The way things moved that were older and larger and more patient than anything built to stop them.

She sat in the barn and understood this clearly for the first time.

Not the intellectual version.

The river version.

The standing-in-it version.

She understood why they were afraid.

She understood why they had spent twenty-three years building a system to prevent it.

She understood why none of the systems had ultimately worked.

Because you couldn't build a system large enough.

Because the thing you were trying to contain was larger than any system.

Had always been larger.

Would always be larger.

Was in fact the thing that systems were built inside of without knowing it.

The ocean doesn't know about the boats.

She and Daniel left at twelve-thirty.

Robert staying with Marcus for the afternoon.

Grace walking them to the car.

The barn lot.

The December cold.

The pale sky.

Grace stopped beside the car and looked at Sarah.

She had something to say.

Sarah waited.

"Tonight," Grace said.

"Yes."

"If they come tonight — "

"They may," Sarah said.

"I know." Grace looked at her steadily. "I need you to know something."

Sarah waited.

"What they did to me," Grace said. "What they tried to do." She paused. "It didn't work. Not ultimately. What I am is not something they could take." She paused again. "What you are is not something they can take."

Sarah looked at her.

"I know that," she said.

"You know it in your head," Grace said. "I knew it in my head too." She held Sarah's eyes. "I need you to know it in the river."

Sarah understood.

The river version.

The standing-in-it version.

Not the intellectual knowing.

The other kind.

"I went this morning," Sarah said.

Grace looked at her.

"Before dawn," Sarah said. "The full version."

Grace was quiet for a moment.

Something moved through her face.

"Good," she said.

She said it the way people said it in this group.

Complete.

Carrying everything it needed to carry in four letters.

"Good," Sarah said back.

Grace put her hand briefly on Sarah's arm.

Then turned and walked back toward the barn.

Toward Marcus.

Toward Robert inside with his mug and his eyes coming home.

Toward Thursday night.

Toward whatever came after Thursday night.

Sarah got in the car.

Daniel drove.

The December fields going past.

The pale sky.

The empty roads.

She looked at them.

Thought about tonight.

About the barn.

About all of them in the circle.

About the full frequency.

About what it would feel like with Robert in the circle for the first time.

About what it would feel like knowing the hold was signed and the timeline was hours.

About what it would feel like to sit in the circle anyway.

To choose the barn anyway.

The full version of choosing.

The both-and.

She felt the pressure behind her sternum.

The warm steady presence of it.

Not warning.

Not pointing.

Just: *here.*

Just: *ready.*

Just: *exactly on time.*

She settled into the seat.

Watched the December landscape go past.

The bare fields.

The stripped trees.

The sky pressing down on all of it with the patient grey weight of a season that had done its work and knew it.

The world resting.

The world always resting between one thing and the next.
The current underneath.
Always moving.
Always moving.
Always moving.

Chapter 27

CHAPTER TWENTY-SEVEN: WHAT THEY'RE PROTECTING

Rachel called at two.

Sarah was at the kitchen table with her notepad.

Not writing.

Sitting with the notepad open and the pen in her hand and the blank page in front of her in the way of someone whose thoughts were moving too fast to be written and too important to be lost.

She answered.

"January fourth," Rachel said.

No preamble.

The Rachel version of a phone call.

"Tell me," Sarah said.

"The board moved it up." A pause. "It's tomorrow."

Sarah set down her pen.

"Tomorrow," she said.

"I got the notification an hour ago. Emergency session. Apparently there's been a formal complaint filed by the facility." Another pause. Shorter. The pause of someone managing something they are not going to allow to manage them. "Hendricks co-signed it."

"Of course he did."

"The charge is patient endangerment." Rachel's voice was level. Precise. The voice she used in professional settings that required the appearance of calm regardless of the internal weather. "Specifically

— unauthorized reduction of prescribed medication leading to patient distress and potential harm."

"Grace," Sarah said.

"Grace."

"Who is going to testify to the distress and harm."

"Hendricks. And a Dr. Pauline Marsh from the facility. She was Grace's attending physician."

Sarah thought about the narrow room.

The narrow bed.

The window that faced a wall.

The specific management of consciousness that Grace had described in the barn.

A physician who had presided over all of that now testifying to distress and harm.

The architecture of it was almost elegant if you didn't mind it being monstrous.

"What does David say," Sarah said.

"He's been on the phone since I called him." A pause. "He says the documentation is solid. The dose records. Grace's medical history before and after. Patricia Wren has agreed to submit a supporting statement." Another pause. "He says the board is not Meridian. That most of the members are independent practitioners who respond to evidence."

"Most," Sarah said.

"Most," Rachel said.

A silence.

The honest silence of two people sitting with the word most and what it left unaccounted for.

"Rachel," Sarah said.

"Yes."

"How are you."

A pause.

Longer than the previous ones.

Not the professional pause.

The real one.

The pause of someone who has been asked a genuine question and is deciding whether to answer genuinely.

"I'm — " She stopped. "I'm not afraid of the board," she said. "I know what I did. I know why I did it. I have the documentation." A pause. "I'm afraid of what it costs if the board doesn't look at the documentation honestly."

"Your license," Sarah said.

"My license," Rachel said. "Twelve years. The work." A pause. "Grace."

The word landed differently than the others.

Sarah heard everything it carried.

Not just Grace's safety.

Not just the group.

The specific thing between Rachel and Grace that had begun in a facility hallway with a reduced dose and a decision made in the full knowledge of its cost and had become something neither of them had a category for and both of them were living inside.

"She knows," Sarah said.

"I know she knows," Rachel said. "That's not — " She stopped. "I don't want her to carry it. Whatever happens tomorrow. I don't want her to feel responsible."

"She won't feel responsible," Sarah said. "She'll feel grateful. And she'll feel angry on your behalf. And she'll sit beside you through whatever the board does and she'll still be there after." She paused. "That's what Grace does."

A silence.

"Yes," Rachel said.

Quietly.

The word landing in the place behind her sternum where the thing lived.

"What time," Sarah said.

"Nine."

"David will be there."

"Yes."

"And me," Sarah said.

A pause.

"Sarah — "

"I'll be in the waiting room," Sarah said. "Not the hearing room. I won't interfere with anything. But I'll be there."

Another pause.

"You have tonight," Rachel said. "The barn. The hold. You don't need to — "

"Rachel," Sarah said.

Rachel stopped.

"I'll be there," Sarah said.

A long silence.

"Okay," Rachel said.

Her voice slightly different.

The contained brightness of her, slightly less contained.

"Okay," she said again.

More settled.

"Get some sleep," Sarah said.

"You too," Rachel said.

She hung up.

Sarah sat at the kitchen table.

The blank page.

The pen.

She picked it up.

Wrote:

Rachel — January fourth. Board hearing moved to tomorrow.

Hold application — signed. Hours.

Robert — at the barn.

Tonight — all of them.

She looked at the list.

The convergence of it.

Everything arriving at once.

The way things did when they were ready.

The way rivers did when the tributaries finally joined.

She thought about Meridian.

About the twenty-three years.

About the forty barns.

About the patience of an organization that had built a system carefully enough that it had never failed.

She thought about the system arriving at its full deployment simultaneously with the group arriving at its full frequency.

Both things.

At once.

The both-and.

Not the intimate both-and of a man who was terrified and staying.

The large both-and.

The structural both-and.

The moment when two things that had been moving toward each other arrived.

She had felt this coming.

Not the specifics.

The shape of it.

The pressure.

The both-and quality that had been building since Tuesday morning on the county road.

This was it.

This was what it had been pointing toward.

Daniel came in from outside.

Stomping his boots.

The cold coming in with him.

He looked at her face.

Read it.

Sat down across from her.

She told him about Rachel.

He listened.

When she finished he said: "Tomorrow."

"Nine."

"I'll drive you."

She looked at him.

"Both," she said. "Tonight and tomorrow."

"Yes," he said.

Simple as that.

Both.

She looked at her notepad.

At the list.

"It's all happening at once," she said.

"Yes."

"Tonight the barn. The hold possibly. Robert in the circle for the first time." She paused. "Tomorrow Rachel and the board."

"Yes."

"And underneath all of it Robert home and the Indiana facility negotiating and the Cobb fraud in front of the court and the fourteen names and the forty barns and — "

She stopped.

Daniel waited.

She looked at the list.

At the blank space below it.

She picked up the pen.

Wrote one more thing.

We are exactly on time.

Looked at it.

"Yes," she said.

To herself.

To the notepad.

To the river behind the cabin doing its work in the December afternoon.

To all of it.

Grace arrived at the cabin at four.

Unannounced.

She came to the door and Sarah opened it and they looked at each other and Sarah stepped back and Grace came in.

They sat at the kitchen table.

Daniel disappeared into the back of the cabin with the specific tact of a man who understood when a room needed to be smaller.

Grace sat across from her.

Hands around a mug of tea Sarah had made without asking.

Made right.

Grace looked at it.

Almost smiled.

"Rachel called you," Sarah said.

"Yes."

"How is she."

Grace looked at her tea.

"She's Rachel," she said. "So she's holding it together and doing everything correctly and not letting anyone see what it's actually costing her." She paused. "Which means it's costing her considerably."

"Yes," Sarah said.

Grace looked up.

"She didn't tell me about the board to worry me," Grace said. "She told me because she doesn't keep things from me." She paused.

"But she told me in the specific way she tells me things she doesn't want me to feel responsible for."

"I know," Sarah said.

"I feel responsible," Grace said.

"I know," Sarah said.

"She would tell me not to."

"She would."

"She'd be wrong."

Sarah looked at her.

Grace looked back.

The eyes fully present.

Fully hers.

"She made a choice," Grace said. "A real choice with real cost. Pretending I had nothing to do with it isn't honoring the choice. It's diminishing it." She paused. "What she did for me was real. The cost is real. I'm going to carry my share of that."

Sarah held her gaze.

"Yes," she said.

"Tomorrow," Grace said. "I'll be there."

"I know."

"She'll tell me not to come."

"Yes."

"I'm coming anyway."

"I know," Sarah said.

Something moved through Grace's face.

Not the smile.

Deeper than the smile.

The expression of someone who has found people worth being found by and is not taking that lightly.

"When did this become my life," she said.

Quietly.

Not complaint.

The wondering of someone looking at something that arrived without their planning it and finding it considerably better than what they had planned.

Sarah thought about the river this morning.

Before dawn.

The cold.

The immensity.

The full version.

"Thursday nights," she said.

Grace looked at her.

"Thursday nights," Grace said.

They sat for a while.

The kitchen.

The December afternoon going toward evening.

The pale light in the windows thinning.

Grace said: "Robert."

"He was at the barn this morning," Sarah said. "He's coming tonight."

Something moved through Grace's face.

The expression of someone hearing something they had worked toward and are now receiving.

"How is he," she said.

"Coming back," Sarah said. "Not all the way. Coming."

"The eyes," Grace said.

"Yes."

Grace nodded.

She knew the eyes.

Had had them.

"It takes time," she said.

"Yes."

"But it comes," she said. "It always comes. If the damage wasn't — " She stopped. "If the time wasn't too long."

Six weeks.

Sarah thought about six weeks versus four months.

About the daughter who hadn't stopped calling.

About David finding her.

About the civil suit and the negotiated release and the terms that weren't justice but were Robert home.

"The time wasn't too long," Sarah said.

Grace looked at her.

"You're sure."

"I felt him this morning," Sarah said. "In the barn. Not the full thing — he's not there yet. But it was there. Underneath. Present." She paused. "He just needs the circle."

Grace was quiet for a moment.

"That's all any of us needed," she said.

"Yes."

"The circle and the time."

"Yes."

Grace looked at her mug.

"Marcus told him about Thursday nights three years ago," she said. "Before the facility. Before any of us knew what any of this was." She paused. "He came twice. Then stopped. Then they moved on him."

Sarah hadn't known this.

"He was almost there," she said.

"Yes," Grace said. "Which is why they moved when they did." She looked up. "They moved on me at the same stage. Almost there. Close enough to be — " She paused. "Close enough to be a threat. Not yet full enough to be — "

"Uncointainable," Sarah said.

Grace looked at her.

The word sitting between them.

"Yes," Grace said. "Not yet uncontainable."

Sarah thought about the river this morning.

Standing in it fully.

The full version.

Uncontainable.

She hadn't used that word before.

It fit.

"Tonight," she said. "With Robert in the circle — "

"I know," Grace said.

They looked at each other.

Both of them knowing.

The way people knew things in this group.

Before the words.

In the place behind the sternum where the knowing lived.

"It's going to be different tonight," Sarah said.

"Yes," Grace said.

"Bigger."

"Yes."

A pause.

"Are you ready for bigger," Sarah said.

Grace looked at her steadily.

The eyes that had been somewhere far away and were fully back now.

Fully present.

Fully hers.

"I've been ready since the parking lot," she said.

Daniel drove them to the barn at six.

The three of them in the car.

The December dark outside.

The fields going past.

Bare and white and patient.

Sarah in the front seat.

Grace in the back.

Nobody talking.

Not because there was nothing to say.

Because what was ahead of them was large enough to be quiet in front of.

The barn appeared through the dark.

The light in the high windows.

The stove smoke rising.

The parking lot.

Cars she recognized.

Rachel's.

David's.

Emma's.

Marcus's truck.

One other.

Older. Dark blue. Michigan plates.

Robert.

She felt the thing behind her sternum.

Warm.

Certain.

Pointing at the barn the way it pointed at things that mattered.

She got out of the car.

Stood in the cold lot.

Looked at the barn.

The light in the high windows.

The smoke.

The sound of nothing from inside yet.

Just — the barn.

Waiting.

The way it always waited.

The way honest spaces waited for the people who needed them.

Patient.

Present.

Holding whatever came in the same way it had always held it.

Without judgment.

Without agenda.

Without any investment in what happened except that it happened honestly.

She breathed.

The cold air.

The December dark.

The barn.

Tonight.

All of it.

She was ready.

She walked toward the door.

Chapter 28

CHAPTER TWENTY-EIGHT: MARCUS TELLS GRACE ABOUT JAMES

She found them at the small table.

Not the circle.

The back corner where the kettle lived and the mismatched mugs and the tin of Earl Grey and the particular privacy of a space within a space.

Marcus and Grace.

Heads close.

His voice low.

She was telling him something or he was telling her something and both of them were in it fully in the way they were in things together now.

Sarah stopped inside the door.

Read the room.

Crossed to the circle of chairs without going near the table.

Sat.

Let them have it.

She found out later what they were saying.

Not that evening.

The following morning.

Grace at the kitchen table with coffee and the expression of someone who had slept on something and was now carrying it in the daylight for the first time.

Sarah sat across from her.

Daniel absent.

Tactfully.

As usual.

"He told me about James," Grace said.

Sarah waited.

"The real version," Grace said. "Not the version he told the group." She looked at her coffee. "There's more."

"Tell me," Sarah said.

Grace looked at her.

"James wasn't the first," she said.

But that was the following morning.

The evening was the barn.

The circle.

Robert in the back corner where he had always sat before they took him.

The same chair.

Nobody had planned that.

He had simply found it the way people found their chairs in spaces they belonged to.

The body knowing.

Sarah had noticed it when she came in from the cold.

Robert.

Back corner.

The chair nobody else had sat in for six weeks.

Waiting for him without knowing it was waiting.

He sat in it with his mug and his careful hands and his eyes that were further along than this morning.

The barn doing something to him that the barn did.

Honest space.

The medicine of it.

Rachel and David came in together.

Rachel with her coat still buttoned in the way of someone who had driven through cold thoughts and hadn't entirely arrived yet.

David with his hand at the small of her back.

Brief.

Gone before anyone would call it anything.

But there.

Sarah saw it.

Grace saw it.

Emma, already in her chair with her clear eyes, saw it and looked at her mug with the expression of someone finding something privately satisfying.

Rachel sat.

Unbuttoned her coat.

Looked around the circle.

Her eyes landed on Robert.

She had met him once.

Before.

Before the facility.

He had been in the barn twice and she had been there once of those twice and they had exchanged the particular nod of two people in the same circle who hadn't yet found their way to conversation.

She looked at him now.

He looked back.

She nodded once.

He nodded once.

The nod of two people who knew, without discussion, what the other had been through.

The compressed acknowledgment of a shared geography.

No words needed.

None adequate.

Emma leaned toward Sarah.

Quietly.

"His chair," she said.

"Yes," Sarah said.

"Did anyone tell him — "

"No."

Emma looked at Robert in the back corner.

At the chair that had been his and was his again.

Something moved through her face.

The architectural mind of her finding the structure in it.

The way things held their shape even when the things themselves were temporarily absent.

"Okay," Emma said.

To herself.

To the fact of it.

Marcus came from the back table.

Grace beside him.

Their hands not quite touching.

Almost.

The almost that had been the language between them since September and was now, since the barn doorway in the snow, something different.

Not almost.

Something that didn't need to announce itself.

Just — present.

The way the current was present in the river.

Not performing.

Just moving.

They were all there by six-thirty.

Eight of them.

Seven in the circle.

Robert in the back corner slightly outside it.

Not excluded.

Not ready yet for the full circle.

The circle accepting this without adjustment.

Making room for the almost-in without requiring the fully-in.

The way honest spaces did.

David opened.

The practical business.

She listened and let it move through her without catching on anything.

The Cobb fraud filing.

The emergency challenge.

The judge's signature.

The timeline.

She had heard it all.

She let the others hear it.

Watched their faces.

Emma with her steady clear-eyed reception of information.

Marcus with the stillness.

Grace with the expression of someone who had already lived the version of this that went wrong and was sitting in the knowledge of that without flinching.

Rachel with the contained precision of a professional managing information that had personal stakes she was not going to perform about.

Robert in the back corner.

Listening.

Very still.

She felt him listening.

Not just with his ears.

With the whole body attention of someone who had been in a room where information was managed and distorted and is now in a room where it is given plainly and is feeling the difference like a change in air pressure.

The relief of honest information.

Even when the information was this.

Even when the information was: the hold is signed and they can come tonight.

Even then.

Honest was better.

Always honest was better.

When David finished Marcus said: "Rachel."

Not a question.

Not a prompt.

The word said in the voice he used for things that mattered and were being insufficiently attended to.

Rachel looked at him.

"Tomorrow," he said.

"It's handled," she said.

"That's not what I asked."

She looked at him.

He looked back.

The patience of him.

The unhurried waiting.

She said: "I'm ready."

"I know you're ready," he said. "How are you."

The circle was very quiet.

Rachel sat with the question.

Sarah watched her sit with it.

The professional composure.

The brisk competence.

The twelve years and the license and the work and the choice she'd made in the knowledge of what it might cost.

All of it present.

All of it held together.

"I'm — " She stopped.

Started again.

"I'm afraid of losing the license," she said. "Not because of what it means for me specifically." She paused. "Because of what I could still do with it. The people I haven't met yet who need someone to do what I did for Grace." She looked at her hands. "I'm afraid of that door closing."

The circle held this.

"And," Marcus said.

She looked up.

"And I'm — " She stopped again.

This time the stop was different.

Not the managed stop of someone choosing what to reveal.

The stop of someone arriving at something they hadn't planned to say out loud.

"I'm grateful," she said.

The word landing differently than anything else she'd said.

"For this," she said. "For the barn. For all of you." She looked around the circle. "Whatever happens tomorrow — I'd do it again. I'd do it a hundred times." She paused. "I just want you to know that."

The circle was very quiet.

Then Grace said: "We know."

Two words.

Carrying everything.

Rachel looked at Grace.

Something passed between them.

The parking lot at two in the morning.

The cold air.

The open sky.

Thank you.

Just that.

Everything.

On the other side of it — this.

The barn.

The circle.

The both of them in it.

The cost.

The worth of the cost.

All of it in the look between them.

Then Rachel nodded.

Once.

The nod of someone receiving something they needed and are not going to diminish by saying more than is necessary.

The nod of someone who is okay.

Not performing okay.

Actually okay.

Underneath the fear and the tomorrow and the board and the license.

Okay.

After the practical business they sat.

The way they always sat.

The stove.

The barn.

The December dark outside.

But different tonight.

The difference that Robert in the back corner made.

Not the full circle.

The almost-full circle.

Something waiting to complete itself.

She felt it.

The frequency of the place building the way it built on Thursday nights.

But slower.

Like a tide that knew it had time.

Emma spoke.

Not planned.

The way things happened in the circle that mattered.

She talked about the grey.

Not the way she had talked about it before — analytically, architecturally, as a phenomenon to be understood.

She talked about it the way you talked about something you had finally finished grieving.

On the other side of the grief.

Looking back.

She talked about thirty-four.

The staircase drawing.

The nothing where the something used to be.

She talked about what she had thought it was.

Tiredness.

Aging.

The ordinary diminishment she had accepted as the price of a certain kind of life.

She talked about what it actually was.

Not her words.

The words she had found since.

The assisted absence.

The managed grey.

The system doing what systems did to people who generated too much light.

She talked about the barn.

The first Thursday.

The second.

The third.

The roots coming in dark.

The glasses she stopped wearing.

The staircase drawing she had looked at three weeks ago and felt something about.

Not the nothing.

The something.

Returned.

She talked about what it felt like to have it back.

Not the pre-grey version.

Something larger.

Something that had been made larger by the grey years the way a river is made larger by the years of rain that feed it.

"I wasted eleven years," she said.

The same words as before.

"And I didn't," she said.

The circle waited.

"The grey years are in me," she said. "I can't remove them and I don't think I want to. They're — information. They're the knowledge of what absence feels like. What managed consciousness feels like. What it feels like to be walked backward away from yourself so slowly you almost don't notice." She paused. "I notice everything now." She looked around the circle. "I design differently now. I see structure differently. I understand what a space can hold and what it can't." She paused again. "The grey years taught me what I was by taking it away. I couldn't have known the full size of it without knowing the absence of it."

The circle was very still.

Sarah felt the thing behind her sternum.

Warm.

The diffuse kind.

Building.

She looked at Robert in the back corner.

He was looking at Emma.

His face.

The eyes.

Something in them she hadn't seen this morning.

Not just present.

Lit.

Briefly.

The pilot light of something that had been turned down very low and was now —

She watched it.

The brief illumination.

The recognition of someone hearing their own experience described.

The relief of that.

The specific particular relief of: *I am not alone in this. This happened to someone else. This happened to people in this room. This is not unique to me. This is not madness. This is something that has a name and a pattern and people who survived it and are sitting in these chairs.*

She watched the relief move through him.

Quiet.

Warm.

The pilot light.

Still there.

Still going.

Marcus spoke next.

He talked about his hand.

Not the fact of it.

The feeling.

The morning it stopped hurting.

He had been at the kitchen table with his coffee.

Ordinary Tuesday.

He had reached for the mug and felt —

Nothing.

Where the pain had been for thirty years.

Nothing.

Not numbness.

Nothing.

The absence of something that had been so constant he had stopped registering it as pain and had started registering it as the baseline condition of his hand.

The texture of his hand.

Just — his hand.

He had sat at the kitchen table for a long time.

He hadn't called anyone.

He hadn't told anyone.

He had sat with it the way you sat with things that didn't have a framework yet.

Carefully.

Without rushing toward an explanation.

Letting it be what it was.

Then he had come to the barn on Thursday night and looked at the group and understood.

Not the mechanism.

Not the how.

The connection.

"I've been thinking about why," he said. "For eighteen months." He looked at his left hand on his knee. "I don't think it was the barn specifically. I don't think it was the group specifically. I think it was — " He paused. Chose. "I think it was the choosing. The repeated choosing of honest space over managed space. The repeated choosing of the full version of things over the comfortable version." He paused. "I think the body responds to that. Over time. I think the body knows the difference between a life lived at the size it was built for and a life lived smaller." He looked around the circle. "My hand knew before I did."

The barn held this.

Grace looked at her own hands.

Emma looked at hers.

Sarah felt the thing behind her sternum.

Stronger now.

The diffuse warmth spreading.

She glanced at Daniel.

He was looking at his hands too.

The expression of a man quietly taking inventory.

Robert spoke.

She hadn't expected it.

Not tonight.

Not this soon.

He spoke from the back corner.

Quietly.

The careful voice, still slightly unsteady at the edges.

"I had a tremor," he said.

The circle went still.

"Left hand. For four years. My neurologist was — he was tracking it." He paused. "Then it stopped."

He looked at his left hand.

Raised it.

Held it in front of him.

Steady.

Completely steady.

"Three weeks before they took me," he said. "The tremor stopped." He looked at Marcus. "I didn't tell anyone. I thought — I thought I'd imagined it. Or it was temporary." He paused. "Then things started — I started noticing things. Knowing things before they happened. Small things." He paused. "I came to the barn. Twice. I sat in the back." He looked at the chair beneath him. "This chair."

Nobody spoke.

"I didn't understand what was happening," he said. "I thought something was wrong with me. That's what they counted on." He paused. "By the time I understood it wasn't wrong — it was the opposite of wrong — they had already started building the case."

He looked at his steady hand.

At Marcus.

At Grace.

At Sarah.

"I'm sorry I stopped coming," he said.

Marcus shook his head once.

The slow certain movement of a man dismissing something that didn't require an apology.

"You're here now," he said.

Robert looked at him.

At the circle.

At the barn.

The high windows.

The stove.

The amber light.

The empty chair where James had sat.

He looked at the empty chair for a long moment.

"James," he said.

"Yes," Marcus said.

"Where is he."

Marcus was quiet.

"We don't know yet," he said.

"But you're looking."

"David is looking."

Robert nodded.

Looked at David.

David met his eyes.

The direct look.

The honest look.

The look of someone who didn't lie on the third question.

"I'll find him," David said.

Robert held his gaze for a moment.

Then nodded.

Once.

The nod of a man who believed what he was told because he could feel the truth of it.

The same way she felt it.

The both-and.

Both ways of knowing.

Both real.

The frequency built.

Slowly.

The way it had been building all evening through Emma's telling and Marcus's hand and Robert's voice from the back corner.

She felt it arrive.

Not suddenly.

The way dawn arrived.

Imperceptibly and then all at once.

The warmth behind her sternum.

Diffuse.

Spreading.

She sat in it.

Didn't reach.

Didn't perform.

Just — let it come.

Let the circle be what it was.

Rachel beside David with the tomorrow in her and the gratitude in her and the full measure of someone who had made a real choice and was living inside it.

Emma with her clear eyes and her eleven years and the architectural understanding of what a space could hold.

Grace with the full version of herself present and insisting and done waiting.

Marcus with the steady patience of him and the left hand and the fourteen grey years and the woman beside him and the full quiet enormity of a man who had built a space for people to find themselves in and had found himself in it.

Robert in the back corner.

The pilot light.

Still going.

Brightening.

Daniel beside her.

Always beside her.

Both-and.

Always both-and.

She felt each of them.

Distinct.

Warm.

Like fingers she knew without looking.

Like the current of the river in the dark before dawn.

And then —

Robert.

From the back corner.

She felt him enter the frequency.

Not dramatically.

Not with announcement.

The way someone steps from the cold into a warm room.

The adjustment.

The arrival.

He hadn't been in this before.

Not this fully.

Not the full frequency.

She felt him feel it for the first time.

Felt his response to it.

The —

There was no adequate word.

Recognition.

The full body recognition of something the system had walked him backward away from and that was now, in this barn on this Thursday night with these people, walking him forward again.

Back toward himself.

Back toward the full version.

The pilot light —

Not a pilot light anymore.

A flame.

Small.

Real.

Present.

His.

She felt it from across the circle.

Warm and certain and unmistakable.

The first real thing since the narrow room.

The first real thing.

She didn't know how long it lasted.

Longer than before.

Much longer.

When it passed it passed gently.

Like the tide going out.

Not taking anything.

Leaving things different than it found them.

The barn was just the barn.

The circle was just people in chairs.

The stove.

The December dark outside.

Nobody spoke for a very long time.

Then Robert said something from the back corner.

Quietly.

So quietly she almost missed it.

She didn't miss it.

Two words.

Said in the voice of a man who had been in a narrow room for six weeks and was now in a barn with people who knew what he was and had come looking for him and had found him.

Said in the voice of a man whose pilot light had just become a flame.

Said in the voice of a man coming home.

"Thank you," he said.

The same two words as the parking lot at two in the morning.

The same weight.

The same everything.

The barn held them.

Outside.

Later.

The parking lot.

The December cold.

She stood beside Daniel and looked at the road.

Three sedans tonight.

Three.

The message being delivered clearly.

We know where you are.

We can come at any time.

We are coming.

She looked at the three sedans.

Felt nothing from them tonight.

Not the compass.

Not the warning.

Not even the both-and.

Just — cars in the dark.

Just — people doing a job in the cold.

She thought about Robert saying thank you from the back corner.

About the pilot light becoming a flame.

About Emma's eleven years and the staircase drawing and the something that had come back larger than the something that had left.

About Marcus's hand.

About Grace in the parking lot and Grace in the barn and Grace in the doorway in the snow.

About Rachel's gratitude and her fear and the both of them real and the both of them hers.

About David stepping through.

About all of them.

All eight of them.

The full circle.

Tonight.

She looked at the three sedans.

We are exactly on time.

More than that.

She looked at Daniel.

"They sent three tonight," she said.

"Yes."

"Because of Robert," she said. "Because of what happened in there."

He looked at her.

"They felt it," she said.

"They can't feel it," he said.

"They measure it," she said. "However they measure it. Whatever instruments they use." She paused. "They know something happened tonight that hasn't happened in any of their other forty barns." She looked at the sedans. "That's why there are three."

Daniel was quiet.

Looking at the sedans.

"They're afraid," he said.

"Yes," she said.

She stood in the December cold and felt the immensity behind her sternum and looked at three black sedans at the end of the road and felt something she hadn't expected to feel.

Not triumph.

Not defiance.

Something quieter.

Something that felt like —

Compassion.

The specific compassion of someone who understood what it was to be afraid of something larger than yourself.

Who had been afraid of this herself.

Who was still afraid, underneath, in the place where the fear lived.

Who knew that fear was real and was not the load-bearing thing.

Who knew that the sedans were full of people doing a job in the cold because someone above them was afraid and had given them instructions because of the fear and they were executing the instructions the way the driver on Tuesday morning had executed his instructions.

She felt the compassion.

Let it be what it was.

Then she got in the car.

Daniel drove.

The December road.

The dark fields.

The stars indifferent above all of it.

They drove in silence.

The good silence.

The silence of two people who had been somewhere together and were carrying it the same way and didn't need to compare notes.

She looked out the window at the dark fields.

At the stripped trees going past.

At the sky.

"Tomorrow," she said.

"Yes."

"Rachel and the board."

"We'll be there."

"And the hold," she said. "Today or tomorrow or whenever they decide to move."

"Yes."

She looked at the sky.

"And whatever comes after," she said.

He reached across.

Found her hand.

"Whatever comes after," he said.

She held his hand.

Looked at the dark sky through the window.

The stars.

The vast indifferent dark.

The current underneath everything.

Moving.

Always moving.

Patient as the river.

Patient as the thing that had no protocol for being stopped because it had never needed one.

Because it was older than the systems built to stop it.

Because it was the thing the systems were built inside of.

The ocean.

The ripple and the ocean.
Both.
Always both.
She closed her eyes.
Felt the warmth behind her sternum.
Steady.
Certain.
Completely unbothered by whatever tomorrow would bring.
She had stood in the river this morning.
The full version.
She would stand in it again.
And again.
And again.
For as long as standing was required.
And after that.
After that she would simply be the river.
The way she already was.
The way she had always been.
The way they all were.
Just — finding out.
One Thursday night at a time.

Chapter 29

CHAPTER TWENTY-NINE: RACHEL'S RISK

She was already dressed when David knocked.

Seven-fifteen.

The January morning dark and cold and the kind of clear that only arrived after a hard freeze — the sky sharp and high and blue-black at the edges, the kind of sky that meant whatever happened today would happen in pitiless clarity.

No grey to soften it.

She had been awake since four.

Not anxiously.

The particular wakefulness of someone who has done everything that can be done and is now waiting for the doing to become the done.

She had read the documentation twice.

David's folder.

The dose records.

Grace's medical history before and during and after.

Patricia Wren's supporting statement.

Two colleagues of David's who had reviewed the case and submitted assessments.

She had read all of it.

She knew all of it.

She was ready.

She opened the door.

David looked at her face.

"You slept," he said.

"Some."

"How much."

"Enough."

He looked at her for a moment with the expression she had come to recognize as his version of concern — not performed, not excessive, just present.

She had come to appreciate that about him.

The precision of his concern.

Nothing wasted.

Nothing performed.

Just — there when it was there.

"Coffee," she said.

"Already had some," he said.

"I'm making more," she said.

He came in.

Gerald assessed him from the kitchen doorway.

Moved toward him.

Sat on his foot.

David looked down at the cat.

The cat looked up at him.

"He does that every time now," Rachel said.

"I know."

"He never did it before you."

"I know."

She made the coffee.

He sat at the kitchen table with Gerald on his foot and the folder in front of him and the expression of someone running through what was ahead one more time.

She watched him do it.

The careful systematic intelligence of him.

The eleven years.

The documentation.

The gap between what was real and what could be proven and his entire career lived in that gap, learning how to close it.

He was closing it today.

She set the coffee in front of him.

Sat across.

"Tell me again," she said.

He looked up.

"You know it," he said.

"Tell me again," she said. "I want to hear your voice say it."

He held her gaze for a moment.

Then he opened the folder.

"The dose records establish a clear clinical rationale for the reduction," he said. "Grace's presenting symptoms at intake were consistent with over-medication rather than the underlying condition documented at admission. The reduction schedule you followed is within clinical guidelines for this class of medication." He paused. "Patricia Wren's statement establishes that Grace's current functional status is significantly improved over her status at admission. Improved cognition, improved affect, improved social functioning. The outcome data supports your clinical decision."

Rachel listened.

She had read this.

She knew this.

She wanted to hear it from him.

"The charge," she said.

"Patient endangerment," he said. "The charge requires demonstrating that your actions put Grace at risk of harm. The documentation demonstrates the opposite. The risk of harm was in the over-medication, not the reduction." He paused. "Hendricks and Marsh can testify to their assessment. We can demonstrate their assessment was incorrect by the outcome."

"They'll say the improvement is unrelated to the dose reduction."

"Yes."

"They'll say it would have happened anyway."

"Yes."

"How do we counter that."

"Timeline," he said. "The improvement correlates precisely with the dose reduction schedule. The timeline is documented. Week by week." He paused. "Clinical correlation isn't causation but it's compelling. The board will see the correlation."

"If they look at it honestly."

"If they look at it honestly," he said.

The word again.

Honestly.

The word that carried the uncertainty.

The word that meant: we have done everything we can do and now it depends on whether the room we walk into is the kind of room that responds to evidence or the kind of room that has already decided.

She had sat across from enough rooms to know the difference.

She didn't know yet which kind this was.

"Rachel," he said.

She looked at him.

"Whatever the board does today," he said. "The documentation exists. The record exists. If they decide incorrectly we appeal. If we appeal we win. It takes longer." He paused. "But the outcome is not in doubt. The only question is how long."

She looked at him.

"You believe that," she said.

"Yes," he said.

She held his gaze.

The precise careful honest gaze of a man who didn't say things he didn't believe.

"Okay," she said.

She drank her coffee.

He drank his.

Gerald remained on his foot with the settled air of a cat who had made a decision about this man and was not revisiting it.

Grace was outside when they got to the parking lot.

Standing by Rachel's car.

Coat. Scarf. The expression of someone who had been there for some time and was not going to apologize for it.

Rachel stopped.

Looked at her.

"I told you not to come," Rachel said.

"You suggested I not come," Grace said. "There's a difference."

"Grace — "

"I'm not going in the hearing room," Grace said. "I'll sit in the waiting area. I won't interfere with anything." She paused. "But I'm not sitting at home while you do this."

Rachel looked at her.

At the expression on Grace's face.

The full version of Grace.

The woman who had been in the narrow room and was standing in a parking lot on a January morning at seven forty-five because someone she cared about had a hearing and she was not going to not be there.

The insistence of her.

The full version of it.

Rachel thought about the parking lot at two in the morning.

Going back into the facility.

Week after week.

The dose records.

The decision made in the full knowledge of its cost.

She had done that without Grace asking her to.

She had done it because Grace was a person in a room who needed help and Rachel was a person who could provide it.

Grace was here for the same reason.

Rachel was a person who needed something and Grace was a person who could provide it.

Simple as that.

The both-and.

"Okay," Rachel said.

Grace looked at her.

"Okay," Rachel said again.

Something in Grace's face.

The full version of something she didn't perform and didn't announce.

She simply stepped forward.

Put her arms around Rachel.

Rachel stood in it for a moment.

Then put her arms around Grace.

Two women in a parking lot on a January morning.

The cold.

The clear pitiless sky.

David standing a respectful distance away looking at his phone with the focused attention of a man who was absolutely not watching this.

After a moment Rachel stepped back.

Straightened her coat.

"Don't make me cry in the parking lot," she said.

"Too late," Grace said.

"I'm not crying."

"Your eyes are doing a thing."

"My eyes are cold."

"Your eyes are doing a thing," Grace said.

Rachel looked at her.

The corner of her mouth.

The thing that lived in the same neighborhood as a smile.

"Get in the car," Rachel said.

The building was on the north side of the city.

Medical district.

The particular architecture of institutional authority — brick, clean lines, the suggestion of permanence and procedure.

Rachel had been in this building twice before.

Continuing education.

A colleague's commendation ceremony.

Both times she had walked in without thinking about it.

Today she felt the building.

The weight of what it represented.

Twelve years.

The license.

The work.

The people she hadn't met yet.

She felt it and walked in anyway.

The waiting area was on the second floor.

Chairs along the wall.

A table with water and the particular magazines of waiting rooms everywhere — three months out of date, nobody's first choice, present because absence would be worse.

Grace and David sat in the chairs.

Rachel stood at the window.

Looked at the January street below.

People.

Cars.

The ordinary business of a city on a Friday morning.

She thought about twelve years.

Not in a inventory way.

Not cataloguing what she was afraid of losing.

Just — feeling the weight of it.

The accumulated weight of twelve years of choosing this work.

Choosing it when it was rewarding.

Choosing it when it wasn't.

Choosing it in the facility hallway with the dose records and the decision made in the full knowledge of its cost.

Choosing it every week.

Week after week.

Grace's eyes getting clearer.

Week by week.

She had known what she was doing.

She had known the risk.

She had chosen it.

She would choose it again.

She turned from the window.

Sat beside Grace.

Grace's hand found hers on the armrest.

Not squeezing.

Not performing comfort.

Just — there.

The plain fact of it.

The same way Daniel's hand was there for Sarah.

The same language.

Different people.

Same language.

Rachel let it be there.

Let herself receive it without deflecting or managing it into something more comfortable.

The full version of receiving.

She was learning this.

From Grace.

From all of them.

From the barn.

One Thursday night at a time.

David's phone buzzed at eight fifty.

He looked at it.

Looked at Rachel.

"Patricia Wren's statement has been received and entered into the record," he said. "Both supporting assessments are in." He paused. "The panel is three members. I know one of them. Dr. Anita Cheung. She's independent. She responds to evidence."

"The other two," Rachel said.

"I don't know them well enough to predict," he said. "One is a GP from the west side. One is a psychiatrist from Beaumont." He paused. "Neither has any documented connection to Meridian."

"Undocumented connections," Rachel said.

"Are possible," David said. "I can't rule it out."

She nodded.

The honest answer.

She appreciated the honest answer.

Even this honest answer.

Especially this honest answer.

"Three members," she said. "Majority rules."

"Yes."

"So we need two."

"Yes."

She looked at the window.

At the January sky.

Sharp and clear and high.

"Anita Cheung," she said.

"Yes," David said.

"She responds to evidence."

"Yes."

"Then we need one more," she said.

"Yes," he said.

She breathed.

In.

Out.

The waiting room around her.

Grace's hand.

David across from her.

The folder in his lap.

Twelve years.

The work.

The people she hadn't met yet.

She breathed.

Let the fear be real.

Let the other thing be real too.

Both at once.

The both-and of a woman who had made a real choice and was sitting in the building that was going to tell her what the choice had cost.

Ready for the answer.

Whatever the answer was.

They called her name at nine-fifteen.

She stood.

Grace's hand released.

She straightened her coat.

Looked at David.

He nodded once.

The nod of a man who had done what he could do and was now at the point where the doing became the waiting.

She looked at Grace.

Grace looked back.

The full version of Grace.

The woman who had been somewhere far away and was fully back.

Fully present.

Fully hers.

The woman who was here in this waiting room because Rachel had gone back into a facility week after week with dose records and a decision made in full knowledge of its cost.

Looking at her.

This is why, Rachel thought.

This is the why.

Not the license.

Not the twelve years.

Not the people she hadn't met yet.

This.

This person looking at her.

Present.

Alive.

The full version.

This is the why.

She walked through the door.

The hearing room was smaller than she expected.

Round table.

Three chairs on one side.

One chair on the other.

She sat in the one chair.

Three people across from her.

A woman in the center — Dr. Anita Cheung, she recognized the name from the nameplate, the face composed and alert.

A man on the left, the GP David had mentioned, reading something in the folder in front of him.

A woman on the right, the psychiatrist from Beaumont, looking at Rachel with the professional neutral expression she recognized from conference room B.

She placed her folder on the table.

Her hands on either side of it.

Steady.

She looked at Dr. Cheung.

Dr. Cheung looked at her.

The direct look of someone who intended to pay attention.

Rachel felt the first thing she had felt since arriving in the building that wasn't fear.

Not hope exactly.

Something more specific.

The recognition of a room that was capable of honesty.

Capable.

Not guaranteed.

But capable.

That was enough.

She opened her folder.

"Thank you for the opportunity to present," she said.

Her voice level.

Professional.

Carrying everything it needed to carry and nothing it didn't.

She had been in rooms like this before.

She knew how to be in rooms like this.

She began.

She was in the room for forty minutes.

When she came out David stood.

Grace stood.

She looked at them.

Her face.

She couldn't control what her face was doing.

She had tried in the room.

She was done trying now.

"They're deliberating," she said.

"How long," David said.

"They didn't say." She paused. "Cheung asked three questions. Good questions. She read the documentation." She paused again. "The GP on the left didn't say anything. The psychiatrist on the right — " She stopped.

"What," David said.

"She asked why I didn't consult with the attending physician before adjusting the medication."

"What did you say."

"I said the attending physician was the person whose over-medication I was correcting." She paused. "She wrote something down."

David was quiet for a moment.

Processing.

"That's a deflection question," he said. "It's designed to shift the frame from whether the dose reduction was clinically appropriate to whether you followed protocol."

"I know," she said.

"And."

"And I followed protocol," she said. "The documentation shows I followed protocol. I documented the rationale. I documented the reduction schedule. I documented the monitoring." She paused. "I did everything correctly. Except ask permission from the person who was causing the harm."

David looked at her.

"You said that," he said.

"Not in those words," she said. "In the documented words." She paused. "But yes."

He was quiet.

"Good," he said.

She looked at him.

"Good," he said again. More certain.

She looked at Grace.

Grace said nothing.

Just looked at her with the full version of herself.

Present.

Alive.

The why.

Rachel sat down.

They waited.

The deliberation took twenty-two minutes.

She counted.

Not to calm herself.

Because she wanted to know.

Twenty-two minutes.

At twenty-two minutes the door opened.

An administrative assistant.

"Ms. Mercer."

She stood.

Walked back through the door.

Sat in the single chair.

Three people across from her.

Dr. Cheung in the center.

The folder closed now.

Hands folded.

The composed alert face.

Rachel put her hands on the table.

Steady.

She was steady.

Whatever came now she was steady.

The full version of steady.

Dr. Cheung said: "The panel has reached a decision."

Rachel breathed.

In.

Out.

Whatever comes now.

I'd do it again.

I'd do it a hundred times.

This is the why.

She held the why in the place behind her sternum where the knowing lived.

Warm.

Certain.

Present.

Whatever came now.

Dr. Cheung said: "The complaint is dismissed."

She sat for a moment.

The room.

The three faces.

The folder.

The window with the January sky.

The words arranging themselves into meaning.

Dismissed.

Dr. Cheung was still talking.

Rachel heard the words in pieces.

Insufficient evidence of patient endangerment.

Documentation supports clinical rationale.

Outcome data consistent with appropriate care.

Complaint dismissed with notation.

She heard all of it.

She heard it from a slight distance.

The specific distance of someone who has been braced for impact and the impact has not arrived and the body is still braced and the unbrace takes a moment.

She thanked the panel.

She said what you said.

She stood.

Walked out.

Grace saw her face before the door closed behind her.

Stood.

Rachel shook her head once.

Not the bad version of a head shake.

The I-can't-speak-yet version.

Grace understood.

Crossed the room.

Put her arms around Rachel again.

Rachel let herself be held.

Fully.

The full version of being held.

Without the managed half-hug of someone who was fine and didn't need anything.

She needed this.

She let herself need it.

She felt David's hand on her shoulder briefly.

Once.

There and gone.

Everything he needed to say.

She stood in the waiting room of the medical board building on a January morning with the pitiless clear sky outside and Grace's arms around her and the decision dismissed with notation settling into her chest alongside twelve years and the work and the people she hadn't met yet.

Still there.

All of it still there.

Intact.

She breathed.

In.

Out.

The full version of a breath.

"Dismissed," she said.

Into Grace's shoulder.

"Dismissed," Grace said.

The word confirmed.

Real.

Both of them saying it.

Both of them in it.

The both-and.

They called Sarah from the parking lot.

David called.

She answered on the first ring.

"Dismissed," he said.

She heard Sarah's breath.

"Tell her," Sarah said.

He handed the phone to Rachel.

Rachel sat in the cold car with the phone and the January sky and Grace's hand on her arm.

"Dismissed," Rachel said.

A pause.

"I know," Sarah said.

"How do you know," Rachel said.

A pause.

Shorter.

"I just do," Sarah said.

Rachel looked at the sky.

The sharp clean January blue of it.

Thought about the knowing.

About all of it.

About the barn and the circle and the frequency and what moved through all of them on Thursday nights.

About the both ways of knowing.

Both real.

She thought about the psychiatrist on the right with her written note and her deflection question and the framework she'd brought into the room that the documentation had been larger than.

She thought about Meridian.

About forty barns.

About all of it.

She thought about Grace in her arms in the waiting room.

About David's hand on her shoulder.

About Sarah's voice saying *I know* before the words arrived.

She thought about Rachel Mercer, twelve years, license intact, the work continuing, the people she hadn't met yet still ahead of her.

She thought about all of it.

"Thank you," she said to Sarah.

"For what," Sarah said.

"For the barn," Rachel said.

A pause.

Then Sarah said: "Thank you for coming."

They stayed on the line for a moment.

Not talking.

The January morning between them.

The cold.

The clear sky.

The work ahead.

The people they hadn't met yet.

The Thursday nights still to come.

The frequency still building.

The current.
Still moving.
Always moving.
"Tonight," Rachel said.
"Tonight," Sarah said.
She hung up.
Sat in the car.
Looked at the sky.
"Ready," she said.
Not to David.
Not to Grace.
To the day.
To whatever came next.
To all of it.
"Ready," she said.

Chapter 30

CHAPTER THIRTY: THE HOLD

They came at noon.

Not evening.

Not the dramatic middle-of-the-night arrival she had half-expected.

Noon.

Ordinary Friday noon with the January sun flat and cold on the snow and the road empty except for the two cars that turned in.

Not sedans.

A county sheriff's vehicle.

And a white van with no markings she recognized.

She was at the kitchen table with her notepad.

She saw them through the window.

Sat for a moment.

The pressure behind her sternum.

Not the compass.

Not the warning.

Something older.

The recognition of the thing you have been told is coming and have prepared for and are now watching arrive and the preparation and the arrival are two different experiences and only one of them is real.

She put down her pen.

Stood.

Picked up her phone.

Called David.

"They're here," she said.

"How many," he said.

"Sheriff vehicle. White van. Two people getting out of the sheriff car. I can't see the van yet."

"Don't resist," he said. "Don't argue. Don't explain. Say nothing except that you want your attorney present."

"I know," she said.

"Say it repeatedly if you need to. Don't let them reframe it. Don't answer questions."

"I know."

"I'll be there in fifteen minutes. The emergency challenge is filed. Patricia's documentation is filed. They know this." He paused. "They're moving anyway because they think speed matters. They're right that speed matters. Which is why the challenge is already in."

"David."

"Yes."

"I know," she said.

A pause.

"Yes," he said. "You do."

She hung up.

She called Daniel.

He answered immediately.

"They're here," she said.

The silence on the other end.

The brief silence of a man absorbing something he had known was coming and had prepared for and was now receiving in real time and the preparation was not the same as the receiving.

Four seconds.

She counted.

The same four seconds as the barn lot in the cold.

Him deciding.

The decision arriving.

"I'm coming," he said.

"You're twenty minutes away."

"I'm coming," he said.

"I know," she said. "David's closer. Fifteen minutes."

"I'm coming," he said again.

"I know," she said.

She let him say it.

It wasn't for her.

It was for him.

The man who needed to be moving toward her.

She understood.

"Drive carefully," she said.

She hung up.

The knock was official.

Three knocks.

The specific cadence of institutional authority.

She opened the door.

Two officers.

The one in front was perhaps forty. Heavy coat. The expression of a person doing a job they had done before and were not enjoying and were going to do correctly regardless.

Behind him a woman she didn't recognize.

Civilian clothes.

Clipboard.

The expression of a person who had been briefed on what to expect and was measuring the reality against the briefing.

Sarah looked at the officer.

"Sarah Mitchell," he said.

Not a question.

"Yes," she said.

He reached into his coat.

Drew out a document.

"I have a court order for an involuntary psychiatric evaluation," he said. "Signed by Judge Harold Weiss." He held it out.

She took it.

Looked at it.

Her name.

Her address.

The signatures.

Hendricks.

Cobb.

The judge's signature at the bottom.

She had known it would have these signatures.

Seeing them was different from knowing they would be there.

She looked at the document for a moment.

Felt the fear.

Real.

Present.

Not the load-bearing thing.

She handed it back.

"I'd like my attorney present," she said.

The officer looked at her.

"The order doesn't require — "

"I'd like my attorney present," she said.

Same words.

Same tone.

Not hostile.

Not frightened.

The tone of someone who has been told what to say and is saying it and means it.

He looked at her for a moment.

"We can wait briefly," he said.

"Thank you," she said.

She stepped back.

"I need to get my coat," she said.

The officer nodded.

She turned.

Walked to the closet.

Got her coat.

Her hands did not shake putting it on.

She noted this.

Filed it.

Not pride.

Just — information.

She was still her hands.

Still her.

Whatever came next.

Still her.

She sat on the couch.

The two officers and the civilian woman in the doorway.

Nobody speaking.

The house around her.

The kitchen.

The table where she wrote.

The window where Daniel found the road empty or not empty.

The fire that had been going most of December.

Not going now.

She looked at the fireplace.

The cold grate.

She thought about the river this morning.

She had not gone to the river this morning.

She wished she had.

She thought about it instead.

The cold.

The dark.

The current moving in the December water.

The immensity coming fully.

The full version.

She found it.

Not the river.

The thing the river had given her access to.

It was there.

Not contingent on the river.

Not contingent on the barn.

Not contingent on Thursday nights or Daniel's hand or any of the external things.

In her.

Hers.

Wherever she went.

Whatever room they put her in.

Whatever medication they —

She stopped.

Let the fear come.

She thought about Grace.

Four months.

The medication that moved you to one side of yourself.

She sat with this fully.

The full version of the fear.

Not managed.

Not diminished.

Real.

And underneath it —

The thing that had stood in the December river before dawn.

The thing that had said *now* five times in a cold barn.

The thing that had felt the sedan in the parking lot before seeing it.

The thing that had been in the circle on Thursday nights and felt each of them distinct and warm and present like fingers she knew without looking.

The thing that was not contingent on any of it.

That was in her.

That was her.

That they could medicate into a corner but could not —

Could not take.

Grace had said it.

In the barn lot.

In the cold.

What I am is not something they could take.

What you are is not something they can take.

She held this.

The full version of this.

In a room that was about to become a different room.

Whatever room came next.

She would be in it.

The full version of herself.

In it.

David arrived in thirteen minutes.

Not fifteen.

She heard his car.

The officer stepped outside.

She heard voices.

Low.

Professional.

David's voice doing what David's voice did — precise, documented, the voice of someone who had the full file and was not bluffing about having the full file.

He came inside.

Looked at her.

"Okay," he said.

"Okay," she said.

"I've spoken with the officer. The emergency challenge is documented with the court. He's aware. He's required to proceed with the order regardless." He paused. "The challenge will be heard Monday morning. First thing." He paused again. "It will succeed. The Cobb fraud alone is enough. With Patricia's documentation it's airtight."

"Monday," she said.

"Monday," he said.

She did the calculation.

Friday noon to Monday morning.

Just under three days.

She looked at him.

"Three days," she said.

"Yes," he said. His voice level. Honest. The voice of someone who was not going to manage this down. "I know."

"Okay," she said.

He held her gaze.

"Okay," he said.

Daniel arrived at twelve twenty-two.

She heard his car before the door opened.

He came through and looked at the officers and looked at David and looked at her on the couch.

He crossed the room.

Sat beside her.

His hand finding hers.

She let herself be found.

The civilian woman with the clipboard was watching.

Making notes.

She let her make notes.

Let her watch.

Let the whole apparatus of it be what it was.

It didn't change what Daniel's hand felt like.

It didn't change what she felt behind her sternum.

It didn't change anything that mattered.

"Three days," she said quietly.

"Three days," he said.

"David says Monday."

"Then Monday."

She looked at him.

The both-and of him.

Terrified and staying.

Always terrified.

Always staying.

"I need you to do something," she said.

"Yes," he said. Immediately.

"Thursday night," she said. "Whether I'm back or not — the barn. Take them to the barn."

He looked at her.

"You'll be back," he said.

"I know," she said. "But if I'm not — the barn. Don't let the circle stop."

He held her gaze.

"The barn," he said.

"The frequency," she said. "Don't let it stop."

"It won't stop," he said.

She believed him.

She believed him with both kinds of knowing.

The intellectual kind and the river kind.

Both.

"Okay," she said.

She stood.

Daniel stood with her.

The officer came inside.

She looked around the kitchen.

The table.

The notepad still open.

The pen beside it.

She went to the table.

Picked up the pen.

Wrote three words at the bottom of the page.

Put the pen down.

Left the notepad open.

She picked up her bag.

She had packed it this morning.

Not anxiously.

The methodical preparation of someone who had been told to prepare.

She had packed it.

Small bag.

Enough for three days.

She picked it up.

Looked at Daniel.

He was looking at the notepad.

At the three words at the bottom of the page.

She watched him read them.

His face.

The complicated thing.

Then past it.

The arrived thing.

Then past that too.

Something she hadn't seen before.

The expression of a man who has looked at three words written by the woman he loves before she was taken from him into a room he can't follow her into and has found the three words are the right three words and is going to carry them for however long he has to carry them.

He looked at her.

She looked back.

"Ready," she said.

Not to him.

To the day.

To all of it.

To whatever room came next.

He nodded.

She walked to the door.

Stopped.

Turned back.

"David," she said.

"Yes," David said.

"James," she said. "Don't stop looking for James."

David held her gaze.

"I won't stop," he said.

She held his gaze for a moment.

Both ways of knowing.

Both real.

She believed him.

"Okay," she said.

She went through the door.

The van was white and clean and unremarkable.

The kind of vehicle designed to be invisible.

She got in.

The door closed.

She looked out the small window.

Daniel in the driveway.

Not moving.

Standing absolutely still in the January cold.

Watching the van.

His hands at his sides.

Not performing anything.

Just — watching her go.

Being the person who watched her go and stayed and was going to be there when she came back.

She held his gaze through the small window.

As long as she could.

Until the van turned.

Until the driveway and the cabin and the bare tree line disappeared around the corner.

Until the road opened up in front of them.

The January fields.

The flat white landscape.

The cold sun.

She sat in the back of the van.

Her bag on the seat beside her.

Her hands in her lap.

Her hands.

Steady.

She was still her hands.

She breathed.

In.

Out.

The full version of a breath.

She felt the thing behind her sternum.

Warm.

Steady.

Patient as the river.

Patient as the thing that had no protocol for being stopped.

Patient as the thing that was older than anything built to contain it.

She sat in the van as the January landscape went past the small window.

Flat and white and cold.

And underneath the flat white cold —

The current.

Always moving.

Always moving.

She was in it.

She was it.

She was going into a room.

She would come out of the room.

The current would still be moving.

She would still be in it.

Nothing that was coming could change that.

What you are is not something they can take.

She held this.

The full version.

In the back of a white unmarked van on a January Friday while the fields went past and the current moved underneath everything.

She held it.

She was ready.

Back at the cabin Daniel stood in the driveway until the van was gone.

Until the road was empty.

Until the sound of it disappeared.

He stood in the January cold and looked at the empty road.

Then he went inside.

He stood in the kitchen.

The house around him.

The table.

The open notepad.

He looked at the three words she had written at the bottom of the page.

He had read them through the window.

He read them again now.

Three words.

The right three words.

He stood in the kitchen with the open notepad and the empty house and the January light in the windows and the road outside and the barn two miles up the road.

Thursday night.

Two days.

The circle.

The frequency.

He picked up his phone.

Called Marcus.

"She's gone in," he said.

A pause.

"Are you okay," Marcus said.

He looked at the notepad.

At the three words.

"Yes," he said.

He meant it.

He was terrified.

He was staying.

He was going to take them to the barn Thursday night whether she was back or not.

He was going to keep the circle going.

He was going to trust David and Patricia and the emergency challenge and Monday morning.

He was going to read those three words every time the terrified part got louder than the staying part.

He was going to be here when she came back.

He was going to be exactly here.
"Thursday," he said to Marcus.
"Thursday," Marcus said.
He hung up.
Stood in the kitchen.
Picked up the notepad.
Read the three words one more time.
Set it down gently.
Open.
So he could read them whenever he needed to.
The three words she had written before she walked out the door.
The right three words.
I am ready.

Chapter 31

CHAPTER THIRTY-ONE: THE ROOM

The facility was not what she expected.

She had expected the narrow room Grace had described.

The narrow bed.

The window that faced a wall.

This was different.

Not better.

Different in the specific way of something that had learned from its mistakes and updated its presentation without updating its purpose.

Clean lines.

Natural light.

A common room with comfortable chairs and windows that faced a courtyard with bare trees and dormant garden beds.

The décor of a place that understood that institutions looked like institutions and had decided to look like something else.

A wellness center.

That was the word on the intake paperwork.

Wellness.

She had read the word and filed it under: the vocabulary of management.

The intake took two hours.

Forms.

The specific architecture of forms designed to establish a record while appearing to gather information.

She answered what she was required to answer.

She said nothing she was not required to say.

She asked twice for her attorney.

The intake coordinator — young, professional, the practiced warmth of someone trained in de-escalation — said her attorney had been notified and could visit during visiting hours.

"When are visiting hours," Sarah said.

"Two to four," the coordinator said. "Daily."

She filed this.

David would be there at two.

She believed this without needing to verify it.

Both kinds of knowing.

The room was on the second floor.

Larger than she expected.

A window.

Not facing a wall.

Facing the courtyard.

The bare trees.

The dormant garden beds.

The January sky.

She stood at the window for a long time after the coordinator left.

Looked at the courtyard.

The bare trees doing their winter work of being bare.

Patient.

Not diminished by the bareness.

Still themselves.

Entirely themselves.

Just — the winter version.

She thought about the river.

About standing in it before dawn.

About the immensity coming fully.

The full version.

She looked at the bare trees.

You are still the river.

Not metaphor.

Fact.

Whatever they gave her.

Whatever they tried.

The river was still moving.

She was still in it.

She was still it.

She turned from the window.

Sat on the bed.

The room around her.

Clean.

Neutral.

Designed to feel like nothing in particular.

Designed to offer no friction and no nourishment.

The managed nothing of a space that wanted to be the only thing you had to look at.

She looked at it.

Noted it.

Filed it.

Then she did something the room had not anticipated.

She closed her eyes.

And went to the river.

Not physically.

Not the barrel forward into imagination that was also not imagination.

Just — closed her eyes and breathed and let the edges of the room stop being the edges of everything.

Let the neutral walls and the clean lines and the managed nothing fall back.

Let the current come.

It came.

Smaller than the river at dawn.

Smaller than the barn on Thursday nights.

But present.

Entirely present.

Not diminished.

Not absent.

The room could not take it.

She had known this.

She felt it confirmed.

The knowing and the feeling of the knowing simultaneously.

The both-and.

She sat on the bed in the room and felt the current moving through her and breathed and let it be what it was.

Small and real and entirely hers.

Entirely her.

Still here.

Still moving.

A nurse came at three.

Young.

Careful.

The kind of careful that meant she had been briefed and was executing the briefing without necessarily understanding all of it.

She had a small cup.

Two pills.

She set them on the bedside table.

"For anxiety," she said. "Standard protocol for new admits."

Sarah looked at the cup.

At the two pills.

She thought about Grace.

About the medication that moved you to one side of yourself.

About present enough to sign.

Absent enough not to understand.

"I'd like to know what these are," she said.

The nurse looked at the cup.

"Lorazepam," she said. "Two milligrams. It'll help you settle."

Sarah looked at the pills.

"I'm settled," she said.

The nurse looked at her.

At the room.

At the perfectly still woman sitting on the bed who had arrived two hours ago in a county transport and had not cried or argued or demanded or performed distress of any kind.

"It's standard protocol," the nurse said again.

"I understand," Sarah said. "I'd like to decline."

The nurse was quiet for a moment.

"I'll need to note the refusal," she said.

"Please do," Sarah said.

The nurse picked up the cup.

Made a note on her clipboard.

Started to leave.

"What's your name," Sarah said.

The nurse turned.

Slightly surprised.

"Andrea," she said.

"Thank you, Andrea," Sarah said.

Andrea looked at her for a moment.

The briefing and the reality of the room not matching the way briefings and realities sometimes didn't match.

Then she left.

David came at two.

She had expected two.

It was two-oh-three when he was shown to the small visiting room off the common area.

She sat across from him.

A table between them.

A staff member visible through the window in the door.

David set a folder on the table.

Thin.

"The challenge is filed," he said. "Monday morning. Nine o'clock. My attorney will be in front of the judge at nine." He paused. "The Cobb fraud documentation is the primary instrument. Patricia's statement is supporting. The challenge is strong."

"Monday," she said.

"Monday," he said. "That means Saturday and Sunday here."

She held his gaze.

"How is Daniel," she said.

"I spoke with him an hour ago," David said. "He's — " He paused. The honest pause. "He's functioning," he said. "He's at the cabin. He called Marcus. He's holding."

She believed this.

"Rachel," she said.

"With Grace," he said. "They both want to come tomorrow during visiting hours."

"Tell them yes," she said.

"I will."

"And Robert," she said.

"At Marcus's," he said. "He's been there since this morning." He paused. "He knows what happened. He wanted to come today."

She thought about Robert.

The back corner chair.

The pilot light becoming a flame.

"Tell him Thursday," she said. "Tell him to be at the barn Thursday."

"Whether or not — " David started.

"Thursday," she said.

He held her gaze.

"Thursday," he said.

She looked at the folder on the table.

"Tell me something I don't know," she said. "Something useful."

He opened the folder.

"Cobb's fraud is more extensive than I initially documented," he said. "I found three additional cases. All Meridian-connected. All wellness hold applications. All with fabricated evaluations." He paused. "My attorney submitted all of them with the challenge. The judge will have a pattern, not an isolated incident."

"Good," she said.

"Also," he said. "The Indiana facility."

She looked at him.

"The terms were finalized this morning," he said. "Robert's daughter signs Monday. He's free to go." He paused. "The other Robert. James. The original James from your group."

She sat forward slightly.

"Tell me," she said.

"He's not in a facility," David said. "He left voluntarily. That's what Marcus knew and hadn't told the group yet." He paused. "James understood what was happening before they could execute the hold. He left. New city. He's been — " He chose the word carefully. "He's been managing. Alone. Without the group." He paused. "I found him yesterday."

She looked at him.

"Where," she said.

"Pittsburgh," he said. "He's working. He's functional." He paused. "He's grey."

She understood.

The managed absence.

The alone-version of what Meridian did.

Not the facility.

The isolated version.

Just as effective.

Just as grey.

"Can you reach him," she said.

"I have an address," he said.

"Write to him," she said. "Tell him about the barn. Tell him about Thursday nights." She paused. "Tell him about Robert."

David looked at her.

"Both Roberts," she said. "Tell him both Roberts came back."

David was quiet for a moment.

"Yes," he said.

She settled back.

Looked at the window in the door.

The staff member.

The corridor beyond.

The clean lines of the managed nothing.

She looked at it all and felt the current underneath.

Still moving.

"Cobb," she said. "When the challenge succeeds Monday. What happens to Cobb."

"He's exposed," David said. "The fraud is on the record. The licensing board gets the documentation. The additional three cases." He paused. "He loses his license. Possibly faces criminal charges." He paused again. "His relationship with Meridian becomes part of the public record."

"Meridian," she said.

David was quiet.

"It damages them," he said carefully. "It doesn't stop them. They'll regroup. They'll find another Cobb." He paused. "This is one case.

One group." He looked at her. "One very visible, very documented, very legally supported group."

She understood what he was saying.

"We're the data," she said.

"Yes," he said.

"The data that comes after," she said. "That they've never had before."

"Yes," he said.

She looked at the folder.

"When this is over," she said. "When I'm out Monday and the challenge is won and Cobb is exposed — "

"Yes," David said.

"We write it down," she said. "Everything. The full account. The barn. The group. The frequency. The protocol they used and how we navigated it." She paused. "The fourteen names. The forty barns." She paused again. "James in Pittsburgh. The three who are still blooming." She looked at him. "We write it down and we make it available."

David looked at her steadily.

"To who," he said.

"To the next group," she said. "To whoever sits in a circle somewhere and starts to feel the thing and doesn't know what it is and doesn't know what's coming." She paused. "So they're not starting from nothing. So they have the map."

David was very quiet.

The visiting room.

The staff member at the window.

The clean lines of the place.

The January light.

"That's what comes after," he said.

"Yes," she said.

He held her gaze for a long moment.

"Yes," he said.

He left at three-fifty.

Ten minutes before visiting hours ended.

The room with the bare trees through the window.

She sat on the bed.

Breathed.

Felt the current.

Smaller than the barn.

Smaller than the river.

Present.

She thought about what she had said.

The map.

She turned it over.

Felt the rightness of it.

Not just fighting the protocol.

Building the counter-architecture.

Not just surviving Meridian.

Making Meridian's work harder for every group that came after.

The forty barns had been alone.

One at a time.

Each one starting from nothing.

Not knowing what was coming.

Not knowing about the others.

Not knowing there was a name for what they were.

What if they had known.

What if the next group knew.

What if the group after that knew.

She sat on the bed in the room and felt the thing behind her sternum expand past the neutral walls and the clean lines and the managed nothing and she understood for the first time the full size of what was actually happening.

Not one group.

Not one catalyst.

Not one Thursday night.

The beginning of something.

The first data point after the threshold.

The first group to reach this stage and document it.

The first map.

She sat with the full size of this.

Let it be what it was.

It was large.

Larger than the room.

Larger than the facility.

Larger than Meridian and their twenty-three years.

It was patient as the river.

And it was only just beginning.

Night came early.

January dark by five.

The courtyard outside her window grey and then darker grey and then just the outline of bare trees against the night sky.

She stood at the window.

Looked at the bare trees.

Thought about Thursday.

Two days.

She would be out Monday.

She believed this.

Both kinds of knowing.

But if she wasn't —

Daniel would take them to the barn.

The circle would hold.

The frequency would do what it did.

And she would feel it.

She knew she would feel it.

Whatever room she was in.

The current moving.

Always moving.

The both-and.

She stood at the window until the bare trees were invisible against the dark.

Then she went and sat on the bed.

Closed her eyes.

Went to the river.

It was there.

Patient.

Moving.

Cold and real and entirely hers.

She stayed in it for a long time.

The room around her.

The facility around the room.

The January night around the facility.

All of it.

And underneath all of it —

The current.

Still moving.

The barn two days away.

The map beginning.

The next group she would never meet.

Reading it.

Starting not from nothing.

Starting from here.

Starting from this.

She breathed.

In.

Out.

The full version.

The room doing its managed nothing around her.

She doing the full version inside it.

Both.

The both-and.

Always the both-and.

She was ready for Monday.

She was ready for Thursday.

She was ready for whatever came after Thursday.

The map.

The next group.

The group after that.

The current reaching.

Always reaching.

Past the forty barns.

Past the threshold.

Into the after that Meridian had no data for.

Into the country that came next.

The country she was the first to enter.

That they were all the first to enter.

That would not be new country for the ones who came after.

Because of the map.

Because of this.

Because of a woman sitting on a bed in a room in a facility in January with the current moving through her and the barn two days away and the full version of herself entirely intact.

What you are is not something they can take.

She held it.

The full version.

The country that came next.

She was already in it.

She had been in it since the river.

Since before the river.

Since the first Thursday night in the barn.

Since the first whisper of the thing that had no name.
She was already in the country that came next.
She was just learning the geography.
One room at a time.
One river at a time.
One Thursday at a time.
The map would show the way.
She breathed.
The dark room.
The bare trees invisible against the January night.
The current.
The barn.
The next book.
The country that came next.
She was ready.

Chapter 32

CHAPTER THIRTY-TWO: THE RIVER — DANIEL

He went before dawn.

Saturday.

He had not slept.

Not meaningfully.

He had lain in the bed on his side of it and felt the other side and at some point the lying became unbearable in the specific way of a body that needs to be moving toward something and is not.

He got up.

Dressed.

The cabin quiet around him.

Her coffee mug on the counter.

Her notepad on the table.

He didn't look at the three words.

He had read them enough times.

They were in him now.

He went out the back door.

The path was frozen solid.

The January dark complete and close.

He knew the path.

Not as well as she knew it.

But enough.

The root.

The place where the trees stepped back.

The dead grass flat and white under his boots.

He had walked this path with her twice.

The September morning early in the barn days.

The November afternoon after the first truck.

He knew the path.

Tonight he walked it differently.

Not toward something.

Away from the cabin.

Away from the notepad and the empty side of the bed and the three days that stood between now and Monday morning.

Toward the river.

Toward the thing she had found there.

He didn't know if he would find it.

He was going anyway.

The river was low and dark and moving.

The same river.

The January version.

He stood on the bank.

Looked at it.

Thought about her standing here before dawn on the day the hold was signed.

The full version.

He thought about the cold barn and the five times and the way he had looked at her afterward.

He thought about the wedding they had never had.

The marriage that had failed.

The careful life before her.

The life after.

The barn.

The circle.

The frequency.

The woman who said *now* before he moved.

Who felt the sedan before she saw it.

Who wrote *I am ready* and meant it in a way he was still learning the full size of.

He stood on the bank.

His hands at his sides.

The January dark.

The river.

He was not going to wade in.

Not in January.

Not without her.

He stood on the bank and looked at the water and tried to find the thing she found here.

He breathed.

Let the cold be what it was.

Let the dark be what it was.

Let the sound of the water moving be what it was.

He stood there for a long time.

He didn't find the immensity.

He didn't find the full version of whatever she found in the water.

He found something else.

Something smaller.

More specific.

The particular quality of a man standing at the edge of something he can't follow her into.

Not the facility.

The river.

The thing in the river.

She went somewhere in the river that he couldn't follow.

He had known this for months.

Had watched her go there and come back changed in the small ways that accumulated into the large way.

Had watched the full version of her arrive Thursday by Thursday.

Had held her hand through all of it.

Had said okay and meant it.

Had been the man who stayed.

He stood at the river's edge and felt the thing he had not let himself feel since the white van turned the corner and the cabin road was empty.

Grief.

Not for her.

Not grief of loss.

The grief of a man who loves someone who is larger than he fully understands and is learning the size of them in the specific painful way of someone who has to let them go somewhere he cannot follow to learn it.

He stood at the river's edge and felt it.

Fully.

The full version of it.

Not managed.

Not diminished.

He was learning this from her.

The full version of things.

Even the difficult things.

Especially the difficult things.

He stood in the January dark and felt the grief and the cold and the sound of the water and found, underneath all of it —

Something.

Not the immensity.

Not the river-version of what she found.

His version.

The version of a man who had stood in cold barns and read the notepad and driven through December snow and said okay forty different times in forty different ways and meant it each time.

The version of a man who understood that loving someone who was becoming something larger than themselves required a corresponding expansion.

Not of the same kind.

His own kind.

The expansion of someone who has to make room in themselves for something they can't fully see yet.

Who makes the room anyway.

Who stands at the river's edge in January dark and makes the room.

He stood there.

Made the room.

Let it be however large it needed to be.

He didn't know the full size yet.

He was beginning to understand it didn't have a fixed size.

It kept getting larger.

He kept making the room.

The sky began to change.

The specific shift of the dark before dawn.

He stood at the river.

Breathed.

In.

Out.

The full version.

He thought about what she had said in the car the night of the first full frequency.

It feels like the right size.

For what.

For whatever comes next.

He thought about what came next.

Monday and the challenge and the barn on Thursday and the map she had talked about with David.

The next group.

The group after that.

He thought about being the person beside the person who made the map.

Not the catalyst.

Not the frequency.

The person who drove and stayed and said okay and made room.

The person who took them to the barn on Thursday if she wasn't back yet.

The person who read the three words when the terrified part got louder.

He thought about what that was.

Not smaller than what she was.

Not larger.

Different.

His own kind of large.

He was beginning to understand that.

The river helping him understand it.

Not the same way it helped her.

His way.

The standing-at-the-edge way.

The making-room way.

He walked back up the path.

The root.

The place where the trees stepped back.

The cabin.

He went inside.

Stood in the kitchen.

The grey pre-dawn light beginning in the windows.

Her mug on the counter.

The notepad on the table.

He looked at the notepad.

He had read the three words enough times that he didn't need to read them again.

He read them again.

I am ready.

He stood in the kitchen and thought about what those words meant from inside the room she was in.

From the facility with its clean lines and managed nothing.

What it meant to write those words and mean them before walking out the door.

What kind of person wrote those words and meant them.

What kind of person he was standing beside.

He stood in the kitchen and felt the full size of her.

Not the version he'd had access to before.

Not the version of the first Thursday night or the barn or the October morning or any of the versions that had arrived one at a time.

The accumulated version.

All of it at once.

The full size of her.

He stood in the kitchen and let the full size of her be what it was.

It was considerable.

It had always been considerable.

He had known it was considerable.

He had not known the full measure until this moment.

Standing in the kitchen at dawn while she was in a room he couldn't follow her into.

This was when you learned the full measure.

When the presence was replaced by the absence and the absence showed you the shape of what had been there.

The shape of her.

In his kitchen.

In his life.

The shape of what they were building together.

The both-and of it.

He stood in the kitchen and let the full size of the grief and the love and the both-and of it be what it was.

Not managed.

Not diminished.

The full version.

He was learning.

He called Marcus at seven.

"I went to the river," he said.

Marcus was quiet for a moment.

"How was it," he said.

"Not what she finds there," Daniel said.

"No," Marcus said.

"Something else."

"Yes," Marcus said.

A silence.

The good kind.

"Thursday," Daniel said. "I need you at the barn early. All of you. I want the stove going before dark."

"I'll be there at four," Marcus said.

"Robert," Daniel said.

"He'll come," Marcus said. "He asked about her this morning."

"Tell him she'll be back," Daniel said.

"She will be," Marcus said.

"I know," Daniel said. "Tell him anyway."

"Yes," Marcus said.

A pause.

"Daniel," Marcus said.

"Yes."

"The river," Marcus said. "What did you find."

He looked at the notepad.

At the three words.

Thought about standing at the edge of something he couldn't follow her into and making room anyway.

His version of it.

The making-room version.

"The right size," he said.

A pause.

"Good," Marcus said.

Rachel and Grace came at two.

He drove them to the facility.

The three of them in the car.

Not much talking.

The January landscape.

The flat white fields.

The sky the same sharp cold blue as the day they took her.

He sat in the parking lot while they went in.

Visiting hours.

He was not listed as a visitor.

She had listed David.

She had listed Rachel.

She had listed Grace.

Not him.

He had understood without asking.

She had known they would need the visits more than he did.

She had known he would be okay.

She had known the right size of what he needed.

He sat in the parking lot and looked at the building and felt the current behind his sternum.

Not her thing.

Not the frequency.

Something quieter.

More specific.

The particular steady warmth of a man who has found his place in something larger than himself and is sitting in a parking lot on a Saturday afternoon being exactly where he needs to be.

Not inside.

Not with her.

Here.

The right place.

His place.

The making-room place.

He sat in the cold car and waited.

They came out at three-fifty.

He watched their faces as they crossed the parking lot.

Grace first.

Her face the face of someone who had been somewhere they recognized and found it different than the first time.

Not worse.

She knew how to be in that recognition.

She had done it before.

She was doing it now with the full version of herself.

The insistence of her.

Present.

Rachel beside her.

Her face the face of someone who had sat across from a person they had fought for and found that person intact.

Not diminished.

Not managed into absence.

Intact.

The full version.

He read their faces.

He understood.

He started the car.

They got in.

He looked at them in the mirror.

"Tell me," he said.

Rachel looked at Grace.

Grace looked at him.

"She sends you something," Grace said.

He waited.

"She said to tell you she went to the river," Grace said. "Inside. She said it worked."

He sat with this.

The January parking lot.

The facility.

The bare trees visible over the roofline.

She had gone to the river inside.

The room had not prevented it.

The managed nothing had not reached it.

He felt the thing in his chest.

Warm.

Certain.

The making-room thing.

He had made enough room.

She was in it.

She was doing it from inside the room.

"Okay," he said.

He meant it.

Fully.

The full version of okay.

He put the car in gear.

"What else," he said.

"She wants to know about James," Rachel said.

"David is writing to him," he said.

"She'll ask again Monday," Rachel said.

"I know," he said.

He drove out of the parking lot.

The January road.

The sharp cold sky.

The fields going past.

"How was she," he said.

A pause.

"Like herself," Grace said.

He held this.

Like herself.

The full version of herself.

In a room designed to prevent that.

Doing it anyway.

He thought about the notepad.

I am ready.

Yes.

She was.

She had been since the river before dawn.

Since the barn.

Since the first Thursday night.

Since before he met her.

She had been ready for a long time.

She was just finding out what she was ready for.

They all were.

"Thursday," he said.

"Thursday," Grace said from the back seat.

"All of us," he said. "Early."

"Yes," Rachel said.

He drove.

The road going toward the cabin and the barn beyond it and Thursday night and the circle and the frequency and whatever came after the frequency.

The map.

The next group.
The country that came next.
He drove toward all of it.
His place in it.
The making-room place.
The staying place.
The beside-her place.
His version of the large thing.
His own kind.
The right size.
Always the right size.
He drove.
Sunday passed.
Slowly.
The way Sundays pass when you are waiting for Monday.
He called David at nine.
Everything was filed.
Everything was ready.
Nine o'clock Monday morning.
He called Marcus at noon.
The barn was ready.
Stove laid.
Wood stacked.
Chairs in the circle.
He sat at the kitchen table in the afternoon with her notepad.
He didn't write in it.
That was hers.
He found a separate piece of paper.
Wrote.
Not a letter.
Not a note.
Something else.

The things he had found at the river.

His version.

The making-room version.

The standing-at-the-edge version.

He wrote it for himself.

Not for anyone else.

Not yet.

Then he thought about the map she had talked about with David.

The next group.

The person beside the catalyst in the next group.

Standing at the edge of something they couldn't follow into.

Learning to make the room.

He looked at what he had written.

Thought about that person.

He folded the paper.

Put it in his coat pocket.

It was for that person too.

He just didn't know it yet.

The map.

Every version of the large thing.

His version.

Her version.

All of them.

The full map.

He sat in the kitchen.

The winter afternoon.

The light going early.

One more day.

The current moving.

Always moving.

Monday morning he was up before the alarm.

Dressed.

Coffee on.

David called at eight-thirty.

"We're at the courthouse," he said. "My attorney has everything. We're ready."

"Yes," Daniel said.

"I'll call you when we're before the judge," David said.

"I'll be in the parking lot," Daniel said.

A pause.

"Daniel," David said.

"Yes."

"She's coming home today," David said.

He heard the certainty in it.

Not performed.

The real kind.

The both-ways knowing.

David was learning that too.

"I know," Daniel said.

He drove to the facility.

Parked.

The January morning.

The sharp cold sky again.

The bare trees over the roofline.

He sat in the car.

The engine off.

The cold coming through slowly.

He let it come.

He was getting better at letting things come fully.

His version of it.

He thought about Thursday.

The circle.

Robert in the back corner.

The frequency building.

And her in the circle.

Back where she belonged.

The full circle.

Nine of them.

The frequency at full.

Whatever that would be.

He sat in the parking lot and felt it ahead of him.

Thursday night.

The full circle.

The full frequency.

The full version of all of them together.

He had not felt it yet.

Not the way she felt it.

Not the both-ways version.

He felt it ahead of him.

The anticipation of something he didn't have the full vocabulary for yet.

Something he would have to stand in to understand.

He was ready to stand in it.

His version.

The making-room version.

The staying version.

The right size.

His phone rang at nine-seventeen.

David.

He answered.

"The judge reviewed the challenge," David said.

Daniel said nothing.

Waited.

"The hold is vacated," David said. "Cobb's fraud is on the record. The hold is vacated effective immediately." A pause. "She can leave as soon as the paperwork clears. Thirty minutes. Maybe less."

Daniel sat in the parking lot.

The cold car.

The facility.

The bare trees.

The January morning.

He breathed.

In.

Out.

The full version.

"Okay," he said.

He got out of the car.

Walked toward the door.

Thirty minutes.

Maybe less.

The current moving.

Always moving.

He was walking toward her.

She was walking toward him.

The both-and.

Always the both-and.

The right size.

The full version.

The country that came next.

He walked through the door.

Chapter 33

CHAPTER THIRTY-THREE: WHAT SHE BROUGHT BACK

The paperwork took forty minutes.

She had expected thirty.

She sat in the discharge room — smaller than the intake room, the same clean lines, the same managed nothing — and signed what she was required to sign and did not perform impatience.

She was not impatient.

She had been in the room for three days.

Forty minutes was nothing.

Forty minutes was the length of a river.

She signed.

The discharge coordinator was not the intake coordinator.

Older.

The careful expression of someone who had been briefed on a situation that had changed and was navigating the change professionally.

She handed Sarah a form.

"This documents your discharge," she said. "Voluntary separation following court order vacatur."

Sarah looked at the language.

Voluntary.

She had arrived in a county transport.

She was leaving because a judge had reviewed fraudulent documentation and vacated an unlawful hold.

Voluntary.

She signed.

Filed it under: the vocabulary of management.

The coordinator said: "Your belongings are at the front desk."

"Thank you," Sarah said.

She stood.

Picked up her bag.

Walked out of the discharge room.

Down the corridor.

Past the common room.

The comfortable chairs.

The courtyard windows.

She paused at the courtyard windows.

The bare trees.

She had looked at them for three days.

They looked back with the patience of things that understood winter.

Still themselves.

Entirely themselves.

Just — the winter version.

She had understood something from those trees.

She would put it in the map.

She walked on.

He was at the front desk.

Not sitting.

Standing.

The way he stood when he was holding something together.

The precise upright quality of a man who has been waiting for forty minutes in a facility lobby and has been doing it without performing the waiting.

He looked at her when she came through the inner door.

His face.

She watched it.

The complicated thing arrived and passed.

The arrived thing arrived and stayed.

Something underneath the arrived thing she hadn't seen before.

Something new.

She would find the word for it later.

She crossed the lobby.

He took one step toward her.

They met in the middle.

He held her.

She held him.

The lobby around them.

The staff at the front desk looking at paperwork.

The January light in the windows.

She let herself be held.

Fully.

The full version.

She had spent three days in a room learning to hold herself fully from the inside.

Now she let him hold her from the outside.

Both at once.

The both-and.

His arms.

Her hands on his back.

The warmth of him.

Real.

Entirely real.

She breathed him in.

Still here.

Both of them.

Still here.

He took her bag.

She let him take her bag.

They walked out into the January morning.

The sharp cold sky.

The bare trees over the roofline.

She stopped on the sidewalk.

Looked up.

The sky.

Blue-black at the edges.

The same sky as Friday.

The same sky as always.

She breathed it.

Cold and real and enormous and indifferent and entirely, completely, unreservedly open.

No ceiling.

No managed nothing.

Just — sky.

As much of it as she wanted.

She breathed it.

Daniel beside her.

Waiting.

Not rushing her.

Never rushing her.

She looked at the sky for a long moment.

Then she looked at him.

He looked back.

The new thing in his face.

She found the word for it.

Larger.

He was larger than he had been on Friday.

Not physically.

The other kind.

She could feel it.

The making-room quality of him had expanded.

Three days.

Something had happened in three days.

She would ask him later.

"The river," she said.

He looked at her.

"You went to the river," she said.

He was quiet for a moment.

"Saturday morning," he said.

"Tell me."

"Later," he said. "In the car."

She held his gaze.

The larger version of him.

"Okay," she said.

They walked to the car.

He told her on the drive home.

The path in the dark.

The standing at the edge.

The thing he had not let himself feel until then.

The grief that wasn't loss.

The making-room version.

His version of the large thing.

She listened.

The way she listened in the circle.

The whole attention.

Without performance.

He talked and she listened and the January landscape went past the windows.

Flat and white and patient.

When he finished she was quiet for a moment.

Then she said: "The piece of paper."

He looked at her.

She looked at him.

"You wrote something down," she said.

His hand went briefly to his coat pocket.

"Yes," he said.

"The map," she said.

He was quiet.

"For the person beside the catalyst," she said. "In the next group."

Another pause.

"Yes," he said.

She looked at the road ahead.

The flat fields.

The bare tree line.

She felt the thing behind her sternum.

Warm.

Certain.

The making-room thing.

Not hers.

His.

She could feel it now.

She had felt it in the lobby.

She was feeling it in the car.

Distinct.

Warm.

Present.

Like the others on Thursday nights.

Like fingers she knew without looking.

His.

Specifically his.

Oh, she thought.

Oh.

She looked at him.

"Daniel," she said.

"Yes."

"It's not just me," she said.

He glanced at her.

She looked at him with the full version of the thing she was understanding.

"The frequency," she said. "The current. The thing in the barn on Thursday nights." She paused. "It's not just the people who are — it's not just the catalysts."

He was very quiet.

"You felt it in the lobby," she said.

He drove.

The road.

The fields.

"I felt something in the lobby," he said carefully.

"Me," she said. "You felt me. The specific quality of me." She paused. "The way I feel the group on Thursday nights. Each of them distinct." She paused again. "You felt me like that."

He was quiet for a long moment.

"Yes," he said.

She sat with this.

The full size of it.

She had assumed the frequency was for the people in the circle.

The ones who were changing.

The catalysts.

She had assumed the people beside them — Daniel, beside her — were adjacent to it.

Present.

Not in it.

She had assumed wrong.

"You're in it," she said.

"I don't feel it the way you feel it," he said.

"No," she said. "Your version." She looked at him. "The making-room version."

He drove for a moment.

"Yes," he said.

"That's in the frequency," she said. "The making-room version is part of the frequency."

He was quiet.

She could feel him absorbing this.

The careful systematic way he absorbed things.

The room in him expanding.

Making room for this too.

"The map," she said. "We were thinking about it wrong."

"Tell me," he said.

"We were thinking catalysts and observers," she said. "The people in the frequency and the people beside them." She paused. "But the person beside the catalyst is in the frequency. Their own version. The making-room version is part of what makes the frequency possible." She looked at the road. "You make room and I expand into it. I expand and you make more room. It's — "

"The both-and," he said.

"The both-and," she said.

He drove.

The January road.

The bare tree line.

The flat white fields.

"The map needs both," she said. "Not just the catalyst's story. Both." She paused. "The piece of paper in your pocket."

He said nothing.

She looked at him.

"That goes in the map," she said.

He held the wheel.

She watched his hands.

The hands of a man who had stood at the edge of the river in the January dark and found his version of the large thing.

"Yes," he said.
The cabin was the cabin.
She stood in the doorway for a moment.
Looked at it.
The kitchen.
The table.
The notepad.
She came in.
Went to the table.
Looked at the notepad.
Her three words at the bottom of the last page.
I am ready.
She looked at them.
Then she picked up the pen.
Turned to a new page.
Wrote:
What I brought back:
The room could not reach the river.
The managed nothing had no access to the current.
The full version is not contingent on circumstances.
It is not contingent on anything.
This is the thing they cannot take.
Not because we are strong.
Because it is not a thing that can be taken.
It can be covered.
Hidden.
Made temporarily inaccessible.
But not taken.
It is what we are.
Underneath everything they can do.
Still moving.
Always moving.

She looked at what she had written.

The map.

The first page of the map.

She kept writing.

Daniel made coffee.

She wrote.

He set a mug beside her.

She didn't look up.

He sat across from her with his own coffee and watched her write.

She was aware of him watching.

She wrote through the awareness.

Let both things be true simultaneously.

Writing and being watched by the person she loved.

The both-and.

She wrote for an hour.

Then she stopped.

Looked up.

He was still there.

Coffee gone cold.

Reading something on his phone.

The steady presence of him.

The making-room presence.

She looked at him for a moment.

He looked up.

She said: "Andrea."

He looked at her.

"The nurse who brought the medication," she said. "I refused it. She noted the refusal." She paused. "She said thank you to me when I was discharged."

"Thank you," he said.

"She whispered it," Sarah said. "In the corridor. She had the expression of someone who had been watching something happen that they didn't have a category for."

Daniel was quiet.

"She's young," Sarah said. "She's in a job that is part of a system she doesn't fully understand." She paused. "She's not the driver on the county road. She's not the driver on Tuesday morning." She paused again. "She's — "

"Tom in the paint aisle," Daniel said.

"Yes," Sarah said. "Or she could be." She looked at her notepad. "The map needs to account for them too. The people inside the system who are not the system." She paused. "The people who say thank you in corridors."

He looked at her.

"You're already thinking about the next group," he said.

"I've been thinking about the next group since Friday," she said.

He smiled.

Small.

The first smile since the van pulled away.

She felt it.

Not saw it.

Felt it behind her sternum like the specific warmth of his.

"Three days in a room," he said. "And you came out with the map."

"I had a lot of time to think," she said.

"And the river," he said.

"And the river," she said.

She looked at the notepad.

At what she had written.

The first page.

The beginning of something.

"David needs to see this," she said.

"Yes."

"And Patricia Wren."

"Yes."

"And Emma."

"The architectural mind," he said.

"Yes," she said. "She'll see the structure of it."

"And Marcus," he said.

"Marcus already knows," she said.

He looked at her.

"He's been building this for years," she said. "The barn. The circle. The honest space." She paused. "He just didn't know it was a map." She paused again. "Maybe he did."

They were quiet for a moment.

The cabin.

The kitchen.

The January light going already.

The short days of the season.

She thought about Thursday.

Two days.

"Tomorrow," she said.

"Yes."

"I want to go to the river."

"I know," he said.

"Will you come."

He looked at her.

Not surprised.

The arrived expression.

"I'll stand at the edge," he said.

"I know," she said. "That's where you're supposed to be."

He held her gaze.

The larger version of him.

The making-room version.

His own kind of large.

"Yes," he said.

That evening Marcus called.

She told him she was home.

He said: "I know."

She said: "How."

He said: "The same way you know things."

She was quiet for a moment.

"Marcus," she said.

"Yes."

"Grace told me what you told her," she said. "In the barn on Thursday morning. Before the full group arrived."

A silence.

"James," she said.

"Yes," he said.

"Not the first," she said.

Another silence.

"Tell me," she said.

He was quiet for a long moment.

The quality of someone deciding.

Not whether to tell her.

How.

"Before James," he said. "Before this group. Before the barn." He paused. "There was another group. Fourteen years ago." He paused again. "I was not the one who built the space. I was the one who sat in the circle." He paused. "I was the one who was changed."

She sat with this.

"You were in a group," she said.

"Yes."

"And it was dismantled."

"Yes."

"By Meridian."

A long pause.

"By whatever they were called then," he said. "The organization has changed its name. The work is the same." He paused. "The group scattered. The space was closed. The people went — different directions." He paused. "I went grey."

"Fourteen years," she said.

"Yes."

"And then you built the barn," she said.

"Yes."

"Because you knew," she said. "What you were building toward."

"I knew what I had lost," he said. "I built toward finding it again." A pause. "I didn't know it would work. I didn't know if the group would come." He paused. "I set up the chairs and waited."

She thought about the circle.

The empty chairs.

Marcus setting them up.

Week after week.

Waiting.

Before she arrived.

Before Rachel.

Before David.

Before Grace.

Before all of them.

Just — chairs in a circle.

An honest space.

A man who had lost something and was building toward finding it again.

"The grey lifted," she said.

"When you arrived," he said. "When the group arrived." He paused. "When Grace arrived." He said her name differently than the others. She heard it. "The last of it lifted."

She was quiet for a moment.

"The map," she said.

"Yes," he said.

"Your part of the map," she said. "The person who builds the space. Who sets up the chairs and waits."

A long pause.

"Yes," he said.

"That goes in the map," she said.

He was quiet.

"The next person who needs to build the space needs to know it can work," she said. "That you set up the chairs and the people come." She paused. "They need to know about fourteen grey years and a barn and a Thursday night and the chairs."

The line was quiet for a long moment.

"Yes," he said.

His voice the voice he used for things that were true and didn't need decoration.

"Thursday," she said.

"Thursday," he said.

"I want to see you," she said.

"You'll see me," he said.

"All of you," she said. "The full group."

"Yes," he said.

"The full frequency," she said.

"Yes," he said.

She felt it.

Ahead of her.

Thursday night.

The full circle.

Nine of them.

The making-room people and the expanding people and all of them together.

The frequency at full.

Whatever that was.

Whatever it would be with all of them present.

She felt the forward edge of it.

The anticipation of something she couldn't fully see yet.

Something she would have to stand in to understand.

She was ready to stand in it.

"Thursday," she said again.

"Thursday," he said.

She hung up.

Sat at the table.

The notepad in front of her.

The first page of the map.

She picked up the pen.

Added a line.

Build the space.

Set up the chairs.

Wait.

They will come.

She looked at it.

Turned to a new page.

Kept writing.

She wrote until nine.

Then she stopped.

Not because she was done.

Because the writing had reached the place where it needed the barn to go further.

It needed Thursday.

It needed the full circle.

It needed whatever happened when all nine of them were in the room together and the frequency did what it was going to do.

She needed to stand in that before she could write beyond where she had gotten.

She closed the notepad.

Looked at Daniel.

He was at the counter.

Making dinner.

The ordinary domestic fact of him.

The extraordinary ordinary fact of him.

She watched him.

The larger version.

The making-room version.

His own kind of large.

"Daniel," she said.

He turned.

She looked at him.

"Thursday," she said.

He understood.

"Yes," he said.

"Whatever happens Thursday," she said. "When the frequency — when all nine of us — "

"Yes," he said.

"It's going to be different," she said. "Bigger than before."

"Yes," he said.

"Are you ready for bigger," she said.

He looked at her.

The larger version of him.

The man who had stood at the edge of the river in the January dark and made room.

Who had written on a piece of paper in his coat pocket.

Who had driven her home and listened and said *yes* in all its forms.

Who was always the right size.

"Yes," he said.

She believed him.

Both kinds of knowing.
She stood.
Went to the counter.
Stood beside him.
Not performing anything.
Just — beside him.
The way the current ran beside the bank.
The way the river ran beside the willows.
The way things ran beside the things they belonged beside.
"Two days," she said.
"Two days," he said.
She picked up the spoon and stirred whatever was in the pot.
He let her stir it.
The ordinary kitchen.
The extraordinary ordinary evening.
The map on the table.
The barn two days away.
The full circle ahead of them.
The country that came next.
All of it.
Both of them in it.
The both-and.
Always the both-and.
Always the right size.
Always moving.
Always.

Chapter 34

CHAPTER THIRTY-FOUR: THE FULL CIRCLE

Thursday came the way things came that had been earned.

Quietly.

Without announcement.

She woke before dawn.

Daniel still sleeping.

She lay in the dark and felt the day arrive and did not rush toward it.

Let it come.

The full version of a Thursday.

They went to the river at first light.

Both of them.

The path frozen.

The January morning dark and close and smelling of cold and the particular stillness of a world that had been holding its breath and was about to release it.

She went first.

He followed.

The root.

The place where the trees stepped back.

The willows.

Bare and patient.

The river low and clear and moving.

She waded in to her knees.

The cold moving through her like a hand at the center of her chest.

Honest.

Present.

Real.

She breathed.

Let the edges of herself become what they became.

The current came.

Smaller than the before-dawn version.

She had expected that.

She was not here for the immensity today.

She was here for the confirmation.

The checking of the instrument.

Still here.

The current said: *still here.*

She said: *yes.*

Both kinds of knowing.

She stood for three minutes.

Maybe four.

Then she waded out.

Stood on the bank.

Dried her feet.

Put her boots on.

Stood.

Looked at Daniel.

He was at the edge.

His boots on the bank.

His hands at his sides.

Looking at the river.

She watched him.

The making-room quality of him.

Still.

Present.
His own version of the large thing.
She could feel it from where she stood.
Distinct.
Warm.
His.
She waited.
Let him have his version of it.
After a while he turned.
Looked at her.
The arrived expression.
Something underneath it she recognized now.
The larger version.
"Ready," he said.
Not a question.
"Yes," she said.
They walked back up the path.
The day passed slowly and completely.
She did not rush it.
She wrote in the morning.
The map.
Three more pages.
The room that could not reach the river.
The nurse who said thank you in the corridor.
Andrea.
The making-room version.
Daniel's piece of paper.
She wrote it all.
Carefully.
Without borrowed language.
Without performing wisdom.
Just — true.

Everything true.

In the afternoon she called David.

"James," she said.

"He responded," David said.

She stopped.

"To the letter," David said. "He responded." A pause. "He's coming."

"When," she said.

"He's driving," David said. "He'll be here tonight." Another pause. "He wants to come to the barn."

She stood in the kitchen.

The winter afternoon.

The pale light.

James is coming.

She felt the thing behind her sternum.

Not the compass.

Not the warning.

Not the diffuse warmth.

Something she hadn't felt before.

Completion.

The sense of a circle that had been open for a long time preparing to close.

"Tell him to come straight to the barn," she said. "Tell him not to stop anywhere. Tell him we'll be there."

"Yes," David said.

She hung up.

Looked at Daniel.

He was watching her face.

"James," she said.

He looked at her.

She felt him feel it too.

His version.

The making-room version expanding to accommodate this.

"Tonight," he said.

"Tonight," she said.

They arrived at the barn at five.

Dark already.

The January dark that came early and stayed late and made the inside of the barn feel more itself.

Marcus had been there since four.

The stove going.

The chairs in the circle.

The amber light.

The smell of the place.

She came through the door and stopped.

Breathed it.

The barn.

The honest space.

The space that Marcus had built and set the chairs in and waited.

She felt the history of it.

All the Thursday nights.

The first whisper.

The building frequency.

The full nights.

The barn had held all of it.

Was holding all of it now.

She could feel it in the walls.

In the high windows.

In the particular quality of the air.

All of this happened here.

All of this is here.

Marcus looked at her from the stove.

She looked at him.

Fourteen grey years.

The barn.
The chairs.
The waiting.
She crossed to him.
Put her arms around him.
He held her.
The steady warmth of him.
The making-room quality.
Not the same as Daniel's.
His own kind.
She felt it.
Distinct.
Warm.
Marcus.
After a moment he stepped back.
Looked at her.
"You're intact," he said.
"Yes," she said.
He nodded.
Once.
The nod of someone receiving confirmation they had needed.
"James is coming," she said.
His face.
She watched it.
The complicated thing.
Then past it.
Then something she had not seen on Marcus before.
Relief.

The specific relief of a man who has been carrying something for a long time and has just been told it is almost over.

"James," he said.
"Tonight," she said.

He looked at the circle.

At the chairs.

At the one that had been James's.

Waiting.

The way chairs waited.

The way honest spaces waited.

"Good," he said.

The full weight of it.

In one word.

They came in ones and twos.

Emma first.

Her clear eyes and her coat and the expression of someone who had been designing something all day and was setting it aside to be here.

She looked at Sarah.

"You're back," she said.

"I'm back," Sarah said.

Emma nodded.

The nod of a woman who had been grey for eleven years and understood what coming back meant.

Rachel and David.

Together.

Rachel's face when she saw Sarah.

The contained brightness of her, briefly uncontained.

She crossed the barn.

Hugged Sarah without ceremony.

Sarah hugged her back.

No performance.

Just — two people who had been through something together on the other side of it.

Intact.

Both of them intact.

David behind her.

His hand on Sarah's shoulder.

Brief.

Everything it needed to be.

Grace and Marcus.

Grace who had been in a narrow room and was standing in a barn and was looking at Sarah with the full version of herself.

The insistence of her.

Present.

Alive.

The full version.

She came to Sarah and held her face briefly in both hands.

The specific gesture of someone who needed to see a person clearly.

She looked.

She saw.

She released.

"Good," she said.

Just that.

Robert in the back corner.

The chair that was his.

The pilot light — not a pilot light anymore.

A flame.

Steadier than last Thursday.

More his.

He looked at her across the barn.

She looked at him.

He nodded.

She nodded.

The nod of two people who had been in rooms they weren't supposed to be in and had come out of them and were here.

Intact.

Both of them.

James arrived at six-fifteen.

She felt him before the door opened.

The pressure behind her sternum.

The compass.

Pointing at the door.

Then the door opened.

He was perhaps fifty-five.

Thin.

The grey visible not in his hair but in his face.

The managed absence Emma had described.

Not gone.

Not the facility version.

The isolated version.

The alone-in-Pittsburgh version.

The grey of a man who had been walking backward away from himself slowly and alone for two years and had received a letter that told him the direction had changed.

He stood in the doorway.

Looking at the circle.

At the barn.

At the amber light and the stove and the faces.

His eyes.

She knew those eyes.

She had her own version of them.

The before version.

Before the barn.

Before the Thursday nights.

Before the current came fully.

His eyes going slowly around the circle.

Landing on Marcus.

Stopping there.

She watched Marcus.

The relief again.

Larger now.

The specific relief of a man looking at someone he had failed to protect and finding them alive.

Changed.

Grey.

But alive.

Marcus crossed the barn.

Stood in front of James.

He said nothing.

James said nothing.

Two men who had been in the same circle fourteen years ago when the first version of this had been dismantled.

Looking at each other.

Then Marcus put his hand out.

James took it.

They gripped hands.

Not shaking.

Holding.

The grip of two people who had survived the same thing from different sides of it.

After a moment Marcus stepped back.

"Come in," he said.

James came in.

He sat in the circle.

Not the back corner.

The circle.

Between Emma and Rachel.

He sat with his hands on his knees.

Looking at the stove.

The barn holding him.

The honest space doing what honest spaces did.
No agenda.
No performance required.
No management.
Just — the barn.
The stove.
The circle.
The warmth.
After a while he breathed.
A long breath.
The kind that empties completely.
The kind that refills differently.
She felt it.
His breath.
Across the circle.
The something in him that had been covered.
Not gone.
Covered.
Responding to the air of the barn.
Beginning.
Just beginning.
But beginning.
They sat for a while without talking.
The full circle.
All of them.
Eleven people.
The catalysts.
The making-room people.
James with his covered something beginning to uncover.
The barn holding all of it.
She looked around.
Felt each of them.

The way she felt them on Thursday nights.

Distinct.

Warm.

Present.

Each one specific.

Each one entirely themselves.

Rachel — the contained brightness.

David — the precise careful intelligence with the larger room now, the stepping-through.

Emma — the architectural clarity, the eleven years behind her, the something larger on the other side.

Grace — the full version, the insistence, the home.

Marcus — the steady patience, the fourteen years, the barn, the making-room in the largest sense.

Robert — the flame, still growing, still his.

Daniel — the making-room, his version, the right size, expanding always.

James — the covered thing beginning.

And she.

The ripple.

The river.

The both.

All of them.

All eleven of them.

The full circle.

She felt the frequency begin.

It came slowly.

Not slowly.

It came the way dawn came.

Imperceptibly and then all at once.

The warmth behind her sternum.

Diffuse.

Spreading.

Further than before.

Further than she had felt it go.

She didn't reach.

She didn't perform.

She sat in the circle and breathed and let it come.

Let it be however large it needed to be.

It came.

Larger than any Thursday before.

Larger than the twenty seconds.

The thirty seconds.

The forty.

She felt each of them enter it.

One by one.

Rachel first.

Then David — his stepping-through more certain now.

Not tentative.

He stepped through.

Emma.

Grace.

Robert.

Marcus.

Daniel.

His version.

The making-room current running alongside the expanding current the way the river ran alongside the bank.

Not the same.

Both necessary.

Both part of the same moving.

The both-and.

And then —

James.

She felt him the moment the frequency reached him.

The covered thing uncovering.

Not fully.

Not yet.

But the first uncovering.

The first contact between the frequency and whatever was underneath the grey.

And it was —

Enormous.

She gasped.

Quietly.

Involuntarily.

The specific surprise of feeling something larger than she had expected.

James sat very still across the circle.

His hands on his knees.

His eyes closed.

His face the face of someone who has been walking backward for two years and has just found the direction reversed.

Reversed.

Forward.

Toward.

The thing he had been walked away from.

Coming back.

Beginning to come back.

She held it.

The full circle.

All eleven of them.

The frequency at a size she had no prior experience of.

No vocabulary for.

She let it be without vocabulary.

Let it be larger than words.

The ripple.

The current.

The river.

All of it.

All of them.

She didn't know how long it lasted.

She stopped counting after sixty seconds.

She stopped measuring.

She was in it.

That was all.

She was in it and it was enormous and it was real and it was the most true thing she had ever stood inside of.

The most true.

The full version of the most true.

When it passed it passed the way the tide passed.

Gently.

Not taking anything.

Leaving everything different.

Changed in the way of things that have been touched by something larger than themselves and carry the print of that touching.

The barn was just the barn.

The circle was just people in chairs.

The stove.

The January dark outside.

But different.

Everything different.

She looked around the circle.

Rachel.

Her eyes.

The contained brightness entirely uncontained.

Unmanaged.

Full.

David.

The precise careful man.

On the other side of the threshold entirely now.

Fully through.

Both ways of knowing available to him.

She could feel it.

Emma.

Looking at her own hands the way she always looked at her hands after.

The architectural mind finding the structure of what just happened.

Already designing.

Grace.

Home.

Always home now.

The full version.

The insistence.

Marcus.

Looking at James.

The relief complete.

The fourteen years and the barn and the chairs and all of it arriving at this.

This circle.

This frequency.

This moment.

Complete.

Robert.

The flame.

She looked at the flame.

It was larger.

Significantly larger than it had been when he sat down.

One Thursday.

One hour.

The frequency and sixty seconds and the thing that had been walked backward from him coming forward again.

His eyes were open.

Wide.

The eyes of a man who has remembered something he thought he had lost.

Something essential.

His.

Daniel.

The making-room current.

She felt it running alongside her.

The both-and of them.

The right size.

Always the right size.

He was looking at her.

She looked back.

His face.

The larger version.

The new thing.

Larger still.

She loved him so completely in this moment that the word seemed inadequate.

She looked at him with the full version of it.

He held her gaze.

The full version back.

Both of them in the current.

Their own versions.

Running alongside each other.

The way they always had.

The way they always would.

And then —
James.
She looked at James.
He was sitting in the circle with his hands on his knees.
Eyes open.
Looking at the stove.
His face.
She had seen the grey when he came in.
She looked at his face now.
Not grey.
Not yet the full color.
But the grey — lifted.
The specific quality of it.
Lifted.
Like weather passing.
Like a season turning.
Like a tide coming in over something that had been dry too long.
He looked up.
Felt her looking.
Looked at her.
His eyes.
She knew those eyes.
The after version.
Hers, after the barn.
His.
After sixty seconds of the full circle.
Sixty seconds.
The beginning.
Only the beginning.
"James," she said.
His voice when it came was careful.

The careful voice of someone whose instrument had been out of use and is warming up.

"What is this," he said.

She looked around the circle.

At all of them.

At the barn that Marcus had built and set the chairs in and waited.

At the map on the table at home, three pages written, more to write.

At the river behind the cabin moving in the January dark.

At the next group she would never meet.

At the group after that.

At the country that came next.

At all of it.

She looked back at James.

"The beginning," she said.

He looked at her.

At the circle.

At the barn.

At the stove and the amber light and the high windows with the January dark beyond them and the stars above that indifferent to Meridian and their protocols and their forty barns and their whole careful architecture of prevention.

He looked at all of it.

And then —

She felt it.

Before she saw it.

The way she felt things.

Both ways.

Both kinds of knowing.

The thing underneath the grey.

His.

Enormous.

Responding.

Waking.

His face changed.

Slowly.

The way light changed at dawn.

Imperceptibly.

Then all at once.

Not a smile.

The thing that lived underneath all smiles.

The original thing.

The full version.

"Yes," he said.

Just that.

Just yes.

The word of someone who has been somewhere far away and has just found the direction home.

Yes.

Yes.

The barn held it.

The circle held it.

All of them held it.

She held it.

The full version.

The full circle.

The full frequency.

The beginning of the country that came next.

The first page of the map.

The first step past the threshold that Meridian had spent twenty-three years preventing.

The after.

The data that had never existed before.

Here.
Now.
Real.
She breathed.
In.
Out.
The full version.
The warmth behind her sternum.
All of them.
Distinct.
Warm.
Present.
All eleven of them.
The barn around them.
The January dark outside.
The stars.
The river.
The current.
Always moving.
She looked around the circle one more time.
Felt each of them.
Held each of them.
Let each of them be the full size they were.
Enormous.
All of them.
Every single one.
She sat in the circle.
The full circle.
In the barn Marcus had built.
In the honest space.
In the frequency that Meridian had no protocol for.
In the country that came next.

In the beginning.
In the full version.
In the moving current of the thing that could not be taken.
In the ripple.
In the river.
In the both.
Always the both.
Always.
She was home.

Did you love *WHAT CANNOT BE TAKEN*? Then you should read *The Voice That Woke Me*[1] by BRAD RABY!

[2]

The Voice That Woke Me

Book One of The Threaded Light Series

Born into the spotlight. Cast into the shadows. Reborn through a question.

In 1939, Brad Marvin was born into a legacy of fame. With a grandmother on the stage and her sister—the celebrated Broadway and Hollywood star **Edna May Oliver**—defining the era's silver screen, his life was promised to be one of culture and prestige.

It did not remain there.

Ripped from his family and separated from his history, Brad and his brother were thrust into a brutal odyssey through the American

---

1. https://books2read.com/u/b5yRgk

2. https://books2read.com/u/b5yRgk

underbelly: two orphanages, twenty-two foster homes, and twelve schools before the fifth grade. In a world defined by starvation, violence, and the fracturing of his own memory, Brad's identity began to slip away.

Then came the winter street that changed everything.

Near death from hunger, Brad was stopped by a stranger whose singular question would spark a spiritual ignition point: *"Are you angry, little boy, because you are poorer than all the other children?"*

What follows is a profound memoir of **spiritual emergence**. From recurring visions of ancient battles to the harrowing "poor farms" of mid-century America, Brad traces the "thread" of his own consciousness. This is more than a story of survival—it is an exploration of how trauma forms the crucible for awareness.

As Brad navigates his brother's descent into psychosis and his own struggle against the violence of his youth, he discovers a gateway to the deeper frontiers of human intelligence, destiny, and the evolving connection between the soul and the modern world.

About the Author

A man of many pasts, farmer, contractor, teacher, fire captain and paramedic. Has built many deep sea boats and sailed the great lakes and ocean. Injured fighting a large fire requiring a rebuild, but still functioning and flipped many homes.

Now retired and enjoying spinning tales as he closed in on 90 years old, 87 and holding.

www.ingramcontent.com/pod-product-compliance
Lightning Source LLC
LaVergne TN
LVHW090547110826
845146LV00001B/43